Degrees 'R' Us

Degrees 'R' Us

Anonymous

First Published 2007
by Impress Books Ltd
Innovation Centre, Rennes Drive,
University of Exeter Campus, Exeter EX4 4RN

Typeset in 10/12 Sabon by Jayvee, Trivandrum, India

Printed and bound in England by imprint-academic.com

British Library Cataloguing in Publication Data
A catalogue record for this book is available from the British Library

ISBN–10: 0–9547586–9–2
ISBN–13: 978–0–9547586–9–1

For Boris

την μεν ματαιολογιαν διωκουσιν οἱ
νεωτεροι · ἡ δε σοφια αὐτων
ἀπολλυται κατα τον κλιμακτηρα
της παιδειας

The young pursue only folly;
By degrees their wisdom is lost.

(attributed to John the Boughtonite)

Author's Note

St Sebastian's University does not exist, and it should not be iden-
tified with any institution of higher education in the United
Kingdom or elsewhere. All characters in the novel are also
entirely imaginary. They have no counterparts in real life.

CHAPTER ONE

St Sebastian's Revisited

The leaves were just beginning to turn when I arrived in Washington DC for the annual conference of the International Academy of Philosophy. It was the start of the autumn term – or the fall semester as our American colleagues have it – but in the lobby of the Hilton Plaza Hotel, teaching and students were forgotten. There were thousands of delegates from all over the world and they were all only interested in each other. The lobby was a veritable babel of talk. Who was going up; who was going down; who had reached the heights of an established Chair at Harvard, Oxford or Berlin, and who had been cast into the outer darkness of yet another temporary post in South Dakota, Salford or Minsk.

I was due to give a short paper on the third day dealing with Immanuel Kant's metaphysics and was listed in the programme as Dr Felix Gass of St Sebastian's University, England. Unfortunately it was too late to get this corrected to 'Glass'. Whilst in Washington I had arranged to visit my old colleague Harry Gilbert and his aristocratic wife Victoria. Harry and I had worked together for ten years at St Sebastian's University in

England. We had not known each other particularly well, since we had been in different departments, but we had always shared common interests. I was still teaching there, but a year ago Harry had moved to Virginia and was now in his second year as the Thomas Jefferson Porpoise Distinguished Professor of Theology at Sweetpea College. He had contacted me when he heard that the Academy of Philosophy was meeting in Washington. He said he was anxious to hear the news from St Sebastian's, and that he would pick me up from the hotel at two o'clock on my first afternoon.

I was not confident that Harry would find me. The lobby seemed to be permanently heaving with shabby-looking academics clutching folders, looking lost, asking for further clarification from the harassed hotel staff and bumping into old friends. There was a constant clatter as old acquaintances were greeted and new deals were proposed. Bearded, distingushed-looking scholars with their breakfast egg still on their ties mingled with learned ladies in spectacles and sensible shoes.

However, as I made my way through the throng, I caught sight of Harry immediately. He was standing near a large potted plant at the entrance reading the conference programme. A plump, greyhaired, somewhat dishevelled figure, he had gone native. He was wearing an American button-down blue shirt, khaki trousers and ox-blood loafers without socks. He seemed pleased to see me and he led me outside where a large red Rolls-Royce was parked just outside the entrance.

'Is that really yours?' I asked increduously. Clearly American salaries were on a more generous scale than British ones.

'Got it when I came, Felix. I knew the brother of the local car distributor in England and he gave me a special deal. Victoria's very scornful of it. She thinks it's vulgar.'

'I think it's great,' I said as we set off. 'I've never been in a Rolls-Royce before!'

As we drove to Sweetpea, Harry told me about the College. I knew that he had had considerable difficulties in his final year at St Sebastian's: the Vice-Chancellor was anxious to retire all senior professors to save money and the word was that there had been an acrimonious fight which ended in Harry's resignation. In fact the debacle at St Sebastian's had been a blessing in disguise.

He and Victoria were enjoying Sweetpea and found the American way of life very congenial. As a Distinguished Professor, there were few teaching responsibilities and most of his new colleagues were pleasant. Victoria had a good job too, she wrote about antiques for the *Washington Post*. I was interested in this because my wife was also a journalist, albeit for the radio.

Harry had been persuaded to undertake one surprising duty. The President of the College had asked him to give talks to alumni groups in all the major American cities. This year his itinerary had included Boston, New York, Philadelphia, Denver, Los Angeles and San Francisco. Apparently this was nothing to do with philosophy or ethics, Harry's academic speciality. I was astonished to learn that the President insisted that he tell the alumni about the ceremony at Buckingham Palace when the Queen had awarded him the Order of the British Empire for his 'Services to Christian Ethics'.

'It's most embarrassing,' he said. 'I have to show them a video of the ritual and wear my medal and then they all ask silly questions which I can't answer about Princess Diana and the erstwhile Mrs Parker-Bowles.'

I was mystified. 'Why does the President want you to do it?'

'Oh it's fundraising. For some reason Americans are transfixed by the royal family and I have taken on mystical significance because I have actually shaken the royal hand. I have to say the gatherings are very successful. The alumni are always attentive and afterwards they write enormous cheques. To date I have raised more than four million dollars in pledges for the college, so there isn't a hope that I'm going to be let off this in the future. Still, the supply of American cities must come to an end sometime . . . .'

After a pleasant journey through the lush Virginia countryside, we arrived at Sweetpea. The college buildings, clad in ivy, were designed in a mock Gothic style. In the centre of the town, overlooking the college green, was a handsome colonial church built in the early nineteenth century. There were students everywhere. Some were jogging; others were sunbathing on the lawn. Harry pointed out the various college buildings as we passed them. A mile distant from the green was a large mansion owned by one Thomas Jefferson Porpoise VI who was the chief patron of the college and who had endowed Harry's Chair. Harry and Victoria's small, colonial clapboard house, which had been lent to them fully-furnished during his tenure as professor, was just inside the estate gates.

Harry led me into the drawing room which was full of beautiful examples of early American furniture. Over the fireplace was a large portrait of Victoria. She was bedecked with diamonds. Apparently it was painted by Julian Bosie, one of Virginia's most fashionable portrait painters who was another protegé of Thomas Jefferson Porpoise. The diamonds, which I have to say were most impressive, were a family heirloom and had been lent to Victoria by her elder brother. I asked if they were still in the house, but Harry laughed and said that he could not afford the insurance. They had been restored to the safe in the family's draughty old castle on the Welsh borders.

'Victoria's due back any time now.' Harry said as he poured me a glass of sherry from a sparkling ship's decanter. 'She's been in New York at the Metropolitan Fall Antique Fair. She's writing an article on New England bureaux . . . Now, tell me about the conference.' Two sleek Siamese cats sauntered about as we chatted, both eventually settling themselves next to Harry on the sofa.

Harry politely asked about my presentation. I told him it was based on a new book which was due to come out before Christmas: *Kant's Critiques Revisited*. 'Probably not many will come to my lecture. Only about a dozen, I expect. But at least St Sebastian's will pay my fare since I'm giving a paper.'

After a quarter of an hour, a taxi pulled up outside. Slim with dark hair, Victoria looked as attractive as I remembered her. The daughter of a baronet, she was unlike any of the other faculty wives at St Sebastian's, her grand pedigree and Harry's inherited wealth had caused considerable resentment among the academic community. I wondered if they were having the same trouble at Sweetpea. We greeted each other, and she went into the kitchen to fetch a fruit cake for tea. 'How was New York?' Harry called after her.

'Wonderful! And I wrote the article on the train.' She returned carrying a butler's tray with pretty cups and saucers and a highly polished Georgian silver teapot. As she began to pour out there was a loud rat-tat on the front door. Victoria ran to open it and kissed the newcomer. He was a tall, craggy gentleman, very upright, but probably in his mid-eighties. Victoria brought him over to be introduced. He was Sir William Dormouse, her father. He was staying at the Porpoise mansion as a guest of Thomas Jefferson, with whom he had become bosom friends. Dressed in an old tweed suit, he walked with a very slight limp and was carrying a walking stick with a carved silver dormouse handle.

He was sat down in the largest armchair and immediately began to talk. He had a grievance and was not going to lose the chance of telling someone new about it. 'I don't know if she told you,' he began, 'But Victoria and I got back from Las Vegas last week. It's my second time there. We stayed at Cleopatra's Palace again. Damned good hotel! They have a champagne fountain in the hall. You just help yourself. And there are plenty of helpful girls around. None of them seemed to be wearing many clothes. It was most refreshing. But this time I got tossed out from the casino.'

'Daddy kept winning,' Victoria explained. 'He's always been good at games and he won enough last time to pay for his trip, but this time it really looked as if he was going to clean them out . . .'

'Well I like cards and I learnt to play blackjack when I was a boy at school. Nothing else to do all day! Harry very kindly gave me a book last Christmas about strategy and card-counting. It explained scientifically how to win. I've been studying it since January.'

Victoria took up the story. 'Daddy hoped he would win so much this time that he would be able to reroof all his tenants' cottages back in Shropshire . . .'

'Damn silly buggers at the casino!' Sir William interjected. 'They thought I was just a senile old fool and they kept betting against me. But I won every time . . . I can tell you, I was making a packet . . .'

'The management got concerned.' Victoria was amused. 'Daddy's stack of chips got higher and higher and apparently they were watching him through their security cameras. Then they sent over a couple of very sinister characters. Honestly they were terrifying. They could have been extras from *The Godfather* films.'

'Probably were in their spare time,' said Harry. He was enjoying the story even though he had obviously heard it several times before.

'Well,' said Sir William indignantly. 'They practically frog-marched me into a backroom. I might have been on court-martial. There was some sort of Mr Big sitting there, a most distasteful fellow; I certainly would not have employed him on the farm. He gave me a glass of disgusting whisky, bourbon or something they called it. The two thugs stood behind his chair like bodyguards while this gangster said he knew I was card-counting. I didn't deny it. I was pleased with myself. I told him that my son-in-law had given me a book about it for Christmas and it seemed a jolly good system. Then they had the impudence to say that card-counting wasn't allowed. Well I can see that they don't want to lose money, but it's still damned unsporting of them. If I want to count cards, it's my right as a British citizen. Bloody Yanks! Anyway, that's what I told them. But they weren't going to listen to reason. This slick mobster gave me my marching orders. Banned from the casino! I've a good mind to write to the White House. This country's meant to be the Land of the Free – I can't understand Americans at all. Rotten bad soldiers! They mess up their wars! And, they don't play fair in their casinos!'

'Well that's the end of the plan for the new roofs,' sighed Victoria. 'I thought we might even be able to afford central heating in the castle.' She handed round more fruit cake. Then she smiled at me. 'So Felix, tell us about St Sebastian's.'

'Well,' I began. 'you probably know we're going to have a new Vice-Chancellor. The old one, Barraclough, has just left. He got himself some sort of job in charge of a government think-tank. He's now responsible for standards in higher education.'

Victoria looked dismayed. 'But he has no standards! Everyone knows he'd do anything for money.'

'I think they were rather desperate and whatever else you say about Barraclough, he was always good at sounding impressive. Anyway, we're all a bit anxious about his successor. He's supposed to start this term. His name's Flanagan and he was brought up in an orphanage in Liverpool. At the age of ten he was shipped

6

off to Australia. Apparently the Australian government was anxious to keep the hoardes of South-East Asians away and were very ready to take on British orphans to swell the European population. So he grew up in some Australian institution run by an order of monks called the Brothers of Mercy.'

'Good God!' Victoria was horrified. 'Have you any idea what went on in those Brothers of Mercy orphanages? There have been loads of newspaper reports recently. I believe some of the ex-orphans are even demanding compensation. It's said that the children were starved and sexually abused by the monks and brutally beaten. They were put to work more or less as slaves on the farms and were treated appallingly. How on earth did this man get the kind of education that enabled him to be a Vice-Chancellor?'

'Not all the orphanages can have been like that,' observed Harry mildly.

'Well somehow Flanagan survived,' I pointed out. 'The word is he was semi-adopted by a neighbouring Catholic priest.'

'The story gets worse and worse,' said Victoria. 'And what exactly was this priest's motivation in befriending a Liverpudlian orphan?

'Who knows? But the upshot of it all was that he did pick up some sort of an education, and eventually he got a BA from the University of Sydney. Then he managed to return to Liverpool where he did his PhD in economics. He was appointed to an assistant lectureship there, and worked his way up the system. After he got his Chair, he went to Ireland where he became Pro Vice-Chancellor at the University of Fandonegal.'

'Isn't that the place that got into trouble with the Quality Assurance Agency?' Harry asked. 'I read they went into partnership with hundreds of rather disreputable institutions. They took their money, did very little checking on the standard of education offered and scattered Fandonegal degrees about like confetti to all their graduates. I read about it in the *Times Higher Educational Supplement* last winter.'

'The article came out just after Flanagan was appointed to St Sebastian's and had given in his notice,' I replied. 'But in any event the whole story died down. Certainly nothing was ever done about it. And it would have made no difference to

St Sebastian's anyway. Our University Council was interested in one thing and one thing only. Flanagan was said to be the moving spirit in getting Fandonegal out of the red – the place had a deficit of over ten million pounds when he started. There was even talk of closure. Now Fandonegal has a very healthy operating profit. All due to him. No one on the Council was interested in the man's scholarship, or his wisdom or his tact in human relationships. They were all dazzled by his financial wizardry. The rumour is he was the unanimous first choice.'

'Let me get this straight,' said Harry. 'When he was at Fandonegal, he made deals with various colleges of higher education world-wide, promising to give them degrees for their courses without too many questions asked. In return they paid Fandonegal a proportion of the students' fees. And I suppose because they could offer Fandonegal degrees, the colleges could attract more students? Was that how it worked?'

'It sounds a jolly good wheeze!' observed Sir William. 'Why doesn't everyone do it? My college at Cambridge is always asking me for money. Why don't they just give out degrees to all these other places?'

'Trinity doesn't give degrees, Daddy,' explained Victoria patiently. 'You have your degree from the University, from Cambridge. And Cambridge still has some standards.'

'Didn't I read that somewhere like the Clapham Happy Clappy Institute of Evangelical African Theology got validated by Fandonegal?', Harry asked.

'So did the Fort William Tartan Institute of Contemporary Folkdance,' I said.

Victoria laughed. 'So you can get a degree in Scottish reeling now.'

'Well,' I said, 'I imagine it's like Sports Studies. They dress it up with some anthropology and physiology and history. It may be that the Fort William Institute is highly respectable and scholarly, but certainly the educational system in Britain has improved no end if the students of all the institutions Fandonegal validated are worthy of BAs.'

'Who does the judging anyway?' asked Sir William. He spoke as if the giving of degrees was like the awarding of rosettes in an agricultural show.

'Well, that's just the point,' I tried to explain. 'If a university goes into a partnership with a college of further education, there should be very careful procedures to check that the students of the college achieve the same standard of scholarship as the students in the university. So all essays and exams should be double marked, once by the staff from the college and once by the academics from the university.'

'And this wasn't happening?' asked Victoria.

'Apparently there was a very cursory system of moderation. According to a *Times Higher Ed.* article, Fandonegal was basically taking the money and no questions asked. But anyway the whole thing died down.'

'But what about the Quality Assurance Agency?' asked Victoria.

'Well no one takes as much notice of the Quality Assurance Agency as they should,' said Harry, 'And when all's said and done, money is money.'

Victoria frowned, 'It's still disgraceful,' she said, as she refilled our teacups.

I continued. 'Anyway, when the article came out, everyone became apprehensive about Flanagan's plans for St Sebastian's. We hope he won't want us to go around validating disreputable institutions. We just don't have time to do it properly.'

'Has anyone met him?' Harry asked.

'Actually a number of us have. His interview took place in the Arts Building, and several of us were having coffee in the corridor next to the kitchen. The Registrar brought him and his wife over, and he introduced us.'

'He brought his wife?' Victoria asked. 'Is that normal?'

'I think the appointments committee wanted to meet her. She's much younger than he is and German by background. Flanagan met her when he was doing some research on the revival of the motor industry in Europe after the Second World War. Her father is a senior executive with Mercedes-Benz.'

'And . . .?' Harry asked.

'Well, to tell the truth, he doesn't look very impressive. He's short, about five foot two I would think, very fat and rather bald. Barraclough at least looked handsome and distinguished. Flanagan nearly crushed my fingers when I shook his hand. His wife followed about three feet behind him. She looked terrified, rather a mousy little woman I thought. They also brought a nasty little Irish terrier with them who bit the Registrar when they left.'

Harry laughed. 'Well that's one good mark for him. I longed to bite poor old Registrar Sloth on several occasions!'

'Damned undisciplined dogs, terriers,' commented Sir William. 'Little buggers always bite. Tell your Vice-Chancellor he should have a border collie. They're clever dogs! Can't do without them on the farm! Never let one down . . .'

'Speaking of the Registrar,' I said, 'you'll be interested to know that there's trouble between him and his wife. You remember Jenny Sloth who works, or rather who does not work, in the library?'

Harry looked at Victoria and they smiled at each other. 'Of course I remember her,' he said 'I had a serious run-in with her in my last year. She was one of the reasons we left St Sebastian's.'

'Well apparently,' I continued, 'Sloth is now involved with one of the secretaries in the Registry, Joy Pickles. Did you ever come across her?' Harry frowned and shook his head.

'She's a blousy blonde who works in the admissions office. She's every bit of thirty years younger than he is, but he has thrown caution to the wind and from all accounts is completely besotted. She drives him into the university every morning and he has set her up in her own house, where presumably he is living too. It's all love's young dream.'

'But what's happened to poor old Jenny?' asked Victoria.

'Well she stays in her job in the library and does even less work than before. At the start of last term I ordered some books for one of my courses and they still haven't arrived. But when I complained, she just wiped her eyes, said everyone was being horrible to her and disappeared into a back room. I hadn't the heart to take it further.'

'Oh dear,' said Victoria. 'I wonder how all this will go down with the new Vice-Chancellor. After all the Registrar is very senior in the university'

'Who knows? The real problem is Joy Pickles. Clearly Sloth has a weakness for incompetent women. Joy has always been hopeless at her job. The rumour is that she was on a final warning, but now, of course everyone is treating her with kid gloves.

As far as the Registrar is concerned she can do no wrong. Heaven knows what admissions will be like. Probably next year we will have no students at all!'

'Well it's all go at St Sebastian's.' Harry got up to circulate the sherry decanter. 'I understand you also had an election for Dean?'

'Yes,' I said, 'There was a contest between John Pilkington who is still Head of the Department of Theology and the revisionist historian Patricia Parham.'

'Oh yes,' Harry replied. 'We heard John lost. He must have been disappointed.'

'He was. It was a very close-run thing. I'm sure you know that Parham is a militant lesbian. Her long-term partner is a cracker-jack car mechanic. I don't know her, but over the years she has built up quite a custom among the university staff and she made it clear that she would no longer repair the cars of any member of staff who did not vote for Parham. I think it was a joke, but John was devastated and said it wasn't fair. Maybe it didn't make any difference anyway, but Parham did win the election and there wasn't anything he could do about it. So he continues as Head of the Theology department.'

Victoria was delighted with the news. She had never liked Pilkington. She told the story about Harry's friend Magnus. He had been a lecturer in Old Testament at St Sebastian's. He had had a large win on the premium bonds and had left the same term as Harry. While he was still at the university, Patricia's partner had repaired his flat tyre. Since it was an act of kindness, Magnus did not feel he could pay her, so he invited her to go to a dance with him at the White Hart Hotel. The mechanic was so outraged by such a sexist invitation that she lashed out at him and gave him a black eye!

'Perhaps Patricia felt guilty about it,' I said. 'I understand that, as Dean, she wrote to Magnus in the spring asking if he would like to come back to teach a Hebrew course for the undergraduates. At that point he was still on his world cruise. He has now apparently got a dancing job on the ship in the New Year as a gentleman host but he's agreed to fill in this coming term.'

'Magnus told us,' Harry said. 'He sent us an email about it last week. He's still recovering from his last cruise; he was continually beseiged by octogenarians who insisted on him being their partner every evening. But he is now such a good dancer that the entertainment director on the ship offered him a job. Magnus said he's signed up for the Christmas Caribbean Cruise leaving from Southampton in December. But before that he's going back to St Sebastian's. To his suprise, he rather misses teaching.'

'He was outstandingly good at it,' I pointed out. 'His courses were always popular.'

Sir William was preoccupied with other matters. 'How much did he win? I've got the full quota of premium bonds, but I've never won more than five hundred in one month. How many does your friend have?'

'Only about a hundred and he won a quarter of a million,' Victoria said. 'It was a Christmas present from his aunt. But Daddy, he really needed the money so he could retire. And after all, you've just won quite a lot playing blackjack.'

'Bloody Hell,' Sir William said. 'A quarter of a million . . . I wonder how he did it. Did he read a book on how to win?'

'There's no such book, Daddy. It's pure chance. Magnus was just lucky. Now, why don't you just have another piece of this nice fruit cake?'

'I think I will. And some of whatever is in that decanter.'

Victoria poured her father more sherry as I continued the saga of St Sebastian's. 'We're also due to have a new chaplain. An Anglican friar, no less! He will teach one course, and will also run the chapel. Apparently he's very high church and is all set to introduce incense and candles.'

'I wonder how that'll go down with the new Vice-Chancellor. He presumably is still a Roman Catholic?' asked Harry.

'I shouldn't think with his experience of the Roman Church that he's anything at all,' remarked Victoria tartly. 'But a friar in religious orders . . . that sounds exciting. Poverty, Chastity, Obedience and all that.'

'Well it's all a bit mysterious . . .' I said doubtfully. 'The University offered him lodgings in the Old Building, but he said he would be living in town. It turns out he's bought an enormous property on a brand-new, very expensive estate. The rumour is he's moving in with his housekeeper. Perhaps friars are very rich nowadays.'

'Are you sure he's still a member of the order?' asked Victoria. 'Lots of monks and friars have left and now are just ordinary priests.'

'No,' I said. 'I saw his curriculum vitae. It makes it quite clear he's still under discipline.'

'Perhaps the house belongs to the housekeeper?' suggested Harry.

'Nonsense!' boomed Sir William. 'She wouldn't be his house-keeper then. You mark my words. I know these High Church johnnies. I won't have them in our church. Short sermons and proper hymns like "Onward Christian Soldiers" and "Fight the Good Fight" is what you need. These bells and smells fellows aren't to be trusted with anything.'

'How exciting!' said Victoria. 'I almost wish we were back!'

After tea Harry took me for a walk around the grounds that he shared with the Thomas Jefferson Porpoise mansion. We crossed over a small bridge and came across Thomas Jefferson himself, a spare, silver-haired gentleman dressed in a dark blazer with a Porpoise crest. He was walking a morose-looking beagle. Harry introduced us and explained that I was a former colleague of his at St Sebastian's and that I was attending a conference in Washington. Thomas Jefferson accompanied us back to Harry's house, but refused to come in since he was due to fly to Nantucket that evening to spend the weekend with his stockbroker and his family.

Victoria was chatting to her father in the kitchen when we arrived back. She was making very desultory preparations for dinner. I was worried about this. In spite of the excellent fruit-cake, I was hungry. However, as soon as we sat down, there was another knock on the front door. A vast black woman dressed in an apron was admitted and was introduced to us as Lucille. She was Thomas Jefferson's cook and she had been co-opted to feed us. Victoria followed her into the kitchen, as Harry passed around the sherry decanter again.

It was not long before the four of us were sitting down at a round mahogany table in the charming dining room. The chair-seats matched the curtains and were of a soft rose chintz. The table had taken on the mellow, deep polish which comes only from decades of elbow grease and the matching mahogany sideboard was decorated with a brass rail and small velvet curtains. Dinner was delicious and was served by Lucille. There was southern chicken, fried bananas, crisp bacon, corn fritters and fresh peas accompanied by a chilled California wine.

'I was thankful Lucille was coming,' said Victoria. 'Emma is such a fantastic cook, you are not an easy person to entertain.'

Emma is my wife and she is a food and cookery journalist for the BBC. It is true that she is an excellent cook, but there was no doubt that Lucille was in the same class.

'Now,' insisted Harry, 'We do want to hear about Wanda Catnip. What happened to her?

The reason that there was a new Dean at St Sebastian's was because Wanda Catnip had resigned. For many years Dr Catnip had been the backbone of the university administration, selflessly and humourlessly serving a succession of Vice-Chancellors, initially as Head of the History department and for the last seven years as Dean. She had not been popular. She was rigid in her views and unimaginative in her management style. Then, nearly two years ago she had her reward. She had been elevated to the heights of a Personal Chair and had became Professor Catnip. It was from that moment that things began to go wrong.

'Well,' I said, 'I don't think she ever really recovered from her disastrous inaugural lecture. She lost her crisp edge and on several occasions in meetings she showed signs of becoming tearful.'

'But why did she resign?' asked Victoria. 'She loved being Dean. Harry and I used to call her Little Miss Bossyboots.'

'It was just never the same again after that lecture. Then at the beginning of last year, she announced that no one appreciated her and that she was fed up with administration. It turns out that she's nearly sixty anyway and Barraclough offered her a good deal if she would take early retirement. She's doing some part-time teaching for the History department, and is said to be busy with a new book about eighteenth-century land tenure. Before I left I saw her in the supermarket accompanied by a grey-haired older woman using a stick who I assumed was her mother. So perhaps she's no longer living alone.'

Harry frowned. 'It does sound dreary,' he said.

Victoria sniggered. 'Can you imagine being Wanda's mother. Poor wretched old lady! I bet she's bullied mercilessly.' She embarked on an uncomfortably accurate imitation of Professor Catnip's mode of speech. 'Come along mother! I haven't got all day! Don't waste my time! You've got to pull your socks up and improve your attitude . . .'

We all laughed and at this point Lucille brought in the most exquisite pecan pie. Decorated with thick cream, it melted in the mouth. I did not dare to contemplate its caloric value.

Over coffee, Sir William asserted himself again. He had been quiet through dinner, concentrating on the food, but now he wanted to demonstrate his blackjack skills. I felt nervous. I am not a natural card-player and I certainly could not afford to lose the kind of money which Sir William expected to win. However, there was no cause to worry. Victoria cleared the table and distributed ten dollars in dimes to each of us while Sir William shuffled a deck of cards. Victoria assured us that it was a fresh pack and there was no possibility of her father cheating. Nonetheless, thirty minutes later, Sir William had roundly defeated us all, and sat smiling over forty stacks of shining dimes which he assembled in a neat row in front of him.

'No wonder they banned him from Cleopatra's Palace,' I said.

'Well, Daddy hasn't given up,' Victoria said. 'I promised we'd visit Atlantic City next weekend before he goes back home.'

'They don't know me there,' the old baronet chuckled. 'I bought some cowboy boots and a cowboy hat, so I'll look less conspicuous.'

It was time for me to go. Before I left, Sir William gave me his address and telephone number in Shropshire. 'Call in any time,' he said. 'We can have another session at blackjack. You can get your revenge!'

Harry drove me back to Washington in the red Rolls-Royce. I was tired after so much talk, but Harry was still interested in his old university. As we travelled through the warm Virginia darkness, he asked me if I were having any difficulties at St Sebastian's. I told him that everything seemed to be all right at the moment, but that philosophy was always in a perilous position. There were only three of us teaching the subject and my two colleagues were both in their late fifties, about seven years older than I. When they left, I might have serious problems. I did not want to retire early, but it was unlikely that the university would continue with philosophy. It was not easy to imagine any vice-chancellor, particularly such a man as Flanagan, being sympathetic to such a non-utilitarian, cerebral subject.

CHAPTER TWO

Outreach to the Ignorant

My conference paper went rather well. There were more in the audience than I had anticipated and there was a very lively discussion afterwards. As soon as the session was over, I checked out of my room. Then I caught a bus to the airport, braved the departures queues, found my aeroplane and flew overnight back to Heathrow. I even managed to get some sleep. Altogether it had been a very successful and enjoyable visit to the United States.

My wife Emma was waiting for me by the arrivals barrier. She looked reassuringly the same – of middle height, brown haired, hazel-eyed, dimpled and smiling when she saw me. But once we reached the car, it became clear that she was worried. As we drove back to St Sebastian's, she told me that she had had two different, but equally disturbing, telephone calls from my philosophy colleagues. Both Malcolm Bridgestock and Jonathan Pike were very anxious to be in touch. Emma had told them that I was away at a conference and so they had both spoken to her.

During the time I was in Washington they had both been summoned by the new Vice-Chancellor for an urgent appointment. Apparently over the summer, Flanagan had formulated a new strategic plan for the university. This had been endorsed by Council at its first meeting prior to the beginning of the academic year. Among many other changes, it had been unanimously agreed that philosophy would be phased out of the university curriculum. Students currently on campus would need to be taught for the three years their courses lasted, but recruitment to the subject would cease immediately. Since both Malcolm and Jonathan were in their late fifties, they were offered a full enhancement to their pensions as well as quarter-time contracts until the current students graduated from St Sebastian's. It had been made clear to them both that if they resisted this, they would not be offered such a good deal in the future. They could well be transferred to another department and they would prob-ably have to teach some new, uncongenial courses.

'And so they're both taking the deal and leaving me in the lurch?' I asked, knowing exactly what the answer would be.

'Yes . . . Malcolm sounded more guilty than Jonathan and beat about the bush more, but ultimately that's what it comes down to.'

'When are they supposed to retire?'

'I had the impression that they'll both be going immediately, but of course they'll still work part-time for three years.'

'So what am I supposed to do?' I asked. 'We've got a full quota of first-year students so our undergraduate numbers are as high as ever. If they are both only teaching quarter-time, there's a huge amount of extra work which will have to be mopped up. We were understaffed with three full-timers. There's no way just one person can do it.'

'It looks like that's what's going to happen . . .'

'But I can't do all that teaching! They'll have to help.'

Emma shrugged. 'I don't know. Malcolm said he was planning to go on a lengthy vist to his daughter in Argentina next month and wouldn't be back until after the New Year.'

'And then what happens when all the philosophy students have graduated? What am I meant to do then?'

Emma shook her head. 'I shouldn't think anyone has thought about it. You know what they're like. No idea of forward planning . . .'

'It seems so unfair,' I fumed. 'The three of us did so well in the

Research Assessment Exercise. The government is giving the university more than sixty thousand pounds a year as a result of the excellence of Philosophy's research.'

The Research Assessment Exercise is the bane of every academic's life. Last year Philosophy was one of the best-rated groups at St Sebastian's. We had gained a very high result – higher even than the Theology department, which was our traditional rival.

'I asked about that.' Emma said. 'I thought perhaps the university would lose the money if the department disappeared, but apparently not. They will argue that there is a department because you're still there.'

'But sixty thousand pounds is more than I earn, quite apart from the fees my students bring in. What it means is that all that money will be used to subsidise a less hard-working department, while I kill myself teaching too much and the students get a raw deal from only having one lecturer. It's not right!'

'It's not the only thing at St Sebastian's that's not right,' observed my wife.

Then Emma told me about our house. I was delighted to hear that the builders had finally, at last, finished their work. For three months they had been building a Victorian-style conservatory on the back of our dining room. It turned out just as I had planned it and Emma knew I would be pleased.

We had lived in the same house for more than twenty years. It was double-fronted and was part of an early Victorian terrace in the centre of St Sebastian's. When I was appointed to the lectureship in philosophy at the university, Emma and I had just married. As a wedding present, my parents had given us the down-payment, and through the years we had gradually paid off the mortgage. When our daughter's fondness for loud pop music had become too much for us to endure, we had extended into the roof, so now Imogen had two rooms and her own bathroom upstairs. Now, of course, she was nineteen. She was away at Cambridge for most of the year, at Beaufort College. It broke my heart when she left, but she was doing exceptionally well reading Social and Political Science and enjoying a lively social life at the university. When she had moved upstairs, Emma had taken over her old nursery for a study and that was where she wrote her articles and planned her food programmes for the BBC.

Meanwhile, I had always preferred to work in the centre of the house with everything going on around me. To Emma's fury, I had increasingly spurned the spare bedroom and had taken my books down to the dining room. For several years now, she had complained about clearing up my papers before she could serve her imaginative meals – hence the need for the new conservatory. It was going to have our dining room furniture and Emma was already planning the exotic vines and creepers which she intended to grow. Meanwhile the dining room was to become my little kingdom. The large Victorian pedestal desk and the handsome wellington chest which I had inherited from my grandfather would at last come down from upstairs, and Emma was sketching out designs for a more comfortable room for our visitors.

We were both interested in house furnishings. I collected old Caucasian carpets, while Emma was fond of Regency furniture and was a compulsive haunter of antique auctions. She was also a passionate gardener. She spent every weekend planting and weeding our square town garden and the flowers and shrubs always bloomed for her.

When we arrived home, I found several letters addressed to me on the hall table. One in particular looked ominous. It had a St Sebastian's crest on the envelope and was stamped Private and Confidential. It proved to be a summons from John Pilkington, the Head of the Department of Theology. It read as follows:

Dear Felix,

As you may have been aware, our new Vice-Chancellor has been busy over the summer with a strategic plan for the university. At its first meeting, it was unanimously approved by the Council. I have been asked to inform you that from now on philosophy will be phased out as a degree subject although the university will fulfil its commitment to the department's current students and so, in effect, the subject will continue for another three years.

Last week the Vice-Chancellor had meetings with your two philosophy colleagues both of whom have agreed to take early retirement in light of this development. Malcolm Bridgestock

20

has indicated that he will be away from the university in the Michaelmas term which will mean that you and Jonathan Pike will have to cover all the philosophy courses. Next academic year, I understand both Malcolm and Jonathan plan to be away in the Lent term.

Given this situation, the Vice-Chancellor and I have discussed the way forward for both you and your two colleagues. We believe it would be in the best interests of the university to amalgamate the Theology and Philosophy departments. What this will mean in practice is that the three of you will become members of the Theology department. However, since Jonathan and Malcolm will be formally retired, they will not be expected to attend department meetings. As you know, there is enormous pressure on space. As a result, they will be sharing an office in the Arts Block. However, there will be no reason for you to move since your room is already located on the same floor as the Theology department.

No doubt you will want to discuss the implications of these changes, and I have therefore scheduled a time to see you in my office on Thursday, directly after the first Theology department meeting which is taking place in Arts Block Seminar Room 3 at 9.30 a.m. Could I ask you please to let my secretary know if this time is not convenient?

Best wishes,

John Pilkington,
Head of the Department of Theology

'So,' I said, 'the three of us are going to join Theology.'

'With that stuffed shirt John Pilkington?' Emma had a low opinion of many of the employees of St Sebastian's. She felt, with some justification, that her friends in the BBC were far more amusing.

'But apparently I am the only one who is expected to attend departmental meetings. Jonathan and Malcolm have been let off the hook.'

Emma looked grave. 'That means you're going to be the only philosopher in the department. I'm sure they want your money, but it doesn't look as if they're wildly keen on a massive philosophical input into their God-centred debates.'

'Well I'm not going to worry about it,' I said resolutely. 'We must wait and see how it turns out.'

On the day the first meeting of the department of Theology was to take place, Emma had a radio programme to organise, so she was up by seven to catch the early train to London. I had a more leisurely breakfast and set off for the university just after nine. I turned down our lane which came out onto the High Street. Like every other town in England, this had been pedestrianised; rents were enormous and all the small, privately-owned interesting shops had been displaced by the standard national chains. The pathway was an ugly shade of pink and the rubbish bins, crammed with fast food cartons, had not yet been emptied from the night before.

Things changed when I went through the Monks' Gate into the cathedral precincts. I wandered round the large green court (only the cathedral clergy and distinguished visitors were privileged to walk on the grass) and I passed in front of the gracious seventeenth-century Provost's House. This has been described as one of the most beautiful houses in England. It was a square Queen Anne building of old red brick, perfectly symmetrical with white-painted small-paned sash windows. It had been inhabited by the various provosts of the cathedral without a break since the middle of the eighteenth century. I knew the present incumbent. As well as running the cathedral, he was the Visitor of the University and took a spasmodic interest in what was going on. However, he was not a particularly effective person. He had previously been the archdeacon of a big urban diocese where the Church was undergoing sharp decline. The rumour was that he had been moved to St Sebastian's because it was felt that he could do less damage there. Victoria Gilbert, Harry's wife, used to do a hilarious imitation of his ingratiating manner and his constant references to 'the dear Archbishop.'

Then, in front of me loomed the great, golden-grey stone mass of the cathedral. Tourists were already gathering in little groups. They were either wandering uncertainly around or were being chivvied by determined-looking ladies with umbrellas. There was the constant click of cameras and a general atmosphere of disorganised reverence. Then suddenly a group of unruly foreign school children swarmed past me, chewing gum and shrieking to each other. The bells struck the quarter hour and I passed under the archway into the cool of the cloisters. Here was order and quiet. Then, as I came out the other side, I walked passed a couple of canons' residences, both on a less grand scale than the Provost's House. I was always amused that an institution which taught that it was the meek who would inherit the earth should have such a clear sense of hierarchy in its housing policy. Finally I passed the cathedral souvenir shop which was already open for business. When I walked out of the precincts through the Trinity Gate, the buildings of St Sebastian's University were directly in front of me.

Established in the reign of Queen Victoria as a training-school for missionaries, the original college was influenced by Oxford-style architecture. Following the ideas of John Ruskin, it was built of local sandstone and decorated with pointed Gothic towers. My office, sadly, was in another building, in a hideous nineteen-sixties construction known as the Arts Block further along the street. Off the entrance hall was a small anteroom which housed the pigeonholes for the academics. My slot was crammed with the letters and periodicals which had collected while I was away, and I hurried to dispose of them in my office.

I unlocked my door and spread the post on my desk. There did not seem to be anything sinister so I abandoned it and searched wildly for the agenda of the coming meeting. Then I set off for the seminar room where the gathering was scheduled to begin at 9:30. I was early and, as I arrived, the departmental secretary, Wendy Morehouse, was just wheeling in a trolley of cups and saucers, coffee pots and a couple of plates of rather sad-looking biscuits. I was not the first. A number of my new colleagues had already arrived.

At the back, tucked in beside the window, sat Magnus Hamilton. He was already dunking a chocolate-chip cookie into his cup. Seven or eight years older than I, he was tall, bespectacled and balding. He had been one of the longest-serving members of the department and had been appointed to St Sebastian's soon after he had finished his doctorate at Oxford. Harry Gilbert had told me something about his background. Apparently both his parents had been killed in a car accident when he was in prep school, and he had been brought up by his aunt who had sent him to Winchester. He had come to the university with superlative references and had been described as possibly the most brilliant Old Testament scholar of his generation. He was also a first-rate linguist. Yet in his years at St Sebastian's, he had published very little and had never been promoted.

However, he was a cult figure among the students. They imitated his mannerisms, told stories of his eccentricities and queued up to take his courses. Undoubtedly he was a first-rate teacher and his classes had always been popular. Several of his ex-students had become distinguished academics on their own accounts and some had even dedicated their scholarly monographs to him with fulsome inscriptions. Then a year ago, to everyone's surprise, he had accepted an offer of early retirement with an enhanced pension. People conjectured as to how he could afford it – particularly after it was known that his first action on leaving the university was to book himself onto an expensive liner for a round-the-world cruise. The rumour went around that he had inherited a vast sum of money from his aunt. Even before I heard about Magnus's triumph with the premium bonds, I knew that that could not be the case. He frequently spoke of the old lady and it was clear that she was still very much alive.

I had always liked him and felt safer sitting near him in this strange company. I made my way around the table to the empty chair directly beside him. Magnus was wearing a rumpled blue blazar and a purple and gold silk tie. He looked slightly heavier than when I last saw him, which was no doubt the result of a great deal of eating aboard ship. Unlike the rest of us, he was deeply tanned. 'Nice to see you, Magnus,' I said as I sat down.

'Bloody Hell,' he glowered, 'I must have been crazy to have let myself be bamboozled into returning to this lot! Just look at them all! Have you ever seen such a miserable-looking crew?'

I muttered something about being in no position to judge. I was just a new boy around here.

Magnus was not to be deterred. 'Look at this agenda,' he muttered, 'A lot of boring nonsense and then the new Vice-Chancellor is coming to waste our time. It's bad enough listening to the Humourless Pilk.' I did not myself feel that our Head of

Department, John Pilkington, would like that description of himself, but I had heard that Magnus was unsparing in his criticisms of his colleagues.

'Have you met him yet?' I asked.

'Who? Oh, the Vice-Chancellor! I just saw him getting out of his car. He's as broad as he's long! He reminded me of a fat dung-beetle!'

I laughed. 'I've seen him too. He isn't very prepossessing, is he? Perhaps he makes up for the shortcomings of his appearance with an abundance of charm, though I didn't see much evidence of it when I met him.'

'Oh then you've spotted him too. Well I wasn't impressed,' pronounced Magnus. 'He spoke to me on the telephone about a month ago, asking me to teach the beginners' Hebrew course. Patricia Parham, our new Dean, put him up to it.'

I smiled. 'I heard from Harry in Sweetpea how you were hit in the eye by her garage-mechanic friend.'

'Damn women!' said Magnus. 'I was only trying to give her a treat after she fixed my flat tyre. It was months before the bruises went away!'

'Anyway,' I wanted to bring Magnus back on track, 'tell me about the phone call from Flanagan. What did he sound like?'

'Exactly what he is. A Liverpool boy made good in Australia. A great deal of fake bonhomie and Down-Under baloney. He didn't quite suggest I was a bonzo cobber to be doing what he wanted, but it wasn't far off. Then once he got down to the real substance of the conversation, he drifted into ghastly phrases like "achieving targets" and "state of the art". He even had the nerve to talk about "financial prudence" and "economic stringency".'

'I don't think that's completely unreasonable, Magnus.' I tried to make a case for our new boss. 'Vice-Chancellors do have to work within very tight budgets.'

'Well they're certainly paying me practically nothing for this Hebrew course, but I've heard on the grapevine that when he negotiated his own salary, it was a very different story.'

'Really?' I knew Emma would be fascinated by this. She always said that if you understood a person's financial situation and their attitude to money, then you knew all there was to know about their character.

Magnus settled in his chair. 'I heard that he demanded a fifty per cent larger salary than his predecessor was getting and drove a very hard bargain. Then, when it was all settled, he had the impertinence to demand a job for his wife on top of it all.'

'His wife?' I was puzzled. 'What was she supposed to do?'

'I don't think she can do anything. Everyone says she's just a little German mouse with no education, but he claimed that she had accountancy qualifications and he wanted a new position created for her in the Bursary.'

'No!'

'Well even our pathetic Council managed to stand up to him over that. But then he argued that if the family were going to lose her income, he must obviously be recompensed. He browbeat them so much and they were so desperate to have him that they gave him an extra twenty thousand pounds on top of what he had already negotiated!'

'No!' I said again.

'I had it on the highest authority,' declared Magnus primly. 'Now I want to hear about Harry and Victoria. I got an email from him saying you went to see them both at Sweetpea. What did you think of the set-up?'

'Well it's all rather amazing. Harry has a fantastic red Rolls-Royce. He picked me up in Washington and drove me over to their house. It was very delightful. The furniture, which I understand came with the house, is stunning and there's an extraordinary new portrait of Victoria on the drawing room wall. She's in a white dress and is literally festooned with diamonds.'

Magnus laughed. 'Yes I've been there and seen all that. The picture was painted by their millionaire benefactor's young boyfriend. The diamonds come from her family. You know she's the daughter of a baronet?'

'Yes, I actually met Sir William. He had dinner with us. He'd just come back from a trip to Las Vegas and was very aggrieved. Apparently he'd been thrown out of Cleopatra's Palace casino for winning too much money!'

It was Magnus's turn to be astonished. 'No! How could they do that? He's just an old man. They can't evict their punters just because they're onto a winning streak.'

'I don't think it was exactly a winning streak. Apparently he was card counting. I don't know quite what that means, but he learnt about it from a book Harry gave him for his birthday. It's all based on mathematics and, if you can do it, it's an unbeatable system. But anyway it's strictly against the rules. They were watching him on the close-circuit television. He was summoned for a sticky interview with the casino owner and then a couple of heavies threw him out.'

'Well I knew he was an absolute card-shark. I lost nearly a hundred pounds playing blackjack with him when I went to visit Harry and Victoria last year. In fact Harry reimbursed me afterwards and I heard later that Victoria introduced a new system so she provides the chips for him to play with when they have visitors.'

I laughed. 'I had the same treatment. He insisted on playing and I was worried about it, but Victoria gave me a stack of dimes which Sir William systematically won off me. He was so successful I half wondered if the deck was stacked, but Victoria assured me it wasn't.'

'Well I can see he would be a nightmare to a casino owner.' Magnus paused for a moment. 'I wonder if he would teach me his system . . .'

At this point our conversation was interrupted. Pilkington called us all to order and reminded us that the Vice-Chancellor would be arriving at ten o'clock. He then very briefly in a few colourless words introduced me as a new member of the team. His lack of enthusiasm was all too obvious. I tried to think positively, but I could not help but feel he was being less than generous. After all I was bringing to his department a dowry of more than sixty thousand pounds per annum.

Then his voice became much warmer. 'Now everyone,' he said, 'I want to introduce you all to a new member of the university. We are very privileged indeed to have as part of the department our chaplain, Crispin Chantry-Pigg. In the time he has to spare from organising and, we hope, revitalising the worship of the university chapel, Brother Chantry-Pigg will be teaching a course on Church vestments.'

With great ceremony, Crispin Chantry-Pigg, who was sitting next to Wendy Morehouse, rose to his feet. He was tall and extremely thin with sparce reddish hair and a long pointed nose.

His hands were yellow and bony and he was dressed in a long brown habit. He cleared his throat, bowed to Pilkington and said in a high, clerical voice, 'If I may, Mr Chairman . . .'

Pilkington nodded and Chantry-Pigg began. 'In the first place, I must indicate my great pleasure, my very great pleasure, in being amongst you as part of such a scholarly company. However, if I may, I must take the liberty in correcting your distinguished chairman in just one particular.'

Magnus snorted beside me. Perhaps the friar did not hear, since he proceeded without a pause.

'He is, of course, quite accurate in referring to me as "Brother Chantry-Pigg". That is the accepted mode of address for a member of my order. However I am, of course, an ordained priest of our beloved Church of England and, since my role in the university is to lead, guide and support the religious life of this venerable institution, I think it would be not unsuitable for me to be spoken of in this context as "Father Chantry-Pigg". Many of you no doubt will have heard of my distinguished uncle, the Reverend the Honourable Canon Hugh Chantry-Pigg. He was the personal priest of the well-known lady-novelist Rose Macaulay and was famous in his own right as an intrepid traveller in the Middle East. I remember so well, as a tiny child, sitting on his knee, playing with his pectoral cross and calling him "Father Uncle". He was always my personal guide and inspiration and I would be honoured to share the same mode of address with him.'

'Well, I'm certainly not going to call him Uncle,' muttered Magnus. I stifled a laugh, but again Chantry-Pigg ignored us.

'Now,' he said, 'I'm sure we would like our Heavenly Father to guide our endeavours. Let me begin our little meeting with a prayer.'

Everyone looked bemused, but we obediently bowed our heads. I glanced sideways at Magnus. 'Is this the usual custom in your department?' I whispered.

Magnus grinned. 'Not in my time,' he said.

Crispin Chantry-Pigg's prayer was in Latin and largely inaudible. It was not short. Magnus did not pretend to participate. He gazed around at his colleagues and continued to dunk his biscuit and drink his coffee. How, I wondered, could I, as a secular philosopher who specialised in the thought of the great Immanuel Kant, possibly fit in amongst such Christian piety?

Eventually the chaplain appeared to have come to an end and everyone muttered 'Amen.'

'Shocking bad Latin!' remarked Magnus loudly as the friar showed signs of sitting down. However, Chantry-Pigg had not finished. He took his chair magisterially and then asked for Pilkington's permission to speak briefly about the chapel. Our chairman had no chance to respond. Slowly and ponderously the friar explained that it was his intention to adopt a more traditional approach to worship than had been the custom in the past. There would be a greater emphasis on the sacramental life and the chapel services would from now on be following the medieval monastic offices.' He continued in a similar vein for another ten minutes while Magnus and I looked at each other.

'The man's a religious lunatic,' Magnus opined.

Even Pilkington began to get restive, and when Chantry-Pigg paused for breath, he cut in apologetically. 'I am so sorry, Father,' he said, 'but the Vice-Chancellor will be here any minute and I have one or two important notices.'

'Of course, of course,' said Father Chantry-Pigg. 'The work must go on. "In the midst of life we are in death" . . .'

Pilkington began to outline the arrangments for the term. There was to be a meeting for the new undergraduates on Saturday afternoon when they would be introduced to members of the department. He hoped that we would all attend. Wendy Morehouse would be baking biscuits and cakes for the occasion. Then we were treated to a little lecture on the importance of recruiting new postgraduate students since the economic health of the department depended on it. Finally, on no account were we to forget the importance of research in the financing of the university.

'It has to be said that the departmental result in the government Research Assessment Exercise was a disappointment . . .' said Pilkington.

Magnus chuckled. 'That's because they left out Harry! Serves them right!'

Pilkington was about to embark on the new arrangements for staff appraisal when he was interrupted. With an incredible amount of noise, our new Vice-Chancellor, Professor Alfred Flanagan, entered the room. Magnus had not been wrong about his bulk – his grey flannel suit barely met around his middle. Round his neck, buried in the folds of flesh, he was sporting the St Sebastian's tie and there was a gold silk handkerchief flowing out of his breast pocket. Magnus looked at the ceiling and groaned. 'This is the fifth Vice-Chancellor I've known here and he's quite the ugliest!'

Everyone except Magnus stood up and was told to sit down again. Pilkington embarked on an effusive introduction, but very quickly Flanagan took control of the room. 'Ladies and Gentlemen,' he began, 'it is a great pleasure for me to come to you as your new Vice-Chancellor. Together I hope we will see many changes and improvements in the university. We need to become cutting-edge and quickly. I may be the Vice-Chancellor, but I am well aware that we must all work as a team. My wife Helga and I have now moved into our new house, and, as soon as we have settled in, we are planning to invite all of you over during the course of the year.'

Magnus leaned over. 'You won't believe this, but they've called the house "Cuckoos' Roost",' he whispered.

'No! Why?'

'Well,' Magnus smiled, 'His wife comes from the Black Forest and collects cuckoo clocks. I've heard the place is littered with them. You're cuckooed at from every side!'

Then, as Flanagan boomed about his qualifications for his new job and left us all in no doubt as to his exceptional ability and expertise, Magnus took out a classic car magazine and ostentatiously leafed through the advertisements. 'I've decided to buy an old Jag,' he murmured as he pointed out a silver grey Mark II. 'Can't let Harry be the only one with a nice car! What do you think?' he asked pushing the picture towards me. Pilkington glared at him and gestured that he should put the magazine away. Magnus took no notice whatsoever.

'Now,' continued the Vice-Chancellor. He was plainly enjoying himself. His voice became even louder and his Australian accent grew more and more pronounced. 'I am sure you have all heard that at my previous university, I started up a great scheme of partnerships with a whole array of institutions of higher learning throughout the globe.' He passed around copies of the postgraduate prospectus of Fandonegal University. On the front was an image of a very ordinary academic-looking building; superimposed on top of it was a group of students from various ethnic backgrounds all grinning at the camera.

'I am proud to say that, by the time I left, there were over twenty thousand long-distance students who had all obtained their degrees from us. They had received all the benefits of a first-rate education, but at places convenient to themselves, and the university gained sufficient funds to restore its financial credibility and stability.'

Magnus looked at the brochure and groaned. 'I suppose he's planning to bring them all here,' he said.

The Vice-Chancellor continued without missing a beat. 'The inspiration for the founders of St Sebastian's was to reach out to the world. And this must be our mission today. Throughout the nineteenth century missionaries from the college went, with no regard for their personal safety, to enlighten the heathen in every country on every continent. Today, through the wonders of technology, we have no need to sacrifice our health and even our lives going out to the highways and byways to spread the word. We can achieve our targets in other ways. Our students come to us through correspondence, through partnerships with local colleges and through the internet.'

Magnus closed his eyes. 'I don't believe what I'm hearing. Where did they find this appalling man? I thought Barraclough was bad enough, but this chap's a positive menace.'

'When St Sebastian's was first established, its priority was outreach.' Flanagan made an expansive gesture to emphasise his point. 'Outreach to the poor, outreach to the unchurched and, most importantly, outreach to the ignorant. This is the tradition I want to draw on. We live in a global community, what is in fact a single village. I intend to channel the benefits that flow from St Sebastian's to all nations. We must think globally. St Sebastian's is going to educate the world. We will be forming partnerships with colleges and institutes on every continent and we will be inviting them to share in the special St Sebastian's brand of enlightenment and education. We will not listen to the kill-joys, to the stick-in-the-muds or to the reactionaries who are always

31

mouthing on about "tradition" and "standards", but have no insight, no imagination and no vision of the future. They belong to the past. We must be true to ourselves and embrace the new world-order. Our new vision must inspire each and every member of the university. It is the responsibility of all of us to embrace this mission and participate in these new initiatives. I promise you the benefits for us all will be incalcuable.'

Magnus buried his face in his hands. 'I don't think I can endure this for much longer,' he moaned.

Pilkington, on the other hand, was thrilled. He sat glowing with rapt enthusiasm. When Flanagan at last came to the end of his encomium, he shook his hand and thanked him extravagantly for coming to address us. He said that the speech was a real inspiration and he was sure that we all felt privileged to be part of this wonderful new initiative. He was certain that, under the Vice-Chancellor's leadership, the new venture would be a huge success and he knew that all his colleagues would be equally committed. He suggested there be a round of applause to show our good will and appreciation of Professor Flanagan's vision for the university. Everyone except Magnus clapped obediently and the Vice-Chancellor took his leave.

I was not sure whether to laugh or to cry.

CHAPTER THREE

Blasts of Incense

After our new Vice-Chancellor had left the meeting, little remained to be said. Pilkington concluded proceedings and I prepared to go to his office for our conference. But before we could gather our things, Pilkington was grabbed by Father Chantry-Pigg, who embarked on an elaborate exposition about the role of the department in future chapel activities. Pilkington gestured that I should go and wait outside his office.

Located on the first floor of the Arts Block, Pilkington's domain looked over the car park. When I arrived, Wendy Morehouse, the department secretary, was photocopying in the hall. The door was open and she told me to go inside. Painted light blue, the walls were covered with tourist posters of Jerusalem and the Dead Sea. In the corner was a large metal filing cabinet with a series of drawers. There were a great many books, which were colour-coded and neatly arranged on the bookshelves in alphabetical order. On the desk was a computer, a printer and a stack of folders including one with my name on it. I was tempted to sneak a look at it, but I heard footsteps in the hall.

It was Wendy clutching a mobile telephone. 'John's going to be late,' she said. 'The new chaplain has several problems. Would you mind waiting outside?'

Next to the photocopier were four chairs lined up against the wall. I sat down and took the *Times* newspaper out of my briefcase. None of the obituaries looked very interesting so I embarked on the crossword on the penultimate page. The seconds passed. The crossword proved to be easier than sometimes and I finished it in less than twenty minutes. Then I got up to stretch my legs and thought I might as well have a cup of coffee from the vending machine. It was as disgusting as usual.

A further ten minutes elapsed before Pilkington arrived. He was out of breath. His tweed sports jacket and polyester green tie were creased, and his tall figure moved clumsily. He apologised for being late. 'Our new chaplain is very talkative,' he said as I followed him into his office.

'He seems very enthusiastic,' I remarked.

Pilkington frowned. 'Yes . . . of course it's splendid that we have a proper chaplain. Apparently he's a protegé of the Archbishop of Cannonbury, which is how the funding became available. But I didn't quite understand about his orientation before I met him.'

I was not very familiar with the different schools of thought within the Church of England, so I was not sure what Pilkington meant. However, since I had just joined the Theology department, I thought I had better learn. I hazarded a guess. 'You mean he's rather high?' I suggested.

'Nothing wrong with the Anglo-Catholic wing of the Church,' said Pilkington briskly, 'but it can sometimes, regrettably, attract some undesirable elements.'

Undesirable elements? Now I was out of my depth.

'I'm not, of course, making any suggestion about Father Chantry-Pigg. But these kind of people can encourage some very silly behaviour among the students. Little mutual admiration groups of young men who are not sure of their sexuality. That kind of thing.'

Light dawned. 'Oh you mean gays. I don't think there's anything to be worried about there. After all, it does no harm for the young to explore the different sides of their natures.'

Pilkington looked very tight-lipped. He clearly did not agree. 'Anyway,' I said, 'it's much more acceptable nowadays. I believe even our new Dean lives with her female partner.'

It was a mistake to mention the Dean. I had forgotten in the excitement of the moment that Pilkington himself had been a candidate in the deanship election and had lost to Patricia Parham. He reddened slightly, sniffed and gestured for me to sit opposite his desk in a metal armchair with a beige rayon seat. He picked up my file and opened it. 'Right,' he said, 'you've come to join us. Your colleagues, too, but I don't think we're likely to see much of them, as you know.'

The telephone rang and Pilkington answered it. 'Yes,' he said, 'He's with me now. I'll be sure to tell him.'

'That's the Registrar's secretary,' he said as he put the receiver down. 'She wants you to go to the Registry after our meeting to fill in some forms since you're changing departments.' He settled himself into his seat. 'Now, Felix,' he began, 'are there any questions you want to ask?'

'Well, frankly I don't understand why you want the three of us in your department. We're not theologians after all.'

John stared out of the window. 'I know you're not and this may be a problem. We must see how it all works out. To tell you the truth, several of us are rather troubled about your background in particular.'

'My background?' Now I really was flummoxed. What could my background have to do with joining the Theology department? I thought back to my parents: my father was a doctor, a dermatologist and my mother dedicated herself to running the house, looking after her family and volunteering for a range of good works. I could not see anything very objectionable in any of that. Perhaps our neat 1930s villa in Hampstead Garden Suburb was the problem? Or could it be my new colleagues were unhappy with the fact that I had won a partial scholarship and had been educated as a day-boy at Westminster School? Perhaps the theologians found something objectionable in private education. I knew Harry Gilbert had gone to Shrewsbury and Magnus to Winchester, so I was not the only one whose parents had paid for schooling. Anyway it was scarcely my fault. I had been thirteen years old when the decision had been made. Maybe they were upset that I had gone to Cambridge. I knew that Pilkington was a graduate of Newcastle University and people could be very odd about that sort of thing . . .

'I'm sorry, I don't understand. What's wrong with my background?' I asked.

Pilkington looked embarrassed. 'Well,' he said, 'as you know, we are a Christian department. Most of us are in some sense committed to the original vision of St Sebastian's as an evangelical missionary college. Of course, its role is different now – we're a modern university as the Vice-Chancellor explained at our meeting. We have a new vocation: to bring educational opportunities everywhere around the globe. Yet there is still the feeling in the department that our first duty is to encourage students in their faith. "*Fides Quaerens Intellectum*", faith seeking understanding, you see . . . That's the purpose of theology, at any rate at St Sebastian's.'

My heart stopped and I stared at him. I had been warned about this, but in my entire career I had never really had to face it before. My family were completely non-religious. The only time in my life I had ever entered a synagogue was to go to the bar mitzvahs of various of my school friends. I had married a non-Jewish woman and my family had loved Emma from the first. Yet it was true that both my parents as children had fled with their families from Germany. They had been lucky. Both sets of grandparents were originally from Berlin and they knew what was going on. With the rise of the Nazi party, they had realised there would be real trouble for anyone with Jewish ancestry. They had settled in England as soon as things became difficult in 1933. In London they had established a new life, cultured, civilised, influenced by their German heritage certainly, but determinedly secular and patriotically English.

'You mean you don't like the fact that I'm Jewish,' I said.

John Pilkington squirmed. He wrung his hands. 'You mustn't take this the wrong way. I have the very greatest respect for the Jewish people. I much admire their ideals of family life. I grew up in Manchester very near to the Jewish area. When I was at university I even shared a flat with someone whose parents were holocaust survivors.'

'In other words,' I interrupted, 'some of your best friends are Jewish.'

'You people are always so sensitive. I knew it would be difficult to talk to you about this. What I am trying to say is that we do see ourselves as a Christian department. We're particularly strong in Biblical Studies.' (I happened to know that the New Testament was John Pilkington's speciality.) 'And we are building our reputation on this. We want to get away from the misguided twentieth-century fashion for phenomenology and world religions. And I must tell you that many of us were alarmed by your latest book. Your criticisms of Kant's religious assumptions were very disturbing . . . .'

'You may not have liked it,' I was still upset, 'but it went down very well with the Research Assessment Exercise . . . .'

Pilkington reddened again. This was clearly another sensitive subject for the theologians.

'I think we were unfairly treated by the RAE . . .'

'Well be that as it may,' I said, 'I'm even more confused than before as to why you agreed to have the philosophers join you. Can we go back to my original question?'

Pilkington continued to look awkward. 'Well there was a considerable financial incentive . . .'

I laughed. 'Ah . . . I see. You were told that if you would take on the three of us, you would get all the Philosophy research money. After all we did better as a department than Theology. Then there are the fees from all the current students. I suppose your department gets all those as well?'

Pilkington tried to look dignified. 'Well those are a diminishing return; the fees will disappear with the last of the students. But the research money lasts at least five years and, with the three of you, that's more than three hundred thousand pounds.'

'And of course, as both Jonathan and Malcolm have taken early retirement, I'm the only one who will cost you serious money.'

'Yes' Pilkington was nothing if not honest, 'I wouldn't have agreed if we had had to have all three of you.'

'So what it comes down to,' I said, 'is you were prepared to cope with one Jewish agnostic, provided he was accompanied by a sizeable dowry?'

Pilkington chose to ignore the bitterness of my tone. 'Well, to tell you the truth, I was reluctant at first, but we're short of funding because we didn't do as well as we deserved in the RAE and the money will come in very useful, but we will do our bit and try to accommodate you within the department. Anyway someone has got to teach all those philosophy students.'

'But, as you say, the philosophy undergraduates will come to an end in three years time. What are you going to do with me then?'

Pilkington frowned. 'That will be a problem. The kind of students we are anxious to attract are generally not interested in philosophical issues. They want to study the Bible, Church history or systematic theology, things like that. But you'll be over fifty-five by then so you'll be eligible to take your pension. I'm sure we'll be able to come to some arrangement when the time comes . . .'

I was speechless. I could not believe what I was hearing. Pilkington quite openly intended to take my money and dispose of me as swiftly as possible. He did not even seem to think he had said anything offensive. He opened my file and pulled out a piece of paper. 'This will be your teaching schedule for the year,' he said in an official tone. 'As you can see, your load will have to be increased since your colleagues won't be working as much as they did in the past.'

I looked it over. My number of classes had nearly doubled from last year. 'Look, John,' I said. 'I don't really mind being in your department. But I can't possibly do all this teaching. That's at least seventeen contact hours a week. I've also got a lot of doctoral students. Is there no one among the theologians who could give me a hand in, say, the beginners' Philosophy of Religion course?'

'I'm afraid everyone is busy,' he said coldly.

'I can't believe that anyone else is teaching even half this kind of a timetable. How many contact hours a week do you have, for example?'

'That's not your affair.' Pilkington closed my file deliberately. 'The work has got to be done and you happen to be the person allocated to do it. Now, unless there is anything else you want to raise, I'm afraid I've a great deal of work to do . . .' The interview had come to an end. There was no point in further argument. As I walked out of the door, Wendy was waiting outside carrying a mug of coffee with 'Boss' written on it and a plate of gingernut biscuits. 'Have a nice day,' she chirped as I made my way down the stairs.

I felt that I needed some lunch, but first I had to go to see the Registrar's secretary. On my way out of the Arts Block, I saw several of my new colleagues standing by the entrance. I knew none of them well and they were absorbed in conversation with each other. They ignored me as I passed.

I crossed the street and climbed up the steps of the Old Building. Passing the chapel, I went up the stairs to the Registry which was located next to the Vice-Chancellor's Office on the top floor. As I turned the corner, I saw the Registrar, Dr Robert Sloth, standing very close to Joy Pickles by the notice board. She was wearing a tight pink sweater and his grey suit looked decidedly rumpled. They were giggling and kissing each other. When they saw me they stepped apart, looking embarrassed. 'I've come to fill in the forms you wanted, Robert,' I said. 'Something to do with changing departments.'

'Oh yes,' said the Registrar. 'My secretary knows all about that. She's waiting for you in there.' He gestured towards one of the open doors. Then he and Joy sauntered off in the other direction, holding each other's hands.

Magnus and I had arranged to meet for lunch. Unlike the rest of the department, Magnus had refused to move to the Arts Block and was to be found in splendid isolation directly below the Registry. I went to his office near the chapel and knocked on the door. I heard a shout commanding me to enter. Piles of books and papers were scattered everywhere; Magnus was sitting by his desk holding a sherry glass and a cut-glass decanter. Just inside the door, standing on a table, was a large Canaanite statue with a huge phallus. Magnus used this as a coat hook. He gestured to me to get rid of my coat and to sit down. Then he poured me a drink and refilled his own glass. 'Thought we needed this after that ghastly department meeting,' he said.

'What did you think of Chantry-Pigg?' I asked.

Magnus rolled his eyes. 'Pompous, self-important little prig.'

'And the new Vice-Chancellor?'

Magnus moaned. 'I'm only thankful I've officially retired!' He stared moodily at his statue. 'Drink up,' he said, 'and let's have lunch.'

I left my briefcase in Magnus's office, and we set off for the Senior Common Room, which was located at the far end of the Old Building. Panelled in dark oak, it was filled with small tables and armchairs. In the corner a waitress served sandwiches and coffee. At one table nearby, the Dean – Patricia Parham – was chatting to her partner Judith. They were an incongruous pair. It was Judith who was the car mechanic, but she was neat and small-boned. Wearing an elegant black trouser-suit, her blonde hair was freshly brushed and her pink lipstick neatly applied. Patricia, on the other hand, was large and untidy. Her hair was cropped and it looked as if she cut it herself. She wore no make-up and her finger-nails were grimy. As usual she was dressed in baggy dungerees and today she sported a badge which read "*I love my fellow-women*".

Understandably, in view of his previous encounter with Judith, Magnus was wary of the pair. He skirted round where they were sitting to reach the counter. There we both ordered cheese sandwiches and coffee and sat in the opposite corner of the room.

'So that's Patricia's lover,' I observed. I had never seen her up close before and was surprised at how attractive she was. 'She doesn't look big enough to have hit you!'

'She caught me unawares,' growled Magnus. 'How was I to know she would react like that? I only asked her to go dancing. I really can't see why being a militant lesbian should stop her from doing the foxtrot!'

'I think she thought you were propositioning her.' I tried to speak soothingly. 'Remember she believes that all men are rapists.'

Magnus was not to be consoled. 'Harry and Victoria thought it was frightfully funny,' he grumbled, 'but it was very serious. I might have lost the sight in one eye. As it was I had to wear an eye-patch for weeks!'

As we were speaking, Pilkington joined the queue for lunch. 'Look, Magnus,' I said, 'I'm not sure I want to run into Pilkington. He gave me a terrible time this morning. It's clear that Theology only took me on because they wanted the Philosophy money.'

'That's the only reason for anything in this place. St Sebastian's may call itself a university, but no one has the least interest in ideas or in transmitting civilisation down the generations. All they really care about is being solvent. They practically sell degrees as it is.' Magnus warmed to his theme. 'In fact I don't know why they don't. The students want the qualifications, but they don't like going to class and they definitely don't want to take any exams. The university is desperate for their fees and would also prefer not to go to the trouble of organising courses. Why don't they just forget about teaching and learning? Cut out the middle-man. That's what I say!'

'Isn't that what's going to happen with Flanagan's new partnerships?' I asked. 'The partner college does the teaching. Well . . . maybe it does or maybe it doesn't . . . The students pay the fees. St Sebastian's takes a large chunk of the money, asks no questions and gives them their degrees.'

Magnus laughed. 'Well there you go! I always said it would come to that! "Degrees Are Us"! That should be St Sebastian's new motto!'

I cut short Magnus's flights of fancy. I wanted to get back to Pilkington. 'You know,' I paused, 'I think he may be a bit antisemitic.'

'I wouldn't be surprised. If this were Nazi Germany, I've no doubt he'd be one of the first to join the SS. He'd love the uniform and the power. He's quite efficient, you know. Why, what did he say to you?'

I recounted Pilkington's reasons why he didn't think I'd fit into the department as Magnus slurped his coffee. Then he bit into his sandwich and crumbs fell on his blazer. 'Just what I'd expect. The department has become a hotbed of Christian evangelism. Both Harry and I got out just in time. I can't imagine they'll get on with Chantry-Pigg in the long term. He's far too high and they're complete bigots about homosexuality.'

I went on to explain what Pilkington had said about the philosophers as well as his hints about early retirement. Magnus's expression was serious. 'Well,' he said, 'I can't say I'm surprised. This isn't the first time. It's just what they did to poor Harry.' I looked puzzled.

'Oh, of course, you won't know the full story. Barraclough,

the old Vice-Chancellor, Wanda Catnip, who was the Dean before Patricia Parham, and John Pilkington decided they wanted to get rid of Harry. That's ultimately why he and Victoria went to Sweetpea, Virginia.'

'But why?' I was bewildered. 'Harry was easily the most distinguished academic in the university. He was always being interviewed by the BBC and even got some sort of an honour from the Queen for his work.'

'That was just the point, wasn't it?' said Magnus gloomily. 'Those boring mediocrities always hated Harry. He was far too clever and interesting . . . and of course Victoria, being Sir William's daughter, and the fact that Harry was rich in his own right didn't help either. Anyway, they decided they'd rather not pay his salary and they made up their minds that he would have to go. They all ganged up on him. There was one discipline case after another. You can't win against that kind of bullying. Everyone knows that. But in the end Harry outmanoeuvred them by getting his Distinguished Chair in the States.'

'I had no idea he had such a bad time,' I said.

'Terrible. I did too! The old Vice-Chancellor kept sending me letters encouraging me to take early retirement. They were even going to make me teach summer school. But then I had a windfall . . .'

'I heard all about it in Sweetpea. You won on the premium bonds!'

'Yes, it was jolly good!' Magnus smiled. 'A quarter of a million. And I've still got the premium bonds so I may have another big prize in the future. You never know!'

'The chances against it are enormous.' I tried to put a damper on Magnus's enthusiasm.

'That's what Victoria said before I won the first lot! Actually, I heard her father was rather annoyed about it. He has had the full quota of premium bonds for years, but he's hardly won anything. He said it wasn't fair.'

'Oh dear!' I said.

'Anyway I took the early retirement deal, and got a nice little cabin on the Queen Christina for their world cruise. The trip nearly killed me. Victoria gave me dancing lessons, and I was beseiged the entire time by old ladies who demanded I escort them to the ship's ballroom. I was known as the best dancer there. That's how I got my new job as a gentleman host on board. I'm due to sail in early December on their six-week Christmas Caribbean cruise.'

'That's amazing, Magnus,' I said.

'All due to Victoria's instruction.' He gazed at Pilkington who had sat down at the table next to Patricia Parham's. 'I'm afraid you may be in for it, just like Harry,' he sighed. Then he brightened. 'But try not to worry. I'll give you a few hints what to do. After all, I'm experienced in these matters!'

I laughed. Magnus always had the capacity to cheer me up. 'Why don't you come to lunch at our house on Sunday week? Our daughter Imogen will be home for the week-end from Cambridge and Emma always cooks when she's at home. I can promise you a good lunch.'

Magnus was delighted. 'That's really kind of you Felix. Thank you. Actually I'm planning to go and see what is happening in the chapel that day. Apparently there's to be some sort of inauguration service for that ridiculous friar at eleven o'clock and I thought I ought to put in an appearance. The vision of a nice lunch will sustain me through it.'

'I'll come too,' I said. 'Now I've become a theologian, I ought to have some experience of the university chapel. Eleven o'clock did you say?'

As I had predicted, once classes started I was very busy indeed. Happily, unlike many of my colleagues, I like teaching. Some of the new students were rather intelligent and I had two outstanding pupils in the second year. I had already taught them and I knew they were good, but once they started on my course on Kant's *Critiques*, I realised that they both had exceptional philosophical minds. Mary and Rosalind were friends. They did all the same courses, their rooms were next door to each other in their hall of residence and they were to be seen wandering round St Sebastian's together. From my point of view, the important thing was that they encouraged each other. They were both fascinated by Kant's subtleties (as everyone should be!) and I could foresee them both doing very well indeed.

In the few breaks I had from teaching, I tried to get to know my new colleagues. Every day I went to the Senior Common Room for coffee and lunch and I made a point of sitting with the theologians. They were not particularly friendly, but they tolerated my presence. I quickly learnt that Flanagan's scheme of partnerships was underway. The Clapham Institute of Evangelical African Theology had already transferred its allegiance from Fandonegal University to St Sebastian's. Two theological colleges had been recruited from Canada, one from India, three from Nigeria and one from Korea.

I was curious about the Korean institution, the Reverend Kwan Christian College of Seoul. India, Nigeria and Canada had all been part of the British empire; no doubt all their students could work in English, but this was not the case in Korea. One day, when I happened to be sitting next to him at lunch, I asked Pilkington how we were marking the students' work.

'It is rather a problem,' he said. 'I'm hoping we'll be able to find a part-time Korean interpreter.'

'But how are you managing now?'

Pilkington shrugged. 'Well . . . the Korean tutors mark the students' work and we just have to accept the grades they give them.'

'The Quality Assurance Agency is not going to be happy with that,' I remarked.

Pilkington was not troubled. 'I've talked to the Vice-Chancellor about it. The QAA is not due to visit us for another four years and I'm sure we'll have sorted out something before then.'

On the Friday evening before the new chaplain's inauguration service, our daughter Imogen arrived home. For her Sociology course at Cambridge, she needed to organise a practical project. She had arranged to go to the local Women's Refuge on Saturday to meet the director and several of the residents. It was lovely to have her home again. She admired my new study and the dining-conservatory and we had a riotous supper together. Emma and I were relieved to see that she was eating properly. There had been a time when she was in the sixth form at school that she had been difficult about food. We had worried about anorexia, but she had grown out of it and now she enjoyed Emma's cooking as much as I did.

On Saturday we pursued our separate interests. After breakfast, Imogen set off for the Refuge and Emma went into

St Sebastian's to buy food for Sunday's lunch. She was working on a programme about Welsh cuisine so I knew the main course would be Welsh lamb, but she was anxious to find some laverbread – apparently a form of sea-weed, and various exotic unpasturised cheeses. She was well-known in both the St Sebastian delicatessens. I stayed at home to work on my new book. I realised that with my current teaching load, I was going to have to work every week-end if I were to meet my publisher's deadline.

On Sunday morning Emma stayed at home to prepare lunch while Imogen and I walked to the University chapel. En route we bumped into the Provost as he made his stately way out of the front door of his beautiful house. I had met him briefly on several occasions at graduation ceremonies, since he was the Visitor of the University. I didn't think he would remember me, but he smiled affably as he hurried by. Then, as we passed through the Trinity Gate, I saw Wanda Catnip, the former Dean, striding ahead of an old lady who I assumed to be her mother. Wanda was complaining loudly that they were going to be late. The old lady trotted breathlessly behind.

As we reached the chapel, Jenny Sloth, the estranged wife of the Registrar, was genuflecting elaborately and making her way to the front seats on the right. Imogen and I chose places at the back on the left. I put my coat over the next-door chair to save it for Magnus. There was no sign of him. Directly in front of us were sitting Patricia Parham, and her friend, Judith. Judith was dressed in a neat navy blue dress and coat for the occasion, but Patricia had remained loyal to her old dungarees. They were busy with the hymn books. Judith found the first hymn and was pointing it out to Patricia like a mother helping a six-year-old child. Patricia did not seem to resent it.

The cathedral bells sounded eleven, the organ struck up and a procession began to file into the chapel. We all stood up. First, in a long blue robe, came a rather effete-looking young man of the kind Pilkington disapproved. He was holding up a large silver cross. Then came two more young men of a similar type; they were enthusiastically swinging censers. There were clouds of smoke and the smell was overpowering. Behind them walked the blue-robed choir. It was at that moment that Magnus appeared.

He barged his way in front of the procession, saw me, waved and appropriated the seat I had kept for him. 'Good God!' he said in a not very quiet voice, 'aren't the smoke alarms working today? What a stench!' Imogen giggled while I tried to ignore him.

I was surprised to see my two pupils, Mary and Rosalind, in the choir. I had had no idea they were religious. After the students had all entered, there was a short pause for effect. Then the Vice-Chancellor marched in. He was in full fig. There was a Tudor hat with a gold tassel on his head. He wore an ample black academic gown with red panels and gold brocade insets and his hood flowed down his back. He looked squatter than ever. After him came the clergy as a not-very-well-matched pair. Both were wearing magnificent white and gold copes, but Chantry-Pigg looked ascetic to the point of starvation while the Provost sported a comfortable Anglican plumpness. The three processed up the aisle. Flanagan sat in a special individual stall near the choir while the clergy placed themselves on two thrones, one on either side of the altar.

It was many years since I had been to a church service, but I had attended Westminster Abbey frequently when I was a boy at school. It all came back to me. First a hymn was announced. Judith directed Patricia Parham to the right place. Imogen, who liked music and had a good voice, sung along with the choir. I spent the four verses of 'Praise my Soul the King of Heaven' looking round to see who else I recognised in the congregation. Since the seating was arranged in two tiers facing each other with an aisle down the middle, I had a view of almost everyone.

Mrs Sloth was very prominent. I could hear her singing from where I was standing. She was looking in the direction of Chantry-Pigg and she had an enthralled expression on her face. On the same bench was Mrs Flanagan. She appeared even smaller than I remembered and was muffled up in an enormous coat with a high collar. Although it was gloomy in the chapel, she was wearing dark glasses.

Wanda Catnip and the elderly woman were sitting opposite. Wanda was briskly following the service, but the older lady looked bewildered and uncomfortable. The liturgy was obviously unfamiliar to her. It was suitable that there was no sign of Registrar Sloth or Joy Pickles. Christianity may have been founded for the benefit of sinners, but at least a small modicum of repentance is required of the lost sheep. However, I was surprised that neither Pilkington nor his wife was in the congregation. I wondered if he were making a protest against the elegant young men in their blue robes, but in fact I was being unfair. I heard later that he was the regular organist at St Sebastian's Methodist Church and thus had a previous engagement.

One figure whom I could not place was a quietly attractive woman in her late forties. She was wearing a sober brown coat and she sang the hymns and followed the prayers. She had an interesting face and I was sure I had never seen her before. I wondered who she was. The Provost intoned a few prayers; we sang another hymn ('Dear Lord and Father of Mankind, Forgive our Foolish Ways!') and then Flanagan bounced up to the lectern. He could barely be seen over the top, but plenty of him was visible around the sides. In his Australian accent he boomed out several verses from the Epistle to the Corinthians about the importance of love. He informed us that love is patient and kind and is not jealous or boastful. It does not insist on its own way and is not irritable or resentful. I felt these were admirable sentiments for a Vice-Chancellor.

Then we came to the important business of the day. The Provost, as Visitor of the University, inducted Chantry-Pigg into the chaplaincy. First there was a great deal of prancing up and down by the precious young men and more swinging of censers. Magnus coughed ostentatiously and announced loudly, 'Not good for my allergies! I shall be complaining to the Health and Safety Committee!' Then the Provost got to his feet to introduce us to our new chaplain. It was clear that our Visitor was very impressed by Chantry-Pigg. We heard how he (the Provost) had had a long, fruitful relationship with the dear Archbishop of Cannonbury, but that our new chaplain's connection was (if possible) even longer and more fruitful. He (Chantry-Pigg) had come to us by special archiepiscopal recommendation and we were all hugely privileged to have him. After repeating this piece of intelligence several times, the Provost sat down and Chantry-Pigg climbed the steps into the pulpit.

I am afraid my memory of the sermon is a little hazy. It certainly went on for a very long time and I must have gone to sleep in the middle. He started off by telling us that his uncle, the Reverend the Honourable Hugh Chantry Pigg, always said that the world was a wedding. I could not imagine what he meant by this; the world seems to me to be totally unlike a marriage. While I was puzzling it out, I must have missed a vital connection. The next thing I heard was that a university should be part of the eternal dance at the heart of things. (What dance? Where?). Then, somehow, we were on the subject of virginity. Chantry-Pigg believed that virginity is very dear to God and he issued some warnings, more in sorrow than in anger, to those who were less than chaste in their day-to-day lives. I thought it a pity that Pilkington was not here to hear this. It would have cheered him up about the effete young men. Then there was a great chunk which I missed and when I resurfaced we were back on the university being a wedding. Then the preacher embarked on some remarks about the importance of confession, the sacraments and faithful regularity in the spiritual life. Finally our attention was directed to a series of pamphlets on Anglican vestments of which our new chaplain was proud to be the author.

When he sat down, accompanied by yet more puffs of incense in every direction, it turned out that we were nowhere near the end. The Provost informed us that our new chaplain had specially requested that his first sevice should be a celebration of Holy Communion. We were severely cautioned that only baptised and confirmed members of the Church should participate. I thought this a little odd since at least half of the congregation were not paid-up members of what Chantry-Pigg persisted in calling 'Our Beloved Church of England' and the chapel was meant to be a symbol of college unity. However, there was no choice. We were stuck. Magnus sighed lustily at intervals and started playing noughts-and-crosses with himself in the back of his hymn book. I tried to think about the next chapter in my book and Imogen fidgeted. It seemed forever before we had the final blessing from the Provost, a rendering of 'The King of Love my Shepherd Is', another final blessing from Chantry-Pigg, the procession in reverse, several more blasts of incense and, at last, blessed freedom.

However, as we stepped out into the hall, we were offered coffee. Judith was smiling and holding out a cup to Magnus.

Magnus did not know what to do. As he said afterwards, it was like being offered a goblet of wine by Lucrezia Borgia. But it was clear that Patricia and Judith were determined to show Christian charity. I left them to it and went to introduce myself to Mrs Flanagan. She looked lost and frightened, but she smiled through her dark glasses at me and we had a pleasant chat about how she was settling into her new house. Then there was a shout of 'Helga'. Flanagan wanted to introduce her to someone and she scurried away like a frightened rabbit.

I looked around for someone else to talk to. Imogen was deep in conversation with the old lady who had accompanied Wanda Catnip. My daughter had always been good at drawing out people and the two were obviously enjoying each other's company. I noticed Mrs Sloth standing on the outskirts of the group of young men surrounding Chantry-Pigg. She looked enraptured and I was reluctant to disturb her. Nearby the Provost and the Vice-Chancellor were discussing a meeting in London they were both due to attend. This was obviously not a conversation for me.

Then I caught sight of the attractive woman I had seen in the chapel. She was standing by herself against the wall sipping her coffee and taking in the whole scene. I went up to her and said, 'I noticed you at the service. I'm Felix Glass. Are you a new member of the university?'

She looked at me, smiled and said in an attractive French accent, 'No! I look after Crispin, your new chaplain.'

It all made sense. Here was the housekeeper! I was fascinated. 'Oh yes,' I said, 'I heard that he had bought a house in St Sebastian's. I imagine he's not very domestic.'

She laughed. 'No, he's not! And the new house is a lot to manage.'

'Oh?' I was curious. 'I did hear you were living in Winchester Close.' Winchester Close was a new development. The houses were very expensive indeed and two firms of builders had gone bankrupt in constructing them.

'Yes!' she said. She did not elaborate further.

'How lovely!' I tried to be encouraging. 'Now you must tell me your name so we know each other when we meet again.'

'I'm Danielle Bousset.'

'Bousset?' I said. I was very fond of French cinema and there was a well-known director of that name. 'Like Jacques Bousset, the director of *En Bon Point*?'

She looked at me strangely. 'Yes. It is spelled the same way . . . Please excuse me, I think Crispin needs his lunch.' And with that she strode purposefully away.

It was time to go. I gathered up Magnus and Imogen and we walked home. Emma was ready for us. The table was laid in the new conservatory, I had recently mowed the grass, and the sun was shining. The garden was full of the autumn flowers that Emma had planted last spring. Magnus and I sat at the table while Imogen served wine from an old silver claret jug which my grandparents had brought with them from Germany.

'Damn silly service! Went on forever!' Magnus announced. He produced a small box of chocolates which he presented to Emma with a flourish. Emma thanked him and remarked how sensible it was that chocolate manufacturers had at last realised it was not essential to put cellophane around their boxes.

Magnus looked embarrassed. 'Actually, that was me! I was rather hungry last night so I helped myself to one or two from the top layer.' It was true. The top layer was half empty.

'Never mind,' said Emma, 'I'm sure the rest will be delicious.'

Imogen embarked on a description of her visit to the Women's Refuge the previous day. Magnus looked bored but he cheered up when Emma's bacon and laverbread pancakes were served. This was followed by exquisite Welsh lamb with caramelised onions, mint sauce, braised artichokes, cabbage boiled in milk and crisply fried potatoes. 'This is utterly scrumptious,' he said as he eagerly accepted a second helping. 'Food wasn't like this when I went on holiday to Wales with my aunt. It rained the whole time and we lived off brown windsor soup and fish and chips.'

Interrupting Imogen's account of how women can be bullied by their partners, Magnus recounted how in his first year at Winchester he had been tormented by a sixth-former named Corkran. This bully had subsequetly gone into merchant banking and Magnus had read in the *Sunday Times* that he had recently been imprisoned for money laundering in Colombia. 'And no more than he deserves!' declared Magnus.

'Bullying doesn't always involve physical violence,' Imogen

explained. 'Emotional bullying is often the worst kind.' She frowned. 'There was an old lady at the service who is clearly being bullied. She's not being hit or anything like that, but she's still miserable. She has her own little house and plenty of friends in Leeds. She wants to sell it and move into a care home, but her daughter won't let her. She insisted that she came down to be looked after in St Sebastian's. She kept on saying how kind it was of Wanda – that's the daughter's name – and that she shouldn't grumble, but she's clearly miserable. I was just about to give her some tips about how to claim extra allowances and home-helps and things like that, but her daughter interrupted us. She was horrible. She ignored me and spoke to her mother as if she were a tiresome three-year-old. I felt really sorry for the old dear.'

Magnus and I looked at each other. 'That's Wanda Catnip, the former Dean,' I said.

'It wasn't anything like that at Winchester,' Magnus ruminated. 'Corkran just kicked me about the study. Damn painful it was too.'

'With women, it's often the insults that hurt most,' Imogen said.

'I wouldn't have cared if Corkran had insulted me – even when I was thirteen, I knew he was a stupid brute and would get his come-uppance in the end. It was just miserable while it lasted.'

Pudding consisted of a steamed treacle confection with a special Welsh ice cream followed by a selection of Welsh cheeses. Magnus loved it. He finished up the cheese tray and looked bloated. He could not even manage one of his own chocolates. 'Can't eat a thing more,' he said. 'The best meal I've had since I don't know when . . . better even than the midnight feast on the Queen Christina. You're a genius, Emma. Quite a tonic after all that smoke and nonsense in the chapel.'

CHAPTER FOUR

A Degree in Casino Management

Over the next few weeks, I was very busy teaching my philosophy courses. My only obvious problem (apart from chronic overwork) was that I kept receiving emails from Joy Pickles, the Registrar's paramour in the Admissions Office, informing me that potential philosophy students were intending to come to the university and would come to see me for interview. Each time I emailed back that there would be no undergraduate philosophy courses in the future so there was no point in the students visiting. After the fourth of Joy's communications, I was tempted to be quite sharp with her, but I remembered in time that she had a powerful protector. So I realised that discretion was the better part of valour and I sent her another emolliant email.

I continued to persevere with my theological colleagues and tried to have lunch with them every day in the Senior Common Room. I did not feel I was making much progress. They were polite, but distant. Magnus, on the other hand, was a delight. He was as morose as ever. He insisted that his Hebrew class was a nightmare. The students either didn't come or failed to do any work. They had disregarded his constant maxim, 'Regular

Hebrew, possible success. Irregular Hebrew, no success at all!' 'But,' as he said, 'what can you expect? They don't learn anything sensible in the schools! No Latin or Greek or proper mathematics. It's just sex education and social studies, whatever that may be!'

One afternoon he phoned and asked me to join him for tea. Only a few academics were in the Senior Common Room when I arrived; Magnus was sitting in the corner reading *The Times*. He had already ordered tea with lemon for both of us and a plate of tea-cakes. 'Just got this in the post,' he said, handing me a large white envelope. It was an At Home invitation from the Vice-Chancellor. It was decorated with a picture of a large Germanic cuckoo and contained the details of a buffet party. 'I was hoping you've got one too and you could give me a lift.'

As it happened, Emma and I had received a similar summons and I said I was happy to pick him up from his flat. 'I can't wait to see Cuckoos' Roost,' he ruminated as he munched through his tea-cakes. 'I thought it might be interesting to go past our revered new chaplain's house on Winchester Close. It's on the way. I'm curious to know how a poor friar can afford that kind of property.'

'Perhaps his Order has bought it for him as an investment?' I suggested.

'Humph!' said Magnus.

That evening I told Emma about Flanagan's invitation and Magnus's reaction. 'I really don't want to go,' I said. 'But Magnus thinks we've got to. He says we can't miss the cuckoo display. Apparently they all pop out at once from all sides.'

'I think we do have to go, Felix. After all he's your new boss. Maybe we'll have a German dinner. I'll be interested to see what she cooks.'

'And Magnus wants to go by way of Chantry-Pigg's new house,' I continued. 'He's curious to know how he can afford to live in Winchester Close.'

My wife laughed. She also was fascinated by in questions of money and how people spent it.

On the appointed evening, we picked up Magnus as arranged. He looked as if he had already had a considerable amount to drink. With much hilarity the three of us drove by Winchester

Close. Only four of the six houses in the development were finished. The other two were still shells. However, they were all enormous, four-square, wooden-framed with mock lathe and plaster. There was a large notice at the entrance to the close advertising them as 'Homes of Distinction . . . Discreet Opulence'. They were described as having six bedrooms (all with ensuite bathrooms), four reception rooms, dream kitchens and landscaped grounds. A jacuzzi came as standard. Nothing so vulgar as a price was mentioned. Apart from one light in an upstairs window, the one belonging to Chantry-Pigg was dark. No doubt our chaplain was out performing some errand of mercy, while his housekeeper was taking a well-earned rest in front of the television.

Cars were already lined up in front of Flanagan's house, which was to be found in another prosperous suburb just outside St Sebastian's. There was a large, dark oak porch with a carved wooden sign in German script on which was written *Cuckoos' Roost*. I pressed the doorbell. Instead of the usual harsh ring, there was an imitation cuckoo sound. A waitress from the university opened the door and admitted us. After removing our coats, we were ushered into a large drawing room full of people. All the furniture was of dark heavy wood. There were long, brown velvet curtains and an indefineable air of Middle-European gloom. It reminded me of my grandparents' old mansion flat in Battersea. Over the draped mantlepiece was a massive cuckoo clock with frolicking rabbits and there were several black and white portrait photographs of elderly over-weight ladies and gentlemen in heavy silver frames. In one corner of the room was a table with a white embroidered cloth; it was laid out with glasses of sparkling white wine.

We all took a glass, and made our way through the throng. The drawing room opened into a dining room; on one wall there were at least ten cuckoo clocks of different sizes. I looked at my watch. It was nearly eight o'clock. I wondered what would happen when the clock struck the hour. On another embroidered cloth on a second black oak table were arranged plates of food including smoked duck, large black sausages, selections of salami, a huge joint of salted beef and an array of pickled vegetables. There were also potato pancakes with apple sauce, and loaves of pumpernickle and rye bread. I looked at Emma who was transfixed. She had just embarked on a series of BBC programmes about European cuisine, and I wondered if Mrs Flanagan's cooking was going to become her next project.

Just before eight Flanagan clinked a wine glass, cleared his throat, and welcomed us all. Helga stood beside him. She was heavily made up, but not wearing her dark glasses. I noticed that her wrist was in a small cast. As he finished, cuckoo clocks began striking the hour throughout the house, accompanied by the racuous sound of cuckoos. I looked at Magnus who rolled his eyes. Several guests began to giggle. When it was over, Flanagan smiled. 'Our birds are singing their welcome, too,' he said, as he signalled for us to form a queue for the buffet.

Emma and I stood next to several academics whom I barely knew. However, there were a couple of theologians and Registrar Sloth and Joy Pickles were of the party. I was thankful that I had not been too critical of the Admissions Office. Clearly Flanagan had arbitrarily divided up the entire St Sebastian's staff, and we happened to be in one of the first groups. Emma wanted to try everything and filled her plate; she then went off to have a discussion about food with our hostess. I was more modest. I took a couple of sausages, several potato pancakes, apple sauce and two slices of rye bread. I made my way to a deep-green velvet sofa opposite a large carved oak court cupboard and addressed myself to my plate. Flanagan went around the room speaking to his guests. Magnus had disappeared.

I was soon being monopolised by the Flanagans' German terrier. He indicated that he was very partial to potato pancakes. I surreptitiously gave him a few bits, but I was interrupted by Flanagan himself who pushed the dog away none too gently with his foot. The dog snarled and cowered. Then he sat down heavily beside me. I looked around desperately for Emma, but she was engrossed in her conversation with Helga. The Vice-Chancellor was clearly determined to have a word, so there was no escape.

'I hear you're the last full-time philosopher in the university,' he said.

I nodded.

'There's something I want to talk to you about,' he began. 'You know there's all this talk in the news about building super-casinos. The more I read about it, the more convinced I am that St Sebastian's needs to be at the cutting-edge. I know there's a demand, whatever all the prudes and killjoys say.'

I had a wild thought that our new leader was about to close down the university and convert all its buildings into some glitzy gambling den. However, he was still speaking. 'The legislation will get through all right. The government needs the tax revenue and no one really cares what a few old women of both sexes say about the evils of gambling. So we need to think how it will benefit the university and I've hit on just the right idea. We'll be world leaders. We're going to have a degree in Casino Management.'

I could hardly believe my ears. St Sebastian's had just dismantled the Philosophy department. The administration had indicated its contempt for the immortal ideas of Plato, Aristotle, Aquinas, Descartes, Hume, Kant, Hegel and all the rest of them. But it was quite prepared to include casino management as a serious academic discipline.

'Vice-Chancellor,' I said hesitatingly, 'I think you've got the wrong person. My field is philosophy. I don't know anything about gambling.'

Flanagan put his hand reassuringly on my shoulder. 'I didn't think you would,' he said, in the manner of a kindly uncle. His Australian accent was very pronounced. 'But I'm sure you know a great deal about the philosophy of chance?'

I was surprised at his perspicacity. 'I suppose I do know something. In fact, I did Mathematics for my first degree at Cambridge and my undergraduate dissertation was on probability and chance. But I gave that up long ago. Probably one of the lecturers in statistics could be more helpful to you now.'

Flanagan patted my shoulder. 'You see mate, you're just the bloke I need. You know all the stuff, but you're far enough away from it to get some persepective.'

'Well actually,' I said, anxious to pass the buck, 'I do know someone who is an expert on blackjack. You may have heard of Harry Gilbert – he was the Professor of Christian Ethics here until about two years ago. Well, he's now a Distinguished Professor at Sweetpea College in Virgina. Anyway, his father-in-law, Sir William Dormouse, is very knowledgable about card games. He won a fortune in Las Vegas. I met him several weeks ago when I visited Harry and his wife. Sir William was there too, but his own house is on the Welsh borders.'

'A Sir, eh . . .' Flanagan was impressed.

'He's a baronet. It was one of his ancestors who did something distinguished . . .'

One of the waitresses came over and refilled the Vice-Chancellor's glass as I told him about Sir Willliam's methods and successes. 'You might want to talk to him,' I continued. 'I doubt if he knows anything about the philosophy of chance, but he's certainly quite an expert at card-counting. He'd also give you an interesting insight as to what the customers in a casino want. I'm afraid I've never even been inside one.'

'We must change that,' boomed Flanagan. He took a pen out of his inside pocket and wrote down Harry's email number on a napkin. I told him that I had Sir William's home address and would send it to him, if he thought it would be useful. I warned him, however, that Sir William, although very spry, was well over eighty.

'I'll be in touch. Thanks for this,' the Vice-Chancellor said as he stood up, accidently scattering drops of wine all over my trousers. As it fizzed, he took a large, white handkerchief out of his pocket, and handed it to me. 'Sorry,' he said, 'I get over-excited.' And he strode off to speak to Joy Pickles and the Registrar who were standing hand-in-hand next to a grand piano near the French windows.

The following Monday, I received an email from the Vice-Chancellor summoning me to a meeting in his office. He said that he had been in touch with Sir William. He wanted to speak to me about arranging a visit to the castle in Shropshire. Pilkington would also be present, he wrote, since the new plans involved the Theology department. I could not imagine what Flanagan had in mind.

On the day of the meeting, I arrived in the department early. In addition to several letters in my pigeonhole, there was a daunting pile of essays from my first-year philosophy students. I went to my office and made a cup of coffee in the kitchen nearby. It appeared that I was the first member of the academic staff to arrive, but I heard Wendy Morehouse in the corridor talking to the cleaner.

Mrs Brush was initially complaining about the mess that had been left in the kitchen. Wendy was trying to soothe her. She promised she would send out an email, reminding everyone that they should wash up their own coffee mugs. Then the subject of the Sloth–Pickles household was raised. Apparently Mrs Brush used to 'do' for the Registrar and Mrs Sloth. That had been bad enough. Mrs Sloth left everything everywhere, but at least the mess could be dusted around. However, the new house was something else. 'I've never seen anything like that, Joy!' came the strident tones of our cleaning lady. 'Cigarette ends in the face cream, dirty tissues all over the floor and the sink blocked with God-knows-what! Jumped-up little trollop! She needs her bottom smacked!'

Just before nine I walked over to the Old Building. In the Vice-Chancellor's parking space there was a vast, silver Mercedes-Benz – presumably a perk from the rich German father-in-law. As I entered the hallway, I almost bumped into Crispin Chantry-Pigg. He was still dressed in his brown habit and was surrounded by his usual entourage of androgynous young men. As I passed, the Reverend Brother let out a braying laugh and his youthful disciples giggled. No one took any notice of me.

The Vice-Chancellor's office was on the floor above the chapel. Flanagan's secretary was sitting at her desk when I arrived. She smiled and told me that the Vice-Chancellor was waiting to see me. Pilkington, she said, had arrived several minutes earlier. Surprisingly the room had not been redecorated for Flanagan. I remembered it from the days of his predecessor. The walls were a pale green, not my favourite colour, and there were acres of emerald green carpet on the floor. In the corner was a Victorian long-case clock. There was also a highly polished reproduction Sheraton table surrounded by dining chairs. However, there was one obvious new addition. Behind the Vice-Chancellor's Victorian pedestal desk was a large cuckoo clock which struck the hour as I entered.

'Come in, Felix,' the Vice-Chancellor shouted. He was seated in a large green leather armchair; Pilkington was opposite on a matching leather sofa. Flanagan gestured that I should sit on the seat facing him. My Head of Department did not look happy as the Vice-Chancellor explained the purpose of the meeting. 'I wanted to see you both,' he began, 'because I intend to establish a new degree course at St Sebastian's. As you will both have read in the news, there is a new government initiative to create super-casinos throughout the country. It's a fair-dinkum opportunity for us. It will renew local economies and create thousands of new jobs.' Pilkington shifted in his chair. It was clear that he was not in complete agreement with our new boss.

Flanagan had got himself into gear and was oblivious to the unease. 'When I heard about these plans,' he continued, 'I asked myself: Who will run these casinos? Who will ensure real excellence? The answer is obvious: our graduates. St Sebastian's will take the lead. Yes, gentlemen, this is our destiny. I have created partnerships throughout the world with many different institutions of higher learning. Your department, John, has been particularly responsive to these initiatives. I am delighted to hear that you have now moved into Korea. It is vital that we plug into these developing Far-Eastern economies. That is where the money in the future will lie!' Pilkington looked a little mollified.

Flanagan was in full flow by now. 'There is no reason why institutes of casino management should be excluded from this glorious spread of knowledge and learning. I have a dream. In casinos throughout the civilised world, the very mention of St Sebastian will bring pride to the hearts of the managers and croupiers alike. They will be our graduates no less than those who have their degrees in the old-fashioned subjects like Mathematics, English, Physics or Theology . . . .'

Pilkington looked increasingly uncomfortable as Flanagan outlined his plans. 'Vice-Chancellor,' he interrupted. 'I'm afraid I don't follow you. Are you suggesting that our university encourages gambling?'

'Come on mate,' said Flanagan, as he stood up and looked out of the window towards the Cathedral. 'It is not our place to either encourage or discourage. This is an individual choice, a moral dilemma, a matter of personal ethics. I am a great believer in human freedom. If members of the public choose to spend their money in casinos, that's their right. Personally, I've no time for roulette. The spinning wheel gives me a migraine and the flashing lights of slot machines are worse. I don't like poker or blackjack. But it's not for me to make decisions for others. If they wish to spend their hard-earned money in this way, that's for them to decide. I don't want to waste my holidays in Blackpool sunning myself on the beach. I've no wish to travel to Disneyland Paris. But I fully respect the wishes of others to do so. Indeed . . .'

'But Vice-Chancellor,' interrupted Pilkington. There was desperation in his voice. 'Gambling is an entirely different matter. It is detrimental to society. It is highly addictive. It imprisons souls. It deprives little children of parental nurture and care. Where there are casinos, there are drug dealers, delinquency, prostitutes and vice. We have to protect our students. All the undesirable elements in the town will be attracted up to the campus. You can't turn a blind eye to these things . . . .'

I was rather impressed by this. Pilkington had always struck me as an exceptionally dull person, but here was real passion. Flanagan had a different reaction. He turned from the window and stared at my hapless line-manager. His mood had dramatically altered. 'Dr Pilkington,' he snorted. 'You have not been invited here to give some undergraduate lecture on the evils of gambling. Save that for your students or your milk-and-water Methodist friends. I am fully aware that there are certain social complications connected with gambling. We here at St Sebastian's in no way condone drug-taking or the exploitation of women. But we are a public institution. If the government in its wisdom sees fit to create super-casinos, then it is not for us to make judgements about our elected representatives. Rather, we're here to cooperate. To set new targets and to meet them. That is why I am proposing we establish a degree course. Even a casino can pursue the ideal of excellence. Let us make sure that our casinos are top-notch in every particular! That's what the government requires of us and that's what we'll deliver!'

'Ah, Vice-Chancellor,' I was embarrassed. I did not feel it would help my relationship with Pilkington if he were to be humiliated in front of me, 'I'm not sure how this concerns me . . .'

'Felix,' he smiled, 'it's you who I want to spearhead this development. That is why I asked you to see me, and Dr Pilkington as your Head of Department. You have connections, and I want to use them.'

'Connections?'

'Yesterday I spoke to Sir William Dormouse. A top bloke if ever there was one! He told me about your recent visit with his daughter and son-in-law. I understand he cleaned up in Atlantic City. Apparently he made enough money to reroof his tenants' houses.'

I stammered something about Sir William having a very clever system in blackjack. Pilkington looked aghast. He had always disliked Harry Gilbert and, by extension Victoria and her father.

'Sir William,' the Vice-Chancellor continued, 'has invited me to come to see him in his castle in Shropshire. He has very kindly extended the invitation to you. We'll be going next Tuesday.'

'That's quite impossible, Vice-Chancellor,' cut in Pilkington. 'Felix is very busy with the undergraduates. He's the only full-time philosophy lecturer we have. And I'm afraid he simply cannot take time off for something unrelated to his work . . .'

'Time, time!' Flanagan exploded. 'Of course he has time. He must make time.' The Vice-Chancellor began to pace like a caged lion as he cross-examined me. 'How many hours do you teach?'

'Well, a lot. Seventeen contact hours a week actually. And then I have twelve doctoral students who need quite a bit of attention . . .'

'Seventeen hours a week!' Flanagan shouted. 'This is a disgrace. Nobody should have such a teaching load. Who told you to do this?'

'Actually,' I said, looking over to Pilkington, 'he did.'

The Vice-Chancellor stood over Pilkington who squirmed. 'You did?'

My Head of Department cowered as he explained that my other two colleagues were part-time, and that all the undergraduate philosophy courses had to be covered. He began to point out that I was the only person really qualified to teach the subject and that in the view of the Quality Assurance Agency, student satisfaction was very important.'

Flanagan was having none of it. 'This is a scandal,' he exploded. 'How dare you exploit your colleagues? How many hours do you teach? Come on, tell me that, man, tell me that!'

61

Pilkington muttered that he was very busy with his administrative duties, but that he was still teaching four hours a week. The Vice-Chancellor's face became redder, 'Four hours a week and you force Felix here to teach seventeen! The sooner you're relieved from your so-called administrative duties, the better! Felix is to teach no more than eight hours. You will distribute his courses round your colleagues. Even theologians can presumably manage first-year philosophy. And you yourself are to take on at least one of his old courses. Four hours indeed!'

'And to whom can I allocate the other courses?' pleaded Pilkington.

'Who? Who? I don't know who. That is your problem. You're Head of Department. Do a simple work analysis. See who's teaching the least. Allocate the work around. I'm not to be bothered with nonsense like that and nor is Felix. We have more important things to do.'

Pilkington was nearly in tears. Wringing his hands, he made one last stand. He cleared his throat, 'I'm sorry, Vice-Chancellor. But I'm afraid I cannot make these changes. Term has started. I can't force my staff to teach courses about which they know practically nothing. I really must protest.'

There was an ominous silence. Flanagan slowly walked round the perimeter of his room and then resumed his place in front of Pilkington. It was the calm before the storm. Suddenly he poked his finger at Pilkington's chest and the tirade began. 'You will do as you are told,' he shouted. 'Your colleagues in Theology are not YOUR staff. They are MY staff. It is not YOUR department. You are merely a temporary, very temporary, department chairman in one not-very-successful-department in MY university. I am not making a request. I am giving an order. If you cannot obey it, then you'll step down from your office now, this minute. I mean it!' The Vice-Chancellor had turned deep purple and a vein throbbed in his temple. Pilkington, on the other hand, had gone deathly pale. He could scarcely clamber to his feet when Flanagan pointed to the door and said 'Get out of my sight! Now!'

I remained seated. I did not quite know what to do, but as soon as the door closed behind Pilkington, Flanagan became a changed person. He smiled warmly , shook my hand and put his arm around my shoulder. 'Now we're in business,' he said, as he showed me to the door. 'I'll be counting on you Felix. My secretary'll be in touch about the arrangements for Shropshire. If you have any more trouble with that long-faced puritan, let me know!'

Dazed I walked back to my office. I had never experienced a scene like that in my whole working life. Emma would be gripped, but how could I possibly justify my new role to her as gambling supremo at St Sebastian's?

When I arrived home that evening, I found a note from Emma in the hall. She had gone to a meeting of the St Sebastian's Garden Club and had left a small, exquisite pigeon pie for me in the oven. I got out a tray and dishes, poured myself a glass of Burgundy, and went upstairs to the bedroom to watch television. At nine I heard Emma's car in the drive. She came upstairs clutching a box of Alpine plants. 'We had the most fascinating lecture about Switzerland,' she said as she put her burden down.

'Emma, I've got to talk to you,' I interrupted. 'I've got a problem with the new Vice-Chancellor.'

'He wants to sack you . . .' She was alarmed.

'No. Nothing like that. It's weird. He wants me to be in charge of a new degree in Casino Management.'

Emma laughed. 'Casino Management? Don't be absurd! There couldn't be a degree in Casino Management! Anyway why you?'

'Well, he seems to think I know something about gambling. We talked about it at his party and I mentioned the name of Harry Gilbert's father-in-law.'

'What does Harry Gilbert's father-in-law know about casinos?' Emma had not heard the story of Sir William's adventures in Las Vegas.

'He's a real card-shark and he has an infallible system for blackjack apparently. Anyway the old boy has invited Flanagan up to his castle in Wales and he wants me to go too.'

'Well you might enjoy a trip visiting the aristocracy.' Emma was a natural optimist. 'What about your teaching?'

'That's just the trouble. The meeting with Flanagan was appalling. Pilkington was there and the Vice-Chancellor insisted that my teaching load be reduced to a reasonable level to accommodate my new duties to the gambling industry.'

'I don't see anything wrong with that,' said Emma stoutly. 'You were teaching many too many hours this term. It can't have done the students any good.'

'Yes, but Flanagan completely humiliated Pilkington. He yelled and screamed and even threatened to demote him from being Chairman.'

Emma was mystified. 'Why did he criticise Pilkington?'

'Pilks is a Methodist and doesn't approve of gambling. He tried to argue his case, but Flanagan went purple in the face with fury. I thought he was going to have a stroke. He raged at him and wouldn't stop. He was like a bulldozer. Pilkington was as white as a sheet by the end. I don't know how I'm ever going to face him again . . .'

Emma smiled. 'I wouldn't worry too much about that. Everyone knows Pilks is a stuffed shirt. And you really have no choice. It's deplorable that the university substitutes Casino Management for Philosophy, but at least it means you'll still have a job when the philosophy students run out in a couple of years' time. And if it's a success, you might even get a chair. Just think: Professor of Casino Management!'

'Very funny.' I was too upset to see the joke. 'But Emma, the Vice-Chancellor was out of control. I thought he might hit Pilkington he was so upset.'

Emma looked thoughtful. 'Well, I'm not entirely surprised. Flanagan was an orphan. He grew up in a Brothers of Mercy home in Australia. Do you have any idea what they were like? The Vice-Chancellor was probably always a fat, little kid who was bullied and teased by the other children and beaten and sexually molested by the Roman Catholic priests. I read an article about those homes. There was a real scandal about them.'

'But what has that to do with him losing his temper with Pilkington?'

'Oh, for heavens' sake Felix! You must know about this.' My wife grew impatient. 'Violence breeds violence. It's battered children who become batterers themselves. It's said to be very common in army families; the cycle of violence goes down the generations. And it was rife in children's homes forty years ago.'

'What do you think I should do then?'

Emma sighed. 'I don't think you have much choice. At least you won't have to teach so many classes.'

Later in the week I received an email from Flanagan's secretary. She said that I was to arrive at Flanagan's house after lunch on Tuesday, and he would drive us both to Shropshire. We were to stay overnight at the castle, and I was instructed to cancel my classes. I then emailed Harry Gilbert telling him what had happened and asking for advice. He was hugely amused by the idea of a degree in Casino Management. He suggested I take at least two hot water bottles on the trip as it would be bitterly cold and he warned me against betting any real money if his father-in-law insisted on playing cards.

The next few days were largely uneventful. Life was far easier with a more reasonable teaching load, but I was disconcerted when I was talking to my Kant class to find three strange sixth-formers knocking on my door. It turned out that they had come for an interview to read Philosophy next year. I couldn't just send them away so I invited them to join the class and said that this would give them an idea of what philosophy was like. My two clever students, Mary and Rosalind, were at the top of their form and there was no doubt that the three newcomers really enjoyed the experience. I felt sad afterwards telling them that their journey was pointless. In fact I was so annoyed with the Admissions' Office in general and Joy Pickles in particular that I wrote her a very sharp note. After all, this was the fifth time she had arranged interviews for a non-existent degree.

The next day, as arranged, I arrived at Cuckoos' Roost at two. Mrs Flanagan answered the door wearing an apron and looking subdued. I was surprised that she was again wearing dark glasses. Flanagan came bustling down the stairs carrying a heavy, leather suitcase. I noticed it had his monogram in large letters on the side. He was dressed in a light brown Harris tweed jacket and dark trousers without a tie. I put my small overnight bag in the boot of his magnificent motor car and helped him with his suitcase. Mrs Flanagan waved as we set out. The Vice-Chancellor fiddled with the air conditioner and the radio and handed me a packet of mints.

When I admired the Mercedes, he looked pleased. 'It's my regular present from Helga's father,' he said. 'He's very big in the

Mercedes company and he gives me the latest model every two years. This one's got heated leather seats.' He turned one of the dials and my seat started to heat up. It was an uncomfortable sensation. Flanagan then told me in detail how he had first met his wife when he was on a research assignment in Germany. He was content just to talk away and no response was expected. I had great difficulty in not falling asleep.

Once we drove onto the motorway, he turned to the subject of his future plans. 'The orphanage is like Eton,' he said. 'It has a top-notch old boys' network. I've been in touch with one of my contemporaries who went with me to Australia. He's a good mate . . . we worked on the Brothers of Mercy farm together – slaved would be a better description. Sylvester Mancini wasn't like me. He never had a chance to go to university – not that he'd have been interested. As soon as he was sixteen, he absconded and worked his way to America. Apparently there were some distant cousins in the Bronx who gave him a job in their waste management firm. The family is huge and has various kinds of business interests, including a chain of casinos. Sylvester married within the family and now has kids of his own. About ten years ago he moved to Las Vegas where he works for his wife's brother. Luigi Mancini is responsible for the Las Vegas branch of the business and Sylvester has ended up managing one of the casinos.'

'What a useful contact!' I said.

Flanagan frowned. I felt I was reviving bad memories. 'Oh well, if you grow up in an institution, you rub shoulders with all kinds,' he said shortly.

I looked out of the window at the changing countryside as the Vice-Chancellor explained his scheme. 'The Mancinis want to expand into Europe; they're excited about the British government's initiative to build super-casinos. They already have a small training school in Nevada for croupiers, hoteliers and departmental managers, but their courses are not yet validated. Sylvester told me that they would love to be able to offer their graduates bachelor degrees and a European experience if at all possible. I made it clear that we don't provide this kind of service for nothing, but he told me that money is no object to the family.'

'But we don't know anything about casino management,' I protested.

'No problem,' Flanagan said. 'We'll just have to hire some experts. But what we can do is offer official validation. It'll be just like all our other partnerships.' Flanagan took a cigar out of his pocket, and pushed in the cigarette lighter. 'Don't mind if I smoke, do you?' he asked.

I did, but I shook my head. Flanagan lit up, turned on the air conditioning and continued. 'Sylvester talked it over with his brother-in-law. He's apparently the boss of the whole outfit. They suggested they transfer a large element of their training operation to St Sebastian's. Each of their staff is to come for a term to receive special instruction. Then, once there are super-casinos in this country, we'll also be recruiting English students.'

'But where will they practise?' My head was spinning. 'Dealing cards and whatnot is a practical skill. It's not enough just to learn about theories of chance.'

'Oh we've thought of that.' Flanagan was very confident. 'The idea is to open a small training casino on campus, which they will bankroll. We'll have to get a gaming licence of course, but I understand from a bloke I know on the town council that that'll be no problem. I thought the best place would be the old squash courts. The building needs to be renewed anyway.'

Flanagan waved his free hand expansively, dropping ash as he continued. He was carried away by his own creation. 'I thought we'd call it "The Golden Arrow" since St Sebastian, our patron saint, was martyred by being shot through with arrows. We could even commission a large picture of his martyrdom. You know how he always stands on a platform being shot at by the heathen. I thought we could get someone to paint the scene, but each arrow should be pinning down a banknote before it goes into Sebastian himself.'

I wanted to laugh, but I managed to hold my voice steady as I said, 'Sir William is very friendly with an American millionaire whose partner is a young portrait painter. He did a very good picture of Victoria Gilbert and I expect he could be commissioned to do something.'

'Perhaps the old man could be persuaded to pay for it, eh?'

'Well you never know,' I said weakly. This was not my area of expertise.

'Of course,' the Vice-Chancellor continued, 'it'll take time to redo the building, but temporarily we can house the casino in the Great Hall.'

I remained silent. The Great Hall was the best room in the university. It was used for important lectures, formal meetings and university feasts. I could not imagine what Pilkington and my other colleagues in the Theology department would make of such a proposal. Magnus, at least, would find it funny. Flanagan looked over and winked. 'Pretty good idea, huh?' he said. 'And you're the one who's going to run it.'

The drive to Shropshire took well over four hours. After Flanagan's extensive description of his plans, he turned on the radio to Classic FM. The announcer was interviewing a Swedish soprano as I fell asleep. An hour later, I woke with a start as we turned into a long pot-holed drive. We went through large gates adorned with stone dragons and past a series of cottages. In the distance a vast grey castle with turrets loomed through the mist. Flanagan was impressed. I heard him mutter to himself, 'Not bad for an orphanage brat!'

Sir William was waiting for us. He was standing on the porch wearing a disreputable barbour jacket and looking at his watch. He waved as we pulled up to the door. I dragged our suitcases out of the back, and we followed our host into the hall.

The castle itself was Victorian, but it was built on the remains of a medieval ruin. We walked through a huge room hung with portraits of various ladies and gentlemen, presumably Dormouse ancestors. Over the massive stone fire-place was a particularly large picture. This, Sir William said, was the first baronet. An icy blast straight from the North Pole blew through the windows, which rattled ceaselessly. We were taken down a long corridor where blood-stained Welsh and English flags were suspended high above our heads. Finally we reached a cosy sitting room with a kitchen at one end. There was a large wood burning stove and a mahogany longcase clock with a brass face. One wall was lined with books. In front of the stove was a battered leather armchair and a brown velvet sofa which looked as though it had been continually clawed by the family cat since the era of the first baronet.

I put our luggage near the door as Flanagan spread himself on the sofa. Sir William took possession of the armchair and I pulled up one of the kitchen chairs. 'This used to be the housekeeper's room when I was a boy,' said Sir William, as he poured us each a glass of madeira. 'Always was the only warm room in the house!'

There was a strong smell of something burning, and Sir William looked agitated. 'My daughter-in-law and my son Billy are away for the week,' he explained. 'Selina left a fish pie in the freezer, but it's a bit tricky. I trust you like brussel sprouts,' he said hopefully.

After considerable fussing, Sir William directed us to a small dining table and served us dinner accompanied by a bottle of claret. Although the fish pie was burned on the outside, it remained frozen in the middle. I hoped none of us was going to contract food poisoning. The brussel sprouts apparently had been put on by the cleaning lady a couple of hours before. They were almost soup.

Over dinner Flanagan told Sir William about his project. Sir William looked amused as the Vice-Chancellor drew a grandiose picture of the proposed Golden Arrow Casino. He chortled, 'We never had anything like that at my college in Cambridge. Would have made the place much more jolly. Where do I fit in with all this?'

'Well,' said Flanagan, 'We were hoping you'd be our patron. I understand you have contact with a portrait painter in the United States and it would be fair-dinkum if he could do a picture of St Sebastian pierced full of arrows.'

'Like a pin-cushion, eh?' chuckled Sir William. 'I suppose I could get in touch with Thomas Jefferson Porpoise. He's always keen for young Bosie to get commissions. Well as long as I can defeat 'em all at blackjack afterwards, I'm happy . . . what about a little game after dinner?'

Flanagan and I demurred, but Sir William persisted. 'No blackjack? Well, what about a round of Scrabble, then?'

We both felt we could manage this and we reapplied ourselves to the food. Sir William refilled our glasses and produced a rice pudding. In contrast to the pie, this was burned all the way through. It also tasted decidedly of the fish with which it had shared the oven. However, it was helped a little by a generous blob of strawberry jam which Sir William put on top of each gooey mess. We did our best to eat what was put in front of us, but we both became more cheerful when Sir William concluded proceedings by producing a whole stilton accompanied by water biscuits in a silver bowl.

After we finished dinner, Sir William cleared the table, dumped the dishes in the sink, and spread out the Scrabble board. Both Flanagan and I were completely routed. Aided by several glasses of excellent claret, Sir William made double our combined score. He was thrilled. Before we were shown to our rooms, Flanagan returned to the subject of the casino. It was his intention, he said, to invite Luigi and Sylvester Mancini to the St Sebastian's University Feast in the second term. This would be a major event in the university calendar and would require an after-dinner speech. 'We'd be honoured if you'd do it,' he said to Sir William.

'Delighted!' said Sir William sweeping up the Scrabble letters. 'Now, let me show you to your rooms.'

I asked if I could borrow Sir William's famous book on card-counting to read in bed. Our host very generously gave it to me. He said he'd already mastered the technique and I was welcome to it. I had a brief fantasy of becoming a brilliant blackjack player and breaking the bank at Monte Carlo. Somehow I felt it would be unlikely.

Then Flanagan and I followed Sir William up a flight of stairs and down a long corridor which led to the other end of the castle. We mounted a futher stone circular staircase up to a landing at the top. The wind continued to whistle and rattle the window-frames. Our rooms were adjoining and looked across open fields. The moon was full and light flooded in. There were no curtains. The bathroom was down the hall.

Sir William gave us instructions how to find our way back to his room for breakfast at eight o'clock sharp. He then said good-night. As I turned on an overhead light, I heard Flanagan curse as he bumped into something. Later, on the way to the bathroom, I ran into him wearing striped red pyjamas and a maroon dressing gown. 'Bloody cold in there,' he said. 'There doesn't seem to be any hot water at all.'

As Harry Gilbert had predicted, the room was bitter, but I filled my two hot water bottles using the electric kettle provided. Once I had got into bed and hugged the bottles for a bit, I felt almost warm enough to sleep. I was just dozing off when there was a knock on my door. Flanagan came in looking dazed. 'I'm sorry Felix mate. I've never been so cold in my life. I've put everything I can on my bed, even the hearth rug, but I think I'm going to die of exposure. D'you think we could wake Sir William and ask for an electric heater or something?'

'You'd probably blow all the castle electrics!' I said. 'Look, Vice-Chancellor,' I said sitting up and pulling one of my hot bottles out from under the covers. 'Perhaps you might like this.'

Flanagan was amazed. 'Where did you find it?' he asked. 'There wasn't one in my room.'

'I've got two. Harry told me to bring them.'

The Vice-Chancellor took a hip-flask out of the pocket of his dressing gown. 'Do you have a tooth glass?' he asked. I gestured towards the bed-side table and he poured me a large measure of whisky. Silently we drank – I from my glass, he directly from the bottle.

Then Flanagan got up to go. 'Thanks, mate,' he said as he stumbled off to his room. 'I won't forget this.'

CHAPTER FIVE

The Depravity of the Clergy

The day after I arrived back from Shropshire, there was a letter waiting for me in my pigeonhole from the Registrar. It was marked Private and Confidential and it looked sinister.

Sloth wrote that it had come to his attention that I had written a highly offensive letter to Joy Pickles about philosophy admissions. He admitted that there had been an oversight. It was regrettable that candidates had had a wasted journey to the university. Nonetheless there was no excuse for the hectoring tone of my letter. Miss Pickles had been extremely upset and had been unable to work for the rest of the day. She was very busy and, as a valuable member of the university administration, she deserved every consideration. If such a letter were ever sent again, I would be facing disciplinary proceedings.

After I received this missive, I went to see Magnus in his room in the Old College. He read the letter and looked concerned. 'You've got to watch out for Sloth,' he cautioned. 'The same thing happened to Harry. Jenny Sloth kept forgetting to order books for the library, so Harry repeatedly contacted her. In the

72

end, she accused him of harrassment and filed a formal grievance: that was the beginning of his troubles.'

I was not pleased. 'So what it comes down to is that Registrar
Sloth's paramours are immune from criticism, however incompetent.'

'I'm afraid so.'

'Perhaps I should apologise and send her a bunch of flowers.'

Magnus was nothing if not realistic. 'I wouldn't think it would
do much good. It would confirm her untouchability and I very
much doubt if she'd even bother to thank you.'

'Oh surely,' I said. 'I cannot imagine Emma or Imogen being
sent flowers, whatever the circumstances, and not writing a nice
thank-you letter.'

'Emma's entirely different,' Magnus pointed out dryly. 'She's
always charming. Joy comes from a different stable. My Aunt
Ursula would say, she has no breeding. Instead of admitting she's
incompetent and trying to do better, she'll just say that flowers
are patronising.'

'You're probably right,' I said, 'but it can't do any harm.' I
took out my mobile telephone, called the florist, and dictated a
friendly apologetic note. Then as Magnus made me a cup of coffee, I recounted the events of my visit to the castle. He roared with
laughter at my tale of the dinner and the sleeping accommodation. At the same time he was appalled by Flanagan's resolve to
have Casino Management in the university.

'It's grotesque!' he said.

I agreed and confessed that I knew nothing about any form of
gambling. I was meant to be the director of this absurd enterprise, but I had never even been inside a bingo hall, let alone a
proper casino. Magnus was ahead of me. As a passenger on the
Queen Christina he was very familiar with blackjack and
roulette, but he admitted that, although there were occasional
sessions on the ship, he had never tried bingo.

'Why don't we all go to the St Sebastian's bingo hall this
Saturday?' he suggested. 'That's the nearest thing this town has
to a gambling den and Emma might enjoy it.'

I promised that I would suggest it at home, but as it happened,
Emma was busy finishing the script of a programme about
Christmas cakes from around the world. She was delighted with

the idea of having the house to herself and she encouraged me to go on the expedition without her.

That Saturday I picked up Magnus from his flat at six and drove into the town. We got lost several times, but eventually we found what we were looking for. Located at the end of a dark lane in the industrial area, Bishop's Bingo and Amusements Casino was a two-story building with crude red, yellow and green neon lights. In large letters the words '!WIN, WIN, WIN!' flashed unceasingly. I had some difficulty in finding a place to park and I was convinced that we would be mugged before the end of the evening, but in the event we arrived inside safely.

In the entrance hall was a row of multi-coloured slot machines with more flashing lights. Several elderly women sat on red velvet stools pushing coins into them. There seemed to be no skill involved. They just kept feeding the money in; they scarcely looked at the dials and they pushed a button mechanically. Then occasionally there was a loud rattle and a cascade of coins came out. I thought that that would be the moment to get up and walk away with the winnings, but I noticed no one did this. They just had more coins to put into the slot.

Behind the reception desk was a white-haired woman in a red velvet uniform with a picture of a Bishop's mitre on the pocket.

'Are you here for the first time?' she asked.

We both nodded sheepishly. 'I'm afraid we don't know what to do,' I confessed.

'You'll need to be members,' she announced taking a wad of papers from under the counter. 'Fill in your names and addresses,' she said. 'And then we'll send you out membership cards.' I had not realised that we were going to have to join a club, but apparently there was nothing to fear. Membership was not selective. There was no nominating, seconding, voting or blackballing. Magnus grinned as he completed his application. 'Perhaps we ought to make Harry a member too,' he suggested. 'Could we have another form please?'

The woman looked at Magnus quizzically and handed over a third form. 'Is your friend coming tonight?' she asked.

'No,' Magnus said. 'But I'm sure he'll want to play some time in the future.'

I was mystified. I thought it highly improbable that Harry Gilbert, Distinguished Professor of Christian Ethics at Sweetpea College, Virginia, would ever voluntarily visit such an establishment. 'It's for his *Who's Who* entry,' said Magnus. 'You list what clubs you belong to at the bottom and you must admit that "Bishop's Bingo, St Sebastians" would look terrific besides the "Acropolis, London".'

I saw his point. 'Now what do we have to do?' I asked the cashier.

She produced two books of tickets with numbers on them. 'Now these are the local bingos,' she said. Then she took out another long strip of paper out of the drawer. 'This one is for the National. That's the really big prize.' She greeted an old lady with dyed golden hair who had just come up to the counter. 'This is Betty,' she said. 'She won a share of the National last week – thirty five thousand pounds it was.'

Betty grinned at us. She purchased a book of tickets and went off humming.

'Bloody Hell,' Magnus mumbled. 'We've got to come here more often. There's a fortune to be made.'

'I should think the odds are heavily stacked against winning a big prize,' I said. 'And, after all, the tickets aren't cheap.' Between us we had parted with more than sixteen pounds to acquire all our pieces of paper.

Then we went into the main hall which was plush with red velvet. The room was divided into small tables at which the players sat and there was a food counter in the corner. The manager wore an ill-fitting dinner jacket and had a gold earring in one ear. He seemed a jolly fellow. We were clearly early and he was preparing plates of rather tired looking salad for his staff.

Magnus and I looked at the tickets with boxes and had no idea what to do. We discussed the various possibilities, but even though we had had thirteen years of higher education between us we could come to no firm conclusion. Mercifully one of the staff saw our bewilderment. She handed us two fibre tip pens, and explained the rules. Magnus got into a muddle over the difference between a Line and a House, but once this difficulty was sorted out, we both felt fairly confident.

We decided we should sample the food. At the sandwich counter an elderly waitress with only two bottom teeth served us very cheap, very nasty, cheese and onions rolls and crisps. The accompanying weak tea was free. 'It's not quite like the casinos in the James Bond films,' remarked Magnus. 'There doesn't seem much chance of a dry martini, stirred, but not shaken.'

Then we had a surprise. At one of the tables in the corner, we saw two familiar figures. 'That's Mrs Brush, the Theology department cleaner,' I said. 'And isn't that other lady old Mrs Catnip, Wanda's mother? She was at the chapel service, remember.'

Mrs Brush smiled and waved for us to join them. We picked up our food and made our way between the tables. 'I've never seen you here before, Dr Glass,' she said.

'We've never been before,' I explained. 'This is our first time.'

'Well, well! This is Mrs Elsa Catnip. Professor Catnip's mother.'

Elsa Catnip wore a purple woolly hat and a hand-knitted mauve cardigan. She smiled when I said that I thought she had spoken to my daughter Imogen after the chapel service. 'Oh yes,' she said, 'a very nice young lady.'

I said that Imogen was disappointed that the conversation had ended so quickly, but that I understood Wanda had wanted to go home. Old Mrs Catnip suddenly looked tired. 'Wanda's very clever, you know, like her father was. She does get a bit impatient.' Then she got up from her seat. 'Before we start,' she said, 'I like to have a look at the blackjack table.'

Gesturing to a corridor alongside the stage, she told us that it was next door and she slowly made her way through the little tables.

When she was out of earshot, Mrs Brush told us about her new friend. 'Poor dear,' she began. 'She does miss Leeds. But that Professor Catnip insisted she come live with her. She can't really do for herself any more – she's eighty-five you know.' I realised this must be about right. If Wanda Catnip was nearly sixty, it was likely that her mother would be in her mid-eighties.

Mrs Brush was relishing the chance for a gossip. 'What Elsa really wanted was to sell her house in Leeds and move into a local old people's home. She had several friends there already and was looking forward to a nice rest. But that daughter of hers wasn't having it.'

'Why would she be against her mother moving into a residential home?' I asked. My mother would have been only too thankful if her parents-in-law had made a similar decision. Instead they had insisted on remaining in the flat in Battersea which brought all sorts of complications of nurses and care arrangements.

'I don't know,' Mrs Brush shook her head. 'Elsa won't say, but I think it's because Professor Catnip doesn't want to lose that house. It's worth a small fortune now and of course it would have to be sold to pay for the home. Well, you know how bossy Professor Catnip is. She likes her own way. She insisted that the house was closed up and that Elsa came to live with her. Between you and me, she treats her like dirt. Elsa has quite a good little pension – but now she gives it all to her daughter. The Professor gives her mother twenty pounds a week for a night out at the bingo, but that's the only treat she has. It's a shame!'

Mrs Brush stopped for a moment and then she took another breath. 'You know,' she said, 'when she was Dean at the university, I had to clean her room. She was a real tartar, always complaining about this or that. One time she even went to the Registrar to say that I skimped my work. Me! I'd never had a complaint before in twenty years! I'm really sorry for Elsa. I met her at bingo and when she let slip who she was, I've tried to be her friend.'

'It sounds as if she needs one,' said Magnus.

Mrs Brush smiled and then looked at her watch. The bingo was about to start. She made as if she were about to go next door to fetch Mrs Catnip, but I volunteered. I was eager to see the casino part of the establishment.

The room was much the same size as the bingo hall and was decorated in the same red velvet. The walls were lined with a series of multi-coloured slot machines. At the far end there was a large roulette wheel operated by a skimpily-dressed blond. Nearby were two blackjack tables. I expected to find Mrs Catnip by the slot machines, but she was standing behind a seedy-looking middle-aged man who was the only blackjack player. In front of him were three stacks of chips in different colours. Mrs Catnip was watching intently and shaking her head. I told her that bingo was due to start. She heaved a sigh and followed me back into the main hall. 'You know, dear,' she said as we passed through the corridor, 'blackjack is far more interesting than bingo. It's not just luck – there's skill in it. That poor man didn't have a clue. I often think I could do very well at it myself . . . I've always had a good memory . . .' and she pottered back to her seat next to Mrs Brush.

Once we understood the rules, neither Magnus nor I found bingo very challenging as a game. But I could understand its appeal. The hall was warm and cosy and everyone was friendly and welcoming. A lonely old age pensioner might well find the atmosphere comforting and there was always the possibility of winning something. Having said that, I was astonished at how much some of the old dears were spending. Many were doing twelve lines of numbers at every game (neither Magnus nor I felt equal to more than six). They participated in every bingo of the evening. Many also smoked fairly continuously and drank several pints of beer. Still it was not for me to judge. I asked Mrs Brush how much an evening could cost a couple and she thought for some of them there would be no change from fifty pounds. Initially I was shocked by this, but as Magnus pointed out, Emma and I would certainly spend that amount if we went to the theatre in London.

For all our efforts, neither Magnus nor I won anything, but old Mrs Catnip did win a line in one of the games and pocketed forty pounds. She, for one, had made a profit from the evening. She was pleased with her win, but was a little anxious I would tell Wanda. I promised faithfully that I would do no such thing. In fact I was not sure that I would confess to any of my colleagues how I had spent my evening.

The next couple of weeks were uneventful. Mrs Brush was particularly chatty whenever we met in the corridor. Bingo had formed a bond. My remaining philosophy classes were going very well and I was reluctantly setting up the new programme in Casino Management. The first necessity was obtaining planning permission to demolish the old squash courts and build a training casino. I had several sessions with the council planning officer, who was already on drinking terms with Flanagan. I did not need to point out that the new venture would provide jobs for local people and inject more cash into the economy – he informed me of these points himself. I felt fairly confident that there would be no objections to our plans.

I was also in correspondence with the Vice-Chancellor's childhood friend, Sylvester Mancini. He was very keen on the proposed partnership between the Mancini training school in Las Vegas and the new degree programme in Casino Management at St Sebastian's. I found it hard to pin him down as to the precise existing syllabus of the training school, but I was overwhelmed to receive a very lavish invitation. Emma and I were asked to stay in the family's fanciest hotel over the New Year. It appeared that this was an especially festive time in Las Vegas. It was to be an all expenses paid trip – first-class flights, limousines to the airport and I was assured we would be the Mancinis' most honoured guests. Sylvester was sure we would enjoy ourselves.

I had reservations about all this. I thought it was improper because there might be a conflict of interest somehow. However, the Vice-Chancellor gave me no choice. He and Helga had had a similar invitation for the late spring and they were certainly going. Magnus expressed his unadulterated envy.

'You'll have a splendid time! It'll be even grander than my Christmas voyage on the Queen Christina and, believe me, that's glitzy enough! Of course, it's even better for you. You don't have to dance with hoardes of ancient American ladies, Emma'll protect you. But there again, you'll miss out on all the presents!' We were sitting in the Senior Common Room when we were having this conversation. Magnus sighed nostalgically and took from his pocket an elegant gold cigarette case which had been a tribute from one of his many admirers. He kept a good supply of mints in it and he offered me one.

'Still,' he continued, 'you'll have to do some gambling. How are you getting on with Sir William's infallible system of blackjack?'

It was true that for several days after our excursion to the bingo hall, I had struggled with Sir William's book on card counting. Entitled *How to Win at Blackjack in Ten Easy Lessons*, it was written by one Ernest Ripper, PhD. Although I was fairly conversant with the various thories of chance, Dr Ripper's system defeated me. After I read the first chapter, I realised that it was a practical course so I bought several decks of cards to try to work out the combinations. It made no difference. The technique seemed to depend on having a photographic memory. You needed to know exactly which cards had been played and which remained. As someone who believed in working things out by logic, I was hopeless at it.

Magnus was no better. He kept the book for a week and ended up pronouncing that the technique was even more difficult than learning ancient Cuneiform. How, we wondered, did Sir William do it? One afternoon, Magnus came for tea and biscuits in my office. I took out the pack of cards and we played several hands. If anything Magnus was worse than I was. I persevered for another two days, but in the end I was frustrated by the whole exercise.

One morning I waylaid Mrs Brush in the corridor.

'Are you still seeing Mrs Catnip at bingo?' I asked.

'Oh yes,' said our cleaning lady, 'and a dreadful state she's in too. She misses her Leeds friends more and more, and that Professor Catnip gives her no peace at home. Nag, nag, nag, she is! She doesn't say much, but I can read between the lines. It's wrong, that's what it is!'

'Well,' I tried to soothe Mrs Brush's indignation, 'I have a little present for her. I understand she's interested in cards and I thought she might like this book on blackjack.'

Mrs Brush looked doubtful, 'Oh I don't think she could ever afford to play blackjack . . . still, you're right. I know she's interested. She always wants to go and look at the tables. It's very kind of you Dr Glass. I'll make sure she gets it; I'll be seeing her tonight.'

The next day, Mrs Brush delivered a note to me. Elsa Catnip must have bought the stationery in the bingo hall. It read:

Dear Dr Glass,

Thank you very much for thinking of me and giving me the book on cards. I have always enjoyed games and I will study it carefully. Perhaps it will make my fortune! I am very grateful for your kind thought,

Yours sincerely, Elsa Catnip.

The card had a pretty flower design, the writing was old-fashioned copperplate and the spelling was impeccable. There was no doubt that Elsa Catnip was a woman of style. Of course Magnus had been right about Joy Pickles. There had been no acknowledgment of my flowers, though the shop assured me that they had been delivered. I had not been forgiven and Joy Pickles had no manners.

During this period I also continued to try to establish contact with my new theology colleagues. As I had feared, however, the scene I had witnessed between the Vice-Chancellor and John Pilkington had not improved our relationship. My departmental chairman now made it clear that not only was I an unbelieving Jew, I was also to be numbered among the loose-livers and gamblers. Whenever I came to sit near him with my lunchtime sandwich, he would look at me as if I were a leper. Then he would make an excuse and leave. My other theological colleagues observed his disapproval and were soon following his example.

I also did not improve my standing in the department when I refused to double-mark some Korean essays. Apparently part of the syllabus of the Reverend Kwan Christian College of Seoul was philosophy of religion. Consequently I was told that one of my responsibilities was to moderate the students' essays in this subject. One day a heap of eighty dissertations in Korean appeared in my pigeonhole. Accompanying them was the usual university mark sheet neatly filled in by the Kwan College teachers with some very creditable marks. It was my role to check a sample of the essays to make sure I agreed with the assessments.

Unfortunately a knowledge of Korean is not among my accomplishments. I telephoned Pilkington to ask him what I was supposed to do. He said I must do as everyone else did. I was mystified. He told me that until the department managed to find a Korean translator, we had no choice but to confirm the original marks. It was just a matter of putting a tick beside each entry on the mark sheet and signing my name at the bottom. I asked when he expected to appoint an interpreter. There was a long pause. It appeared that the department had many other pressing things on which to spend its money and a Korean interpreter was by no means the first priority at present.

I was appalled. I did not say anything on the telephone. Instead I put all the essays in a very large envelope and sent them back to the departmental secretary, Wendy Morehouse. I included a note pointing out that, due to my linguistic deficiency, I was not qual- ifed to check the asseessments. Formally I heard no more of the matter, but Magnus told me that he had overheard Pilkington describe it to Wendy as 'typically unhelpful behaviour.'

I was not the only person to be rejected by the Theology department. Our new dean, Patricia Parham, was also not popu- lar. Initially I thought this was because she had defeated Pilkington in the Deanship election, but Magnus indicated to me that there was also strong disapproval of Patricia's personal lifestyle. Same-sex relationships were condemned in the Old Testament in the Book of Leviticus and the St Sebastian's theolo- gians believed that nothing had changed in the three thousand years since the Bible was written.

Patricia did not seem to mind their attitude. Indeed she was rather amused. One lunchtime she joked to me that the disap- proval of Pilkington was the one thing that she and Father Chantry-Pigg shared in common. It was certainly hard to think of any other quality. Our new chaplain remained pompous, humorless and self-important while Patricia was funny, straight- forward and pleasant to everyone. The friar was still to be seen round the building with his entourage of obsequious young men. He had even brought a group of them into the Senior Common Room for a meeting. Pilkington had told him very sharply on that occasion that students were not permitted there. Chantry- Pigg had not repeated the experiment.

One day Patricia told me that her partner Judith had started spending one evening a week volunteering at the Women's Refuge. She had heard from the woman in charge that my daughter Imogen was intending to write her undergraduate thesis on battered women and would be working in the Refuge herself over Christmas. I confirmed that this was the case and we agreed that there was no excuse whatsoever for domestic violence. Magnus was rather sceptical when I told him about this conversation. After all, he maintained, he had been battered by Judith, but I said that I thought that that was rather different.

There was one person, however, who seemed to be thriving under the new regime. At the start of term Jenny Sloth, the Registrar's rejected wife, was very tearful and miserable. She had always been hopeless at her job in the library. She was responsible for ordering books, but this was a task that was rarely done. Indeed it used to be said that solely because of Mrs Sloth's inadequacy, the library was the only area in the university that consistently underspent its budget. Registrar Sloth's desertion had not improved her performance.

By November, things had changed. I had ordered new books for my Kant class. As a matter of form, I emailed Jenny a couple of times to remind her, but, just as I was about to formulate the third tactful missive, I had a note from her that they had arrived. I was astonished. I made a point of going over to the library to thank her and I found her looking very smart. Her hair had been freshly dyed and waved. Her clothes were flattering to her figure and looked new. Something had happened.

I remarked that she was looking very well and she smiled, 'It makes all the difference to be appreciated.'

'Oh?' I said.

'I've just been appointed Trustee of the Chapel. Father Chantry-Pigg says he very much approves of my choice of prayers and hymns. Of course, I always try to pick his favourites. He works so hard and he's such a wonderful man. The chapel has completely changed since he's been here.'

'How splendid.' I tried to enter into her enthusiasm. 'You must be working with all those nice young men who seem to hang around there. I'm sure you help them a lot.'

'They're very nice boys,' said Jenny defensively. 'I know people have the wrong idea about them and Father Crispin,' she blushed a little, 'but it's completely untrue. They just don't know him as I do . . .'

I was curious about this conversation. It seemed that Jenny Sloth did not share the general belief in Chantry-Pigg's homosexuality. She was certainly besotted by him. On the other hand, the man was almost a caricature of the kind of gay Anglo-Catholic priest portrayed in novels. He had all the qualifications – the sense of superiority, the arrogance, the little in-jokes and the flurry of effeminate disciples. Well, I thought to myself, love is blind.

Consequently I was very surprised one rainy afternoon when I called in to see Magnus. While we were chatting, there was a knock on the door. It turned out to be Mary, my philosophy student and she looked as if she had been crying. 'I hoped I'd find you with Dr Hamilton,' she said. 'I'm sorry to bother you, but I do need to talk to someone. Are you busy?' Rosalind stood behind her in the doorway and both girls looked anxious.

'Do you want to see me, too?' I said. 'Is it private?'

The girls came into the room. I noticed that they were both well brought up and averted their eyes from Magnus's phallic statue. They sat down together on the sofa. 'We're so thankful to find you together,' Rosalind said. 'You both teach us and we thought we'd be able to tell you what's happened.'

Mary blew her nose as Rosalind explained. 'Mary was in the vestry with Father Chantry-Pigg,' she said, 'and he tried to kiss her. He lunged at her from behind.'

'Oh dear,' I said.

'Well, Mary didn't intend to do anything about it. She doesn't want to cause trouble. But it just isn't right. He's the chaplain. And he's always going on about chastity and virginity and all that . . . Anyway, you're our teachers and we thought you'd know what to do.'

Mary started crying again. 'It's all my fault. Normally I'd be careful about being by myself in a closed place with a man. But you don't expect it from a friar in his habit and anyway he always shows much more interest in the boys than in the girls. I always thought he was . . .' She was embarrassed and stopped.

'You always thought he was gay?' Magnus asked gently.

Mary nodded. Magnus and I looked at each other. 'Listen, Mary, Rosalind,' I said, 'you were absolutely right to come to see us. But I'm afraid there may be a problem. You see, Father Chantry-Pigg will in all likelihood deny that anything happened. So it would be Mary's word against his. There was nobody else there, was there?'

'No,' Mary sniffed. 'The other members of the choir had just gone. I had volunteered to collect the music and put it back. I knew he was in the vestry with me, but I didn't think anything of it. Anyway, just as I had finished, he came behind me and grabbed me. He was quite rough. I thought maybe he was pulling me away from some falling books or something, but when I turned around, he tried to kiss me. I really had to squirm and push to get away from him.' She lapsed into tears again. Rosalind patted her shoulder and looked appealingly at us both.

Mary took a deep breath. 'Anyway I managed to get away and I ran out of the room. I just don't understand it. He doesn't like me.'

'How do you know that?' asked Magnus.

Mary smiled rather damply. Rosalind took up the story. 'She corrected him after one of his sermons. He said that the pre-Socratic philosopher Parmenides taught that the world was in a state of constant flux. Well we knew from your Introduction to Philosophy course, Dr Glass, that it wasn't Parmenides, it was Heraclitus. Parmenides said the opposite. We thought he'd want to know. I had to see someone after the service, but Mary went up to him and told him,' she giggled.

'He was furious,' said Mary. 'He didn't even thank me. He just said something like "Oh detail, detail!" and stormed off.'

Magnus had been listening intently as Mary told her tale. 'Dr Glass is right,' he pronounced. 'The problem is that Chantry-Pigg will deny the whole thing if you confront him. Ultimately it's your word against his and in this country you are innocent until you are proven guilty.'

'But he can't get away with it,' Rosalind objected. 'And he'll do it to other girls.'

'I shouldn't think Mary is his first victim,' pointed out Magnus.

Mary and Rosalind looked at each other. 'A couple of girls have dropped out of the choir already,' they said.

Magnus explained how the grievance procedure worked. 'The university authorites are obliged to investigate any student complaint. But they will decide that you simply don't have any proof. It isn't even as if you can go to Clifford Maxwell or someone and threaten to sell your story to the newspapers. Even the tabloids won't take a story without firm evidence. They're too frightened of an expensive libel action.'

'Who's Clifford Maxwell?' Rosalind asked.

'He's a famous publicist,' I told her. 'Believe it or not I was at school with him. He makes millions for his clients because the newspapers love juicy scandals. They'd adore your story . . . I can just see the headlines – "Frisky Friar's Fornicating Fun". But without definite proof that you're telling the truth, even the most scurrilous rag won't take the risk. And St Sebastian's University certainly won't.'

'But you believe us, don't you?'

'Yes,' I said, 'I do.'

'Anyway,' Magnus cut in, 'the only thing you can really learn from this is not to be alone in a room with Chantry-Pigg. That's my advice.'

'I wish we could help more,' I said.

When Mary and Rosalind had left, Magnus snorted. 'Well, well, our holy friar isn't as chaste as he pretends. Could have fooled me. I thought he preferred choirboys.'

'You don't think there's anything we can do?' I asked.

'Nope. Chantry-Pigg will deny everything. And blame the girls. Better to keep quiet.'

'I do feel sorry for Mary.'

'Rosalind is quite tough, I think.'

'But she wasn't the one Chantry-Pigg tried to seduce.'

'Of course not. No doubt he chooses his victims carefully. Anway, it's not really about sex. It's about power.'

'What do you mean?'

'Mary's an attractive girl. But she challenged the friar – that business about the pre-Socratic philosopher showed him up. And he didn't like it. So he tried to humiliate her.'

'But he tried to kiss her,' I objected.

'Yes, but he terrified her. He wanted to show her who was boss. Sexual harassment is a form of bullying. I've read about it.'

'How do you know about this, Magnus?'

'Really, Felix. You're as bad as Harry Gilbert. You both know a lot about philosophy and ethics. But neither of you has a clue about human beings.'

That afternoon I had promised to do some shopping for Emma before I went home. I was standing in the queue in the delicatessen when I saw Chantry-Pigg's housekeeper, Danielle Bousset. I had not bumped into her since we had met at the inaugural service in the university chapel. After what I had heard from Mary and Rosalind, I was embarrassed to come in contact with her again, but I was fascinated by her purchases. She was asking for a half-kilo of their best smoked salmon, a small jar of beluga caviar and a bottle of the most expensive balsamic vinegar. The bill was more than a hundred and fifty pounds.

I turned away as she passed and hoped she did not notice me. I really did not want to have a chat. How could a friar, who was vowed to poverty afford to eat like that?

When I arrived home, I was curious to know more about our new chaplain. I turned on my computer, went to Google, and typed in his name. There were over a hundred and fifty entries, mostly dealing with his pamphlets on clerical dress. I could find no references to money, sexual irregularities or harassment.

Then it struck me that there might be something about Danielle Bousset. To my astonishment there were more than eight thousand entries. Most seemed to be connected with Jacques Bousset, the film director who had won many prizes for his *En Bon Point*. It seemed that Jacques had been married to a woman named Danielle. There had been an acrimonious divorce and the French newspapers had been full of it. Since there was a more famous Danielle Bousset, there seemed little chance of my finding out anything about the chaplain's housekeeper from the internet and I was about to turn the machine off.

Then I caught sight of a photograph. It was illustrating one of the more lurid articles and it was of the same woman who had stood before me in the queue in the St Sebastian's delicatessen. There was no doubt about it. Chantry-Pigg's housekeeper was the ex-wife of Jacques Bousset.

I turned back to the Google list of articles. Finally I picked one in English from a respectable magazine. It was a lengthy biographical study of Mrs Jacques Bousset. Apparently Danielle had been a student in Paris which was where she had met her husband. At that stage he had been a young, avant-garde film director.

Rejecting the nihilism of French existentialism, Danielle became a devout Roman Catholic. She trained as a radiographer and supported her husband financially for twenty years while he directed several unimpressive films. There had been no children. Danielle had longed for them and her religion forbade contraception, but Jacques would not hear of it. He said he was dedicated only to his art. Then came his most famous film – *En Bon Point*. It was wildly successful at the Cannes Film Festival and ultimately won the Oscar in Hollywood for the best foreign language film.

It was the end of the marriage. While Bousset was shooting the film, he was having an affair with the 21-year-old star. By the time Danielle found out, the girl was pregnant and Jacques was demanding a divorce. Despite her deep resistence, Jacques had little difficulty in persuading the Roman Catholic authorities to grant an annulment to the marriage on the grounds of Danielle's supposed unwillingness to have children. He had also done his best to argue that the marriage was over before he had started shooting the film and that therefore she was not entitled to any of the proceeds.

At that point she had gone to the courts. Numerous friends testified that the fundemental idea behind *En Bon Point* was hers. They told of Jacques' cruelty, his neglect of his wife and the real story of their childlessness. Even in the world of movies, it was a major scandal. In the end, the French divorce courts gave her a very generous settlement. There was no doubt that Danielle Bousset was a very rich woman. So here was the explanation. The house in Winchester Close must belong to her. She did not need to make money from her tenant and she could afford to conduct housekeeping on a very lavish scale. But how had she met Chantry-Pigg? Why was she willing to do this for him? What exactly was their relationship? And what did the order of friars feel about all this? I could find no answers to these questions on the internet.

I printed out the article and phoned Magnus. He was still in his office. 'You won't believe what I've discovered,' I said. 'Danielle Bousset, Chantry-Pigg's housekeeper, is the ex-wife of Jacques Bousset, the famous film director.'

'Never heard of him.'

'He directed *En Bon Point*,' I said.

'Oh I went to see that with Harry.' Magnus was interested. 'He loved it. He's always been sensitive about his weight and a film about the sexiness of fat men was just his cup of tea!'

'You're missing the point,' I said rather desperately. 'She's loaded. That's why Chantry-Pigg can live in such a grand house. It must belong to Danielle.'

There was a pause. 'It's hard to imagine they're lovers . . . what do you think?' Magnus asked.

'I don't know, Magnus. It's a mystery.'

'I wonder what she sees in him,' Magnus pondered.

'Well, he's religious. Maybe that's what she needed after Bousset.'

'Skinny, pompous, self-important and phoney,' said Magnus. She can't possibly need that. That man shouldn't be living in a luxury house. He ought to be defrocked and drummed out of his order.'

We had given our best advice to Mary and Rosalind. There was nothing to be done about Chantry-Pigg's behaviour and I tried to forget the incident. Then one afternoon a week later, as I was marking essays, there was a knock on my door. Both girls asked if they could see me. 'You might want to contact Dr Hamilton,' Rosalind said triumphantly. 'We've got something to show you.' I phoned Magnus and he agreed to come over – he had just finished his Hebrew class and said he needed a drink.

When he arrived, I put on the kettle, but he indicated that something stronger was required. I poured him a glass of sherry and offered the same to the students. 'So what's the news?', he asked.

Rosalind pulled a small tape-recorder out of her bag and put it on my desk. 'You said we needed evidence. So we got some.' She then turned it on and we listened to a muffled conversation beginning with a female shriek.

Then there was a rather noisy kiss. 'Father Crispin,' came Mary's outraged voice, 'I don't think you ought to do that . . .' There was the sound of clothes being ruffled and another louder shriek. 'Please, Father Crispin, don't do that . . .' pleaded Mary's voice.

Then it was Chantry-Pigg's turn. 'Don't be silly, you know you want it, you know you do . . . Stop wriggling! Do what you're told!' There was another confused sound, perhaps of a chair falling over and the sound of running. In the background, Chantry-Pigg could be heard roaring: 'Come back, you stupid little bitch . . .'

Mary dissolved into tears. 'He was horrible,' she said.

Rosalind put her arm round her friend. 'You were really brave!' She patted her shoulder and looked at us, 'We've got him, haven't we? They'll have to believe us.'

Magnus nodded. 'Yes,' he said. 'That's pretty conclusive. What do you want us to do?'

'We don't know. What does happen next?'

'Well,' I said, 'I think the best course of action is to see the Vice-Chancellor. Do you want me to go as your teacher?' I asked.

The girls nodded. They handed over the cassette tape, finished their sherry and left. I promised I would tell them the outcome.

The next day I made an appointment to see Flanagan. He had several meetings, but said I could come for five minutes. When I arrived, he had a stack of books on his desk about gambling as well as a travel guide to Las Vegas. 'This is for you mate,' he said handing me the guidebook. 'Sylvester's excited about your visit.' Unlike me, Flanagan was entirely committed to the enterprise. On his desk was a miniature roulette wheel with the Mancini logo.

'Vice-Chancellor,' I said. 'I've got to talk to you about something serious.'

'Yes, yes. Now I've been in touch with the planning officer. There's not going to be any trouble about the squash courts and I want to talk to you about the interim arrangements for the Great Hall . . . .'

'No, Vice-Chancellor, it's nothing to do with Casino Management. It's about Father Chantry-Pigg.'

Flanagan changed gear. 'What's the problem with that windbag?' he asked.

'You need to hear this.' I took out the tape recorder. 'He's molested one of my students, a young woman. She came to me to complain. I said that there was nothing to be done. Although I believed her, I pointed out that he would deny it and it would be her word against his. Anyway, he tried again and this time she was carrying a tape recorder. The evidence is quite conclusive. Do you want to hear it?'

All of a sudden, Flanagan looked ten years older. He shrunk in his seat, but he nodded his head. I played the damning evidence.

'Play it again,' he demanded as soon as I turned it off. We listened a second time and he shook his head. 'I'm sorry Felix. This is all too reminiscent of my childhood. There's nothing you can't tell me about the depravity of the clergy. I experienced it all first-hand.' Then he brightened. 'Well at least I can get rid of this bastard.'

He thought for a minute. 'It must be completely water-tight. According to the university statutes, in cases like this I have to set up an investigative panel presided over by the Visitor.'

'But the Visitor is the Provost of the cathedral. He'll support Chantry-Pigg.'

'He can't. Not with that evidence. Then Chantry-Pigg must have his immediate line-manager. That's the Trustee of the Chapel, that stupid sheila Jenny Sloth. She'll do what the Provost tells her. Then, to make sure, the third member must be a senior university officer. Let's have Patricia Parham. She's the Dean and she won't stand for any nonsense.'

We both smiled. Flanagan became serious again. 'My secretary will organise a day next week for the hearing. She'll be in touch. Tell your little girl not to worry. She'll have to tell her story, but she can bring in a friend and you should be there too. Tell her that the university will not tolerate this type of behaviour. We're on her side.'

CHAPTER SIX

It was Irremediably Disgusting

The Vice-Chancellor moved fast. Mary and Rosalind had to submit a formal complaint against Chantry-Pigg. This would be accompanied by a transcript of the tape recording of the incident. Father Chantry-Pigg, they declared, had twice made advances to Mary in the chapel vestry. The tape recording was of the second encounter which they submitted as proof of their allegation. They also explained that after both occasions they had met with Magnus and me. As soon as Flanagan received this, he set up the hearing.

As their philosophy teacher and a senior member of the university, I was to be their representative. The Provost, in his capacity as Visitor of the University, would preside and the other members of the panel would be the Dean – Patricia Parham – and the Trustee of the Chapel Committee –Jenny Sloth. The meeting was to be held in the Vestry since this was where the alleged events had taken place. The Vice-Chancellor made it clear that he wanted to be kept informed at every stage.

Chantry-Pigg was asked to respond to Mary and Rosalind's allegation. His defence was a classic. He first outlined in detail his educational background and religious training. He pointed out that he had been a student of the current Archbishop of Cannonbury when the Archbishop had been Principal of Highminster Theological College. He was certain, he stated, that the Archbishop would be willing to write a testimonial on his behalf. During his ordination training, he had been awarded the Anselm medal for a dissertation on the subject of clerical vestments; subsequently he had written a number of pamphlets and learned articles about this sadly neglected topic. Once he had joined his order of friars, he had been appointed spiritual director to the Anglican order of the Little Sisters of the Pyx in Oxford. During his career, he stressed, there had never been a word of complaint against him nor a single hint of impropriety.

After five pages, he turned to his short career at St Sebastian's. He acknowledged that both Mary and Rosalind had been active members of the choir, but he had always been worried about Mary. There was a danger with impressionable young girls, that they became over-enamoured with their pastor. It almost certainly was the expression of a need for a father-figure, which sadly, all too often in these degenerate days, they lacked at home. Mary had made it clear that she was in love with him. She hung about the chapel constantly and always wanted to discuss his sermons. On one occasion she was particularly persistent and insisted on exploring some philosophical detail. He had had no alternative but to rebuff her. No doubt this current complaint was the result of her feelings being hurt on that occasion.

In any event, he insisted, nothing had happened in the chapel vestry. The transcript could only be a forgery. There could be no genuine tape recording of a conversation with Mary, because none had taken place.

Mary was incensed by this defence. As it happened, she came from a very secure loving home and she lived with both a mother and a father. In any event, Chantry-Pigg was telling one lie after another. She was very distressed to discover that a clergyman could be so dishonest. As she said to me, 'I don't see how I can ever go inside a church again. I will never be able to trust the priest.'

On the day of the hearing, I arrived early. I had never been in the vestry before. It was next door to the chapel and shared the

same musty smell. It was panelled in light oak. A modern crucifix hung on the wall over a Victorian flat-top mahogany desk
stacked with papers and an array of prayer-books. In the corner
was a large wooden table surrounded by six chairs that had been
arranged for our meeting. At one end of the table was placed an
old Welsh Eisteddfod throne carved with a dragon and the date
1899. It was intended for the Provost and I wondered how the
university had acquired it.

Just before eleven, Mary and Rosalind arrived. They looked
very smart. Mary had on a dark red sweater and a black skirt;
Rosalind was in an emerald green trouser suit. Both were wearing discreet make-up. Patricia was the next to enter just as the
cathedral bell was striking the hour. She looked as though she
had been working on her car – there was grease on the cuffs of her
denim jacket. Underneath she was wearing a mauve woolly
sweater, slightly grubby blue jeans, and large silver hoop ear-
rings. She was followed by Jenny Sloth, trim in a navy blue suit
and high heels. Jenny did not look friendly.

We assembled ourselves around the table and waited in
silence. It was ten minutes before the Provost and Chantry-Pigg
came in together. The friar was wearing his brown habit and the
Provost was in cassock and dog collar. They had obviously been
in conference together and I began to feel uneasy.

The Provost took possession of the Eisteddfod chair. He
extracted gold-framed spectacles from his top pocket, and he
opened a file that he brought with him. 'Perhaps we should begin
with a prayer,' he intoned. I looked at Patricia who made a face.
He then recited a lengthy invocation in which he asked God to
guide us in judgement. The details escaped me, but he found it
necessary to enlist the help of all the saints in Heaven to look
down on our deliberations.

Chantry-Pigg did not look as subdued as I would have
liked. He sat wrapped in his robe staring at Mary and Rosalind.
The girls were uncomfortable under his gaze. 'Ladies and gentlemen,' the Provost began, 'we are here to examine the complaint
lodged by these two students against the chaplain of this university, Father Crispin Chantry-Pigg. You have before you the
accusation made by these undergraduates and Father Chantry-
Pigg's response. Now before we go any further, I must point out

that in these kind of proceedings, tape recorded evidence is inadmissable. My fellow panellists must wipe from their minds the contents of the transcript which they have received among their papers. Furthermore I must insist that the original tape recording be handed over to me immediately and I will destroy it.'

Mary and Rosalind looked shocked. 'But Provost,' I objected, 'the statement made by these students is based primarily on this tape recording.'

'Tape recordings are notoriously suspect.' The Provost was adamant. 'There is every opportunity for distortion and forgery. How can we know for certain whose voice is on the recording? These girls may have made use of an imposter. I cannot have a man's reputation destroyed on the basis of such unreliable evidence. Now I will not discuss the matter further. That is my ruling on the subject.'

Patricia was not having it. 'I must object,' she interrupted. 'You cannot simply dismiss the tape recording. At the very least, the panel should hear it and be allowed to judge for itself whether it is a recording of a real happening.'

'That is precisely my point, Madam Dean.' The Provost was not going to budge. 'The panel will not hear it. Nor should they consider any transcript of its contents. As I said, tape recordings are inadmissable. There can be no guarantee whose voice is upon them. Therefore I require that the original be handed over to me immediately.'

'But . . .' Rosalind interjected.

'There is no "but", young lady. I tell you quite frankly I am appalled that a privileged young person like yourself should bring such a case against your very distinguished chaplain. It is profoundly unlikely that any friend of the dear Archbishop could behave in the way you have alleged. I believe you have used one of your evil-minded friends to imitate Father Chantry-Pigg. I can only hope you can show the panel better evidence than you have produced so far. I have been assured that the tape recording is a malicious forgery. If this proves to be the case, then in my opinion you and your friend should be expelled immediately from the university. You will have made damaging and potentially libellous charges against a man of God and such behaviour cannot go unpunished. That will be my recommendation to the Vice-Chancellor.'

'I'm sorry, Provost,' Patricia was persistent. 'You appear already to have made a judgement about this case. And we haven't yet had an opportunity to consider it.'

'We are considering it. As chairman, it is my view that the students' accusation is itself under scrutiny. They have offered no proof of what they allege.'

'But they have provided a tape recording of what took place,' I said.

The Provost looked at me with loathing. 'I'm sorry Dr Glass. You are clearly incapable of listening to what I have just said. The evidence you refer to is inadmissable. It must be set aside. It has no place in these proceedings. I cannot expect someone of your background to understand. Of course I have the greatest respect for the Jewish people, but you cannot begin to appreciate what an admirable man you have in Crispin Chantry-Pigg. He comes from a distinguished clerical family. I believe you people do at least recognise the importance of family. He has an impeccable record as a caring and effective pastor. How could I explain to the dear Archbishop that this man's reputation and career was destroyed on the word of two evil-minded young Jezebels. It would be a calumny.'

Without a pause the Provost took out a letter from his file; I could see that there was a gold mitre on the top and the address of the Archbishop's palace. He handed out copies and cleared his throat. 'As you will see, this is the original testimonial for Father Chantry-Pigg when he came to St Sebastian's from no less an authority than the Archbishop himself. Now,' he continued, 'this meeting is not to be adversarial. Both parties shall be given an opportunity to state their case. Then the panel may cross-examine their statements.'

Mary and Rosalind looked shocked. 'But Provost,' Mary said, 'without the tape recording, it is just my word against his.'

'That is true. But you should have known this.'

'But Dr Glass told us that our tape recording was essential to our case. Without it, you won't believe us.'

'Well, that may be. Now, do you have anything to add to what you wrote in your statement?'

Mary's answer was inaudible. She was on the edge of tears. The Provost then turned to Chantry-Pigg. 'And you, Father Crispin, is there anything you would like the panel to hear at this stage?' Chantry-Pigg was not one to lose the opportunity of making a speech. He opened his mouth, but Patricia cut across him.

'Forgive me, Provost,' she said, 'you are deliberately making it impossible for Mary to make a case. I would like to know what evidence you would accept for misbehaviour on the part of the clergy. Would a video be enough? Presumably you would say that it was set up with actors. Would independent witnesses be sufficient? I imagine that unless the Archbishop himself were the source of the testimony, you would not accept it.'

'I am not dealing with theoretical questions, Madam Dean. The point is that these two girls have made a serious accusation against one of God's ministers, but they seem to have no evidence whatsoever for their claims.'

Crispin Chantry-Pigg seemed to have forgotten that it was his conduct which was on trial. He put up his hand, 'Mr Chairman, if I may . . . Obviously it grieves me to hear such a charge. But it is very important that everyone should be allowed to speak. We have not yet heard from my valuable Trustee of the Chapel, Mrs Jenny Sloth. If she might be permitted . . .'

The Provost immediately turned to Jenny. His manner was ingratiating towards her. His tone softened. 'Of course. The admirable Mrs Sloth. What do you think of this sad matter, my dear?'

Jenny was overwhelmed. She blushed and then she looked to Chantry-Pigg for guidance. He smiled reassuringly at her. She turned back to the Provost. 'All I can say, Provost, is that Father Crispin is the most wonderful man. He has done so much for the chapel. I just can't believe that these ungrateful little hussies can bring themselves to tell such lies about him. But of course girls nowadays . . .' She wiped away a tear. It was clear she was think-ing of Joy Pickles. 'Girls nowadays . . . they have no respect for the bonds of sacred matrimony, running about half-dressed, stealing other women's husbands . . .'

I had heard enough. 'I was under the impression that Mr Chantry-Pigg is not married,' I said.

'Nonetheless,' interjected the Provost, 'He is a wonderful addition to our community, and we are indeed grateful to have him here. Thank you for your contribution, Mrs Sloth.'

Patricia was determined to fight to the last. 'I'm sorry, Provost, but I insist that we hear the tape recording and judge for ourselves.'

'I am not going to satisfy your prurient interest, Dr Parham' said the Provost, 'and there is an end of it. The original recording and all copies must be given to me. Now!' He glared at Mary and she meekly handed over the tape recording. 'Thank you. That is the end of the matter. We will hear no more of it.'

Patricia was furious, 'If you refuse to allow us to hear it, then I will formally object to the procedure you have adopted. As Dean of the university, I am totally opposed to this course of action, and I want my objections noted.'

'That is your right, Madam Dean.' The Provost put on his gold spectacles again and read out the regulations regarding the disciplinary procedure. The panel members were to make a recommendation concerning any action to be taken. The majority decision would prevail and there was no appeal against it.

He then asked Jenny Sloth for her view. She said that of course Father Chantry-Pigg was innocent so nothing should be done. She only regretted he had been put through such a horrible experience. Patricia reiterated her objections and said advice must be sought concerning the admissablity of the tape recording. The Provost then said he agreed with Jenny Sloth. Their two opinions consituted a majority. Father Chantry-Pigg was thus exonerated of all charges and it was to go on record that the university authorities had complete confidence in its chaplain.

With that the Provost stood up. He gestured to Chantry-Pigg and Jenny Sloth that they should leave the room with him. Then he turned to Mary and Rosalind. 'I will be recommending to the Vice-Chancellor that your places here should be terminated. You are unworthy to be members of this university,' he declared and with considerable dignity the three of them left the room.

'A bloody disgrace!' Particia snorted. Mary began to cry; Rosalind was furious. 'I don't understand it,' she stormed. 'I thought the university was supposed to protect its students.'

Patricia shook her head. 'I will be going to see the Vice-Chancellor this afternoon,' she said. 'That was a travesty. Don't worry. We're not going to allow anything to happen to you two.'

Partially reassured, the two girls set off in the direction of the Student Union as Patricia and I made our way to the Senior Common Room. We were both stunned. There was still a possibility that Flanagan might intervene. But the Provost, as Visitor of the University, was technically his boss. Probably the most sensible thing would be to concentrate on damage limitation. At least Mary and Rosalind must be protected.

Afterwards I set off for home. I thought I needed to calm down and I did not want to meet my smug theological colleagues in the Senior Common Room. As I walked down the High Street, I passed the Amalfi, our local Italian restaurant. To my astonishment, the Provost, Chantry-Pigg and Jenny Sloth were having lunch at a table in the window. They were laughing and clearly enjoying themselves. Chantry-Pigg was pouring out what looked like a bottle of champagne and the Provost had tucked his napkin into his dog collar and was eating snails. They were too preoccupied with their triumph to notice me.

I was outraged. The moment I arrived in the house, I telephoned the Vice-Chancellor's secretary to make an appointment. She was out, but I left a message on her answerphone. Later in the day I received an email. Patricia Parham had already been in touch and Flanagan wanted to see us both at half-past ten on the following morning. He was due at a Senate meeting at eleven o'clock, but he was able to fit us in briefly beforehand. I then contacted Mary and Rosalind and asked them to come and meet us outside Flanagan's office so we could let them know the outcome of our discussion.

The next morning I started off for the university at ten. As I passed through the cloisters, I saw the Provost on his bicycle heading toward town; his cassock flapped in the wind as he passed through Trinity Gate. He looked as if he did not have a care in the world. I felt murderous, but I tried to remind myself that not all clergy were as appalling as Chantry-Pigg and the Provost. Harry Gilbert was ordained and several of the school chaplains at Westminster had been good, kind men.

I collected my post from my pigeonhole in the Arts Block, and crossed the street. Several of my theology colleagues were standing chatting outside the Old Building; they looked in my direction but made no gesture of recognition. As the cathedral struck the half hour I knocked on the Vice-Chancellor's door. From inside Flanagan shouted: 'Come in Felix.' Patricia was already sitting on the sofa and Flanagan was at his desk playing with his roulette wheel. He gestured for me to sit in the arm-chair.

'I received a note from the Provost,' he said. 'He told me the case was dismissed.'

I nodded. 'It was a disgrace. The Provost refused to hear the tape. He said it was inadmissable evidence. Then he insisted that it be given to him and destroyed. He just wouldn't listen to reason.'

Flanagan nodded. 'Patricia has just told me.' He was icy calm. It was as if he were keeping himself tightly in check. In many ways it was even more disconcerting than when he had lost his temper.

'Look, Vice-Chancellor,' I said, 'there's no way I can accept the result. Nor can Patricia. It's against natural justice. You can't just dismiss evidence. I can't imagine what the Provost was thinking.'

'What exactly did he say?'

'He stated that tape recordings were notoriously unreliable. They could be falsified. He insisted that it probably wasn't even Chantry-Pigg's voice on the tape.'

The Vice-Chancellor snorted. Patricia was pink in the face. 'When I tried to demand that we heard it, he accused me of being prurient.'

'He said that it was a priori impossible that the dear Archbishop could have recommended someone who would behave like that . . .'

'And he called those nice young women evil-minded little Jezebels . . .'

'And he told them that he was going to recommend that they be sent down from the university,' I concluded.

Flanagan stood up. He walked over to the window and looked out in the direction of the cathedral. I could see he was trembling. 'I blame myself.' It was as if he were talking to himself. 'I should have known what would happen. Why didn't I see it?' He turned around and spoke directly to us. 'It was just like that with the Brothers of Mercy. You could never win against them. Whatever the evidence, the authorities refused to believe it. Even today the Church always protects itself.'

As he spoke the colour suffused his face. He was flushed with anger. 'I'm sorry, both of you,' he said. 'But there's nothing we can do. The Provost is the Visitor of the University and the decision of the panel is final.'

'I just don't believe it.' Patricia was determined not to let the matter go. 'Surely there can be an appeal?'

Flanagan shook his head. 'Not if the Visitor is involved.'

'But what about Mary and Rosalind? Surely you're not going to send them down? It would a travesty of justice.'

The Vice-Chancellor seemed to relax. He took a deep breath. 'No,' he said. 'They were never on trial so they cannot be found guilty. If they have not been found guilty, I cannot expel them and that's the end of the matter. You can tell them from me that they are safe. Also warn them to keep out of the Reverend Friar's way. In my experience people like him are extrememly vengeful, but the whole thing will die down in a few days.'

'It's appalling!' Patricia was still incenced.

'Yes it is. If I had my way I'd get rid of that wretched man today, if not yesterday. But I can't, dammit. We must just hope that there are enough other complaints that I can write to the Archbishop some time in the future. Anyway, about those nice little girls, I'll give Pilkington a ring, as head of their department. He must be told that no action can be taken against them whatever the Provost says.' Flanagan sat down at his desk and shoved the roulette wheel to one side – it fell off into his wastebasket and cracked in two. 'Damn,' he said picking up the pieces. 'Damn, damn . . .'

'Perhaps you can glue it back together,' I volunteered.

The Vice-Chancellor picked up the telephone and gestured for us to go. Outside Mary and Rosalind were waiting. Patricia and I took them down to the Junior Common Room, bought them some coffee and explained that they were in no danger. Mary began to cry. Rosalind put her arm round her and made a vow. 'I'll get even with that Chantry-Pigg,' she said, 'if it's the last thing I ever do!' Patricia and I left them there.

Several days later I was working at home; Emma was in the kitchen trying out a new receipe for whisky-baked alaska. The post arrived and she came into my study. 'Look at this,' she said.

It was an invitation from Pilkington to an end-of-term Christmas party. On the front was a nativity scene with glitter. Inside was a pious Christmas greeting and a hand-written note about the date and time of the party. 'Really, Felix,' Emma said passing over the card, 'your colleagues have no taste.'

'Well, I'm not going,' I announced.

'I think you must.'

'But why? After Pilkington's comments about my Jewish background, I really don't see why I should.'

'These are your new colleagues, Felix,' said Emma gently. 'You've got to try to be friendly.'

'It'll be ghastly. I'm telling you.'

'Well, at least Magnus will be going. You can talk to him.'

I picked up the telephone to offer Magnus a lift to the Pilkingtons. He sounded amused. 'Sorry Felix,' he said. 'You and Emma are on your own. I'm just going out to deliver Pushkin to his catsitter.' Pushkin was Magnus's cat. He was famous throughout the university for only eating the most expensive cat food and refusing to use all but the most rarified cat litter.

'I'm off on my cruise in a couple of days' time,' he continued, 'And I have to make sure Pushkin is settled in before I set off. Then it's lobster all the way for me while you'll be getting tinned pineapple and plastic vol-au-vents from Maureen Pilkington!'

Emma was horrified to hear about the food. 'It can't really be like that,' she said, but she cheered up at the thought of Magnus as a gentleman-host on the Queen Christina.

'It's hard to imagine,' she said.

'I understand from Harry and Victoria that he's a fantastic dancer. He's pursued by all the old ladies who want a partner. So he won't be at the party and I won't have anyone to talk to. As a matter of principle, none of the theologians want to have anything to do with me now that I've taken over the casino project and anyway they're furious that they have to do some of my teaching.'

'You can always talk to me.' Emma was comforting. 'Anyway

I'm curious to meet your new colleagues and their wives. So, you'll just have to put up with it.'

'Please, Emma . . .'

'No, Felix,' Emma was unusually firm. 'We're going. After all, you'll have to work with these people in the future.'

I could see there was no escape, so I wrote a note to Pilkington to let him know we were delighted to accept his kind invitation . . .

In the meantime I heard from my publisher that advanced copies of my new book were due. At the beginning of December, six shiny volumes arrived in a large parcel in the post. They looked very nice. The cover was blue with *Kant's Critiques Revisited* in large gold letters. I had been told that only a hardback would appear in the first instance, but no one had mentioned the price. I was astounded to see that the book cost sixty pounds. Who, I wondered, would ever pay that amount? When I phoned my editor to ask about this, he tried to be reassuring. As a scholarly monograph, it was aimed initially for a library sale. If it did well, then they would consider a paperback edition.

I thought Flanagan might like to see my work even though it had nothing to do with casino management and I put a copy in the internal post for him. I also sent one to Pilkington as Head of my department. The Vice-Chancellor's secretary sent me a brief note saying that Flanagan appreciated my kind thought and that he hoped he'd have a chance to read the book during the Christmas holiday. There was no response from Pilkington. In class I mentioned that my latest work had just appeared and that I had given a copy to the library. The students looked pleased, but I doubted if anyone would peruse it.

I knew it was not the kind of volume to appear in an ordinary neighbourhood bookshop. It was not even the kind of work to provoke a reaction in the upmarket Sunday papers. I had been told by the *Journal of Philosophical Studies* that although they intended to cover it, they were at present two years behind with their reviews. There was such complete silence that I felt as if I had spent three years of my life on a project only to have the manuscript dropped in the deepest and remotest area of the Pacific Ocean. It was not an encouraging thought.

Then, just before Pilkington's party, I received an email from Magnus with a photograph. He had gone to Southampton to begin his cruise and he was already sailing the ocean waves In the picture, he was seated in the first-class dining room surrounded by a group of elderly women in glittery costumes. Magnus himself was wearing a dinner jacket with a red bow tie and was slightly out of focus. Accompanying the photograph was a message:

Here I am at the gala first night dinner. These are some of the ladies I told you about. The average age must over eighty. We're just beginning our cruise, so they are still quite sprightly. On my left is the widow of one of the former directors of Shell. Have a look at her ruby necklace – biggest I've ever seen. Unfortunately one of my fellow hosts fell off a ladder before we set sail. He was trying to fix his Sky television dish, so we're one man short and I've got several extra duties. Anyway we've just finished dinner – eight courses, and I'm stuffed! They now want to go off to the casino, and then dancing. I'll need the entire day tomorrow to rest up from the ordeal.

Now, Felix, I've had a thought. You know that Harry has a great friend who's the Bishop of Bosworth. I emailed Harry and asked him to ask Charles (the Bishop) about Chantry-Pigg. Harry says the friar has had quite a checkered career. There was lots of gossip about him and various ladies when he was living with his order. The Church of England rumour is that he was sent to St Sebastian's to get him away from the latest conquest.

Anyway Charles is going to poke the drains to see what else he can dig up. I've also got lots of free time during the day, so I'm going to do some research on the internet about Madame Bousset. I'll let you know what I come up with. Perhaps there might be a little story here for *Private Eye*! Got to go now. I managed to sneak away to the computer room to send you this email. But one of the ladies has just found me and insists that I take her to play roulette. A gentleman-host's life is not a happy one! Lots of love to Emma

Magnus.

On the afternoon of Pilkington's party I went to pick Imogen up from the station. She had permission to leave two days before the end of term to do some research at the Women's Refuge. I was delighted to see her. She was carrying two suitcases, both filled with books; they were so heavy I had difficulty lifting them into the boot.

On her duffle coat my daughter had pinned a badge I had never seen before. It read: WOMEN ON TOP. 'Have you got a spare one of those?' I asked.

Imogen looked puzzled. 'Do you really want to wear one?'

'It's not for me,' I said. 'It's for Magnus on his cruise. I think he's going to need it.'

After Emma and Imogen had greeted each other rapturously, we all sat down and had a cup of tea. Then six o'clock was approaching and it was time to brace ourselves for the Pilkington's annual Christmas party. Neither Emma nor I were certain how everyone would be dressed. I thought it was better to err on the side of conservatism so I climbed into my dark blue corduroy suit and I put on my old college tie. Emma eschewed the garments she would have chosen for a BBC office party and was very sedate in a black silk skirt and a soft cashmere sweater. I hoped we would look like model members of the Theology department.

I drove slowly and reluctantly to the Pilkington residence. It was on a small modern estate on the outskirts of St Sebastian's. By the time we arrived there was already a long line of cars parked in front of the bungalow. One of the department's graduate students opened the door to us and showed us into the open-plan living room. I was curious to see the house and it was very much as I had imagined. The carpet throughout the ground floor was of a beige abstract design and the curtains were of the same neutral shade. The furniture was late 1970s modern and must have been new when John and his wife Maureen had married.

There was no doubt that they were were married. There was a large picture of two youthful-looking Pilkingtons dressed as a bride and groom on the side-board. The kindest thing that could be said of the composition was that the flowers were pretty. Flanking this were several other photographs of our host. In each he was receiving some kind of academic degree from a benign dignitary. There were also pictures of two children, a boy and a girl, at various stages of childhood or adolescence. I looked round the room to see if the originals were present at the party, but, wisely perhaps, they had absented themselves.

In one corner of the room was a mahogany cabinet with a collection of dolls from various parts of the world. There were several book-cases mainly full of organ music and the upholstered armchairs and sofa were of a dark sludge green. Magnus had told me to check on the downstairs lavatory. Apparently Harry Gilbert had always been fascinated that it was knicker-elastic pink and Magnus wanted to be able to report to him that nothing had changed. I thought I had better complete this task early so I made my way through the crowd. I was not disappointed. It was both an extraordinary colour and quite radiantly clean. I almost felt I should recommend it for some television commercial.

All my theological colleagues seemed to be there. I greeted them as I passed. They all smiled wanly, but no one was about to include me in their conversation. Maureen Pilkington, in a neat two-piece mauve costume, was handing out canapes from a large tray; they seemed to be pieces of cheddar and pineapple on orange sticks. In the corner Pilkington was responsible for the dispersal of alcohol. He handed me a glass of anonymous red. I took it into a corner and sipped it. It was irremediably disgusting so, after holding on to it for a few minutes and looking brightly at the assembled company, I left it on top of the book-case and started circulating.

First I went into the kitchen. This was fitted out in beige laminate and on every surface large platters of canapes were waiting to be distributed. I played a game with myself to decide which was the most horrible-looking. There were chipolata sausages on sticks, moist and pink on one side and burnt on the other. There was a large bowl of a mysterious white dip with limp pieces of celery and carrot to dunk into it. On another plate were small vol-au-vents which looked as if they were made of plastic; they were filled with a pink sauce and a very occasional shrimp. Then the pièce de résistance were tinned asparagus spears wrapped in very thin, sweating pieces of ham. I longed to discuss this display with Emma.

On the refrigerator was a poster from the St Sebastian's Methodist Church announcing a Whist Drive. I wondered if Mrs

Brush and old Mrs Catnip would be attending. Then over the kitchen table was a notice board filled with miscellaneous post cards. There was an outside light so I could see the view. Immediately in front of the window was a clothes line, a bar-beque and a small lawn. Over the fence at the end of the grass was another house, precisely like the one I was standing in. I could see someone working in the kitchen opposite.

I knew I had to make an effort. I returned to the living room where Emma was circulating among the wives. She never had trouble at parties. In contrast the husbands stood in small groups clustered against the wall. No one was anxious to talk to me, and I stood for a few moments in front of the French windows by myself. Then I caught sight of Chantry-Pigg. He had just entered the room and before he could be monopolised by Mrs Sloth who was walking purposefully towards him, I intercepted him. He was forced to stop as I blocked his path. He looked disconcerted to see me. His crucifix swung from his belt and his brown habit radiated a slightly spicy smell. 'Lovely party, isn't it?' I said.

'It is indeed,' he intoned and made as if he would move on, but I was determined. 'Have you brought Madame Bousset with you? I was eager to continue a conversation I had with her after your inauguration service.'

The friar looked even more uncomfortable. 'How did you know her name?' he asked.

'She told me when I spoke to her.' I looked at him out of the corner of my eye. I was going to make him guess how much I knew. 'I expect she misses France,' I said, 'England is miserable at this time of year'

'It is indeed!'

'And where does she come from originally?' I persisted.

'I know very little of the former life of my housekeeper,' declared Chantry-Pigg. 'She is, of course, at home, attending to her duties . . .'

'Good heavens,' I said, 'is she still working at a quarter to seven in the evening?' I thought of the enormous divorce settlement Danielle Bousset's lawyer had achieved for her. 'She really is a treasure!'

'She is indeed.' And Chantry-Pigg stepped round me into the welcoming conversational ambit of Mrs Sloth.

I was a little puzzled why Jenny Sloth was at the party. She had no claim to be a theologian; as far as her work was concerned, she was barely a librarian. Presumably the Pilkingtons felt sorry for her in her deserted state and had invited her as an exercise in Christian charity. Or maybe she was a close friend of Maureen Pilkington . . . .

Anyway it was clear that no one was going to talk to me. Surprisingly, Pilkington had abandoned all his reservations about Chantry-Pigg. He greeted him effusively and made sure he was provided with wine and food. There was a great deal of animated conversation and it seemed as if the two had become best friends. I was shocked. I knew that the Vice-Chancellor had told Pilkington about the sexual harassment case. Presumably my Head of Department was so relieved that the friar was not corrupting the young men of the university, he was prepared to overlook his behaviour towards the young women.

I had had enough. Even though we had been there only half an hour, I really did not want to stay any longer and I started looking for Emma. But before I could gather her up, there was a commotion at the front door. There was a blast of fresh air; everyone turned to see what was going on and we heard an Australian bellow of greeting. The Vice-Chancellor had arrived.

Flanagan was wearing an enormous camel-hair coat and was exuding excitement and bonhomie. Behind him trailed Helga. She had abandoned her dark glasses, was heavily made up around her eyes and looked miserable. She was walking with a very slight limp that I had not noticed before. The graduate student who had opened the door relieved them of their coats and Maureen Pilkington came forward and guided them into the room. The Vice-Chancellor took a glass of wine off Pilkington's tray and headed in my direction. 'Felix mate,' he said, shaking my hand, 'I thought I'd see you here. Let's sit on this sofa.' I realised that he had been drinking before he came to the party, but there was no escape. I could feel the entire company looking at us and I wondered what they thought about the scene.

'Well, Felix,' the Vice-Chancellor began, overwhelming me with his alcohol-laden breath, 'I understand you're off to Las Vegas for the New Year. I've just had a letter from Sylvester. He tells me they've booked the top suite for you and your wife at the Ziggurat.'

I leant as far back into the sofa as I could and nodded. Two days previously I had received a letter from the Mancinis with two first-class return air tickets. We were to arrive in Las Vegas on the evening of December 30th. All expenses would be covered for the trip and one of the Mancini staff – a certain Wolfie Goldberg – was to meet us at the airport and take us to the hotel. The first night we were to have dinner with Sylvester himself at his house and we would be given our full programme then.

As I was telling Flanagan about the arrangements, another of Pilkington's postgraduates came over with a plate of selected canapes. They looked even worse than in the kitchen. Flanagan gazed at them and shook his head. 'Looks awful,' he said, 'Just get me another drink, would you mate?' The student scurried away.

'Now Felix, I've several pieces of good news. First of all, I've been in touch with our friend Sir William Dormouse. He tells me that his rich pal – that Porpoise bloke – has arranged for the young artist to do a large portrait of St Sebastian for the Great Hall.'

'Probably the person who painted Harry's wife,' I suggested. 'I saw it when I visited Sir William's daughter and son-in-law in Sweetpea. It was quite something.'

'Quite something is what I'm hoping for,' boomed Flanagan. 'Anyway, he's started work on it already and he'll send it to the university as soon as it's finished.'

'For the casino?' I asked.

'Right! It'll strike all the right notes. A giant St Sebastian pierced with banknotes and golden arrows. Absolutely top-notch for the Golden Arrow Casino! Of course, until we get the squash courts fixed, it'll go in the Great Hall. A good change from all those dull portraits of my illustrious predecessors.'

'What are you going to do with the pictures of the old Vice-Chancellors?' I asked.

'Put them on a bonfire if I had my way.' He saw I looked aghast. 'No, they can go in the Senior Common Room for the time being. Put our colleages off their lunches.' He guffawed loudly. I was very aware that everyone in the room was listening to the conversation.

'Anyway,' I said, 'they'll all go back to the Great Hall when the new casino is ready.'

'Oh no they won't.' Flanagan was in full flow. He looked around for Pilkington. 'John, you need to hear this . . . and get me another drink, would you?'

The graduate student appeared as if by magic and another glass of red wine was put in the Vice-Chancellor's hand. John Pilkington came over and Flanagan looked up. 'I've got some very good news. I've just heard from a friend on the local council that the university has been awarded a licence to perform civil marriages and commitment ceremonies. That's where the money lies nowadays. From now on the Great Hall will be given over to that purpose.'

There was a stunned silence in the room. The Great Hall was the glory of the university. All important lectures and dinners were held there. It gave our students a small glimpse of the traditional university experience. They could imagine they were back in a time when students were undergraduates, when the term was for tutorials, the vacations for reading parties and no one even thought of supporting themselves with a part-time job. In the Great Hall even the staff could enjoy the illusion that they were scholars in a university, not wage-slaves striving after targets in an education factory.

The Vice-Chancellor was impervious to the sensation he had caused. 'I heard there's a shortage of marriage venues in the St Sebastian's area, now the Church no longer has a monopoly.' He looked spitefully at Chantry-Pigg. 'We think that we'll be able to clean up. We'll do as many as four or five ceremonies a week. If the couple want religion, they can always use the chapel and our caterers will do the wedding breakfasts. It's a winner, a real little earner . . .'

The whole party stood like statues. Then Chantry-Pigg cleared his throat. 'With all due respect, Vice-Chancellor, you seem to be taking the sacrament of marriage very lightly . . .'

Flanagan brushed him aside. 'We must move with the times, Crispin, we must move with the times. Anyway, it won't just be weddings. We're doing commitment ceremonies as well. There's a big demand. If we're to hit our targets, we must diversify. Diversification . . . that's the name of the game nowadays!'

Pilkington looked as if he were about to faint. 'Commitment ceremonies . . . You mean between homosexuals . . . I really think . . .'

I realised that Flanagan was very drunk by this time, but no one was about to cross him when he demanded yet another glass of wine. 'You've no business to think, John, that's my job. Weddings and commitment ceremonies, that's what we're at. St Sebastian's will be famous for them. I want none of your po-faced Methodist principles here! I'll have another glass of that red stuff please . . .'

Helga came forward. She looked frightened, but she put her hand on Flanagan's arm. She was obviously used to dealing with this situation. She said in her German accent, 'Alf, I think it's time for us to go home. We both need an early night.' She turned to our host and smiled, 'Thank you for a lovely party Dr Pilkington.' There was a short tense moment. I thought the Vice-Chancellor was going to argue the point, but then he nodded, heaved himself up and stumbled towards the door. The party had come to an end.

On the way home Emma shook her head about the food. 'I've never seen anything like it,' she said. 'I didn't know you could still buy tinned asparagus. And all that grease! Honestly I could almost hear everyone's arteries screaming for mercy!'

'It was dreadful,' I agreed.

'Do you think Maureen Pilkington would be offended if I sent her a BBC helpsheet on healthy eating?' my wife asked.

CHAPTER SEVEN

New Year with the Mafia

We were sitting down to breakfast the next morning when Imogen and Judith, Patricia Parham's partner, came through the front door. We knew that Imogen had spent the night on duty at the Women's Refuge and it seemed that she had met Judith there. Judith was also a volunteer. They both looked sleepy as if they had been up most of the night and they were clearly worried.

Emma provided them both with orange juice, coffee and toast and Imogen began the story. 'It was a fairly quiet evening. There were the five usual women and their children. They live in the Refuge for the time being while they're waiting for injunctions against their partners. Anyway they'd just gone up to bed and I was having a session with Jan, who's the senior paid worker – she's being really helpful about my dissertation . . .'

'I was upstairs, settling one of the children who had ear-ache,' Judith broke in. 'Anyway there was a ring at the door bell . . .'

'Jan went to answer it,' Imogen continued, 'and Liz, the other paid worker, went out to join her. I peeked through the door and it was Mrs Flanagan, the Vice-Chancellor's wife. As soon as Jan had taken her into the kitchen, which is the only warm place in the house, I shot upstairs to warn Judith.'

'You see, it's all meant to be confidential,' explained Judith. 'If we happen to know a woman who comes in, then we have to make ourselves scarce. Well both Imogen and I met Mrs Flanagan after that awful priest's inauguration ceremony. I'm not sure she'd remember us, but it'd be very embarrassing if we met again at a university social occasion.'

'So we stayed upstairs and let Jan and Liz cope with the situation. It was serious. Helga was crying and she was in real pain. Apparently Professor Flanagan had kicked her and she had fallen down the stairs. Jan had to drive her to the casualty department at the hospital. She was bruised all over; she wrenched her shoulder trying to save herself on the bannister; a couple of ribs are cracked and she has sprained her ankle badly. She was lucky. They initially thought it was broken.'

'What time was this?' asked Emma.

'About eleven.'

Emma and I looked at each other. 'We saw them last night at a party,' I said. 'Professor Flanagan was very drunk. Helga persuaded him to go home but he was quite docile when they left.'

'That's not all,' said Judith. 'After Jan had put her in the car and they had gone to hospital, we didn't feel like going to sleep so we had more coffee and Liz told us that this wasn't the first time. She looked back in the record book and Helga's been in three times since September.'

'Why doesn't she leave him?' I asked.

Emma looked thoughtful. 'I must admit I was worried about her. I thought there might be something odd. When we went to that party at Cuckoos' Roost, she and I had a good chat. She had made a really splendid German feast and I wanted her to come on my programme to talk about food from the Black Forest. She seemed to be very pleased with the idea.'

'What happened?' asked Imogen.

'It was strange. I rang up a couple of times. She was completely different, monosyllabic and shy. She was anxious to get off the phone as soon as possible and she made it clear that she didn't want anything to do with me. I couldn't understand it. She was so friendly at the party.'

'That's how it often is,' said Judith. 'Violent men terrorise their wives. They undermine their confidence and want them entirely to themselves. What they're doing is isolating them and cutting them off from any female support or help . . .'

'Anyway you haven't heard the end,' Imogen interrupted. 'At seven in the morning there was a tremendous hooting outside the front door and someone leaned on the doorbell for a couple of minutes. I looked out of the window and there was the biggest Mercedes-Benz you've ever seen in your life with the Vice-Chancellor stamping beside it. I heard Jan trying to persuade Helga to stay in the Refuge, that she'd be safe there, but then I heard Helga say, "No, No! He really does love me. It was my fault. He just doesn't know his own strength sometimes", and she limped out of the house, climbed into the car and off they went.'

'That's what happens,' said Judith resignedly. 'These women are so beaten down that they believe that it's their own fault that they're battered. It's really sad . . . '

Emma was conscience stricken, 'I wish I had known. Perhaps I could have helped the poor woman, but I don't expect there's anything anyone can do.'

After Judith had left and Imogen was having a bath, Emma took me on one side. 'Be careful of the Vice-Chancellor, Felix. You know he's a bully. You saw how he treated John Pilkington. Judith's story just confirms it. No wonder Helga's so frightened. But it'll have bad implications for the university. I've seen it in one or two departments in the BBC. Once there's a bully in charge, a whole bullying culture takes hold and it sweeps through the entire organisation. Do look out . . .'

It was time for me to leave for the university. I had a busy day so I gave Emma a kiss and set out on my way.

When I arrived in my room, Mrs Brush was emptying the waste-paper basket. I asked her how she was and then enquired after old Mrs Catnip. Mrs Brush was full of it. 'Well,' she said, 'you'll never guess. Elsa didn't play bingo last night. She'd had a small win last week and she decided she'd try blackjack. She said she'd been reading up about it. Well . . . she won more than a hundred pounds.'

I thought of Sir William Dormouse. Clearly Mrs Catnip was another cardsharp. How did these old people do it? Mrs Brush was in full flow. 'She's always had a very good memory you know. Even at bingo she always remembers all the numbers that are called in every game. I think that's why she's good at cards. She won every hand yesterday.'

'Did she say anything about a book I gave her?' I asked.

'She mentioned something about learning how to count cards . . . I really don't remember . . . but she'll make a fortune if she goes on like this . . .'

'She ought to be careful not to let on that she has a system for winning. You remember Professor Harry Gilbert?'

'Oh yes. I never got to clean his room, but I know he had some nice things. A real gentleman, he was. Always said "Good Morning". I heard he went to America . . .'

'He did. The reason I mention him is because his father-in-law, Sir William Dormouse, is an expert on blackjack. He wins every time. Anyway he was thrown out of the casino in Las Vegas because he won too much money. Mrs Catnip must be careful.'

'I'll tell her. Thrown out of the casino because he won too much! Well I never! . . . She'll be tickled pink!' And with that Mrs Brush picked up her cleaning equipment and stumped off to her duties.

When I was alone, I turned on my computer. There were two emails from Pilkington. The first said that the department had entered into three more partnerships. We were now going to award degrees to two Bible colleges in Japan and to a Lutheran seminary in Sweden. I was sure the Vice-Chancellor would be pleased with this, but I wondered how we were going to assess written work in Swedish and Japanese.

The second email was marked URGENT. It read as follows:

Dear All

You will be aware from the Vice-Chancellor's comments at our annual Christmas party that the university intends to transform the Great Hall into a wedding venue. It will no longer be available for university functions.

Some of you may be disappointed with this. Yet, given the financial situation, it is important that the university should make full use of its facilities. Hence, I believe (with some reluctance) that we should welcome this proposal since it will raise some much needed revenue.

However, I do also think that we have a moral duty to resist the suggestion that civil commitment ceremonies for homosexual couples should be conducted on our premises. St Sebastian's was founded as a Christian missionary college. Our founders would turn in their graves at the thought of such a desecration of their vision. Quite apart from the ethical question, such ceremonies are a betrayal of our whole tradition. I have discussed the matter with our chaplain, Father Chantry-Pigg. He shares my whole-hearted opposition to this plan.

Attached to this email is a copy of a petition which I am circulating round the department. The original is in the secretarial office and I would be grateful if you would take the time to come in to sign it by the end of the week. It will then be delivered to the Vice-Chancellor. I cannot believe he will continue with this venture if he finds the Theology department unanimous in its opposition.

With Best Wishes

Dr John Pilkington,
Head of Department

I was sorry Magnus was away on his cruise ship. His comments would have been a tonic. As it was, I deleted the email off my machine. I certainly was not going to sign such a petition.

I told Emma about it at dinner that evening. We were eating a cheese soufflé which was a delight. Emma was incensed. 'What a bigot!' she declared. 'His wife can't cook; their house is a disaster; and his opinions are appalling. Really, Felix, I don't understand your new colleagues. Are they all like that?'

'Maybe. They won't talk to me, so I really don't know them. But from what I've seen, I think they will probably all sign this idiotic petition.'

'But surely the Vice-Chancellor won't pay any attention.'

I laughed. 'I shouldn't think so!' Then I became serious. 'Actually, you have to hand it to Pilkington. He's brave. He knows what Flanagan's wrath is like, but he still sticks to his principles.'

Emma snorted. 'I wish he'd be brave about something sensible.'

It turned out that I was the only member of the Theology department not to sign the petition. Pilkington informed my colleagues of this fact in another email. I felt hostility all around me. At coffee and lunch-time I was isolated and everyone turned aside if they happened to pass me in the corridors. I looked forward more and more to Magnus's return.

Then, just before the winter break, we all received a Christmas card from Flanagan. On the front was a German woodcut of a cuckoo clock with a Christmas greeting. Inside the Vice-Chancellor had scribbled a personal message: 'Enjoy yourselves in Las Vegas. Remember me to Sylvester. Best regards, Alf and Helga.' Also in the envelope was an enclosure.

It was a glossy pamphlet. At the top was a company logo of an arrow piercing a heart with 'Mixed Blessings' written in fancy lettering underneath. At the bottom of the page Mixed Blessings was described as a subsidiary company of St Sebastian's University specialising in high-class catered events.

Inside the text read:

St Sebastian's University is proud to announce the establishment of Mixed Blessings, a wedding and partnership service based on our beautiful, historic campus in the centre of the medieval town of St Sebastian's. The university Great Hall is licenced for all civil wedding and partnership ceremonies. It can hold up to 250 guests and with its oak-panelled walls and arched ceiling it provides an elegant setting for your special day.

The famous American artist Julian Bosey has been commissioned to paint a magnificent portrait of the Christian martyr St Sebastian which will provide a unique backdrop for photographs. Together with the beautiful quadrangle and gracious lawns outside, the setting and ambiance are unique in the county.

The catering service is of the highest international standard. Our experienced banqueting manager will sit down with you personally to ensure that you have exactly what you want on this great day in your life. Choice extends beyond food. If you opt for a religious service, the magnificent Gothic chapel is at your disposal. If you prefer a secular celebration, the local registrar will conduct exactly the type of ceremony you prefer.

Our hand-picked staff are ready to discuss all your requirements, including table decorations, musical entertainments and anything else to make your great day unique and memorable. We can direct you towards our own carefully selected firms of photographers, printers, florists and car hire services, all of whom will offer you our generous Mixed Blessings discount. Of course, if you prefer, you can bring in your own specialists. Everything is designed to make your celebration as splendid and care-free as possible.

The Vice-Chancellor, Professor Alfred Flanagan, and other officers of the university cordially invite you to let Mixed Blessings at St Sebastian's give you the best possible start to a lifetime of commitment and happiness.

At the bottom of this were a series of photographs. There was a picture of the Great Hall; another of a bride and groom standing in the quadrangle; a third of a lesbian couple both wearing massive white wedding dresses; and a close-up of two handsome young men holding hands. I shook my head and laughed. It was clear that the Vice-Chancellor had taken no notice at all of the petition. What, I wondered, would Pilkington and the department of Theology do now?

The three of us had a very happy Christmas at Emma's parents. They were no longer young, but they still loved having Emma, her two brothers and all the grandchildren to stay. Emma took charge of the cooking. After we had recovered from all the cheer and over-eating, it was time for our trip to Las Vegas.

It was an extraordinary interlude, wholly different from our usual life. There was no nonsense about catching a train to the airport. A massive limousine drew up at our front door and took us directly to Heathrow. We were shown to a plush first-class lounge where everything was, as they said, 'complimentary'. We helped ourselves to excellent orange juice, coffee and rolls. Then we read all the daily newspapers as we waited for our flight to be announced. Our suitcases had been whisked away, but we were assured that they would turn up like a couple of obedient dogs when we arrived at our destination.

At half past ten precisely our flight was called and we made our way to the gate. First-class passengers were invited to enter before everyone else; I was curious to see who would be seated near us. Ahead of us in the queue was an elegant woman wearing a headscarf and sunglasses, accompanied by a huge black man who looked like a bodyguard. Neither of us knew who she was, but Emma was convinced she had seen her on television in a BBC drama where she had played a sinister murderess.

We took our seats and, even before we cruised down the run-way, we were served very good champagne and canapes. As Emma observed, it was a far cry from the Pilkingtons' party. It was also somewhat different from my last trip across the Atlantic Ocean when I was crammed in the back between a young mother and baby and a very large gentleman who overflowed his seat. An attentive hostess hovered about refilling our glasses. Once air-born, orders were taken for lunch. We both chose wild mush-room soup followed by seared salmon with a rocket salad. For pudding I had cherry tart and cream with a spoonful of ripe stil-ton to follow; Emma chose fresh mango trifle. The meal was served on real china plates and we ate with silver knives and forks. I felt very sorry for the hoardes behind us with their plastic portions wrapped in cellophane.

Afterwards, I adjusted my seat so it was completely flat and I fell into a dreamless sleep. Meanwhile Emma worked on a pro-gramme she was preparing. I awoke a couple of hours later and found I had a choice of entertainment. Among the many films on offer was Jacques Bousset's *En Bon Point*. It was as funny and clever as I remembered. I tried to imagine the director being mar-ried to a woman who was content to spend her time devising expensive meals for the cadaverous Crispin Chantry-Pigg. It seemed impossible.

It was a very long flight, but we both managed to sleep for part of the time and we felt refreshed when we finally arrived in Las Vegas. It was still light outside and there was a spectacular desert sunset. As promised our luggage appeared as if by magic; we were eased through immigration and customs and Wolfie

Goldberg was there waiting to meet us. He had been described to us as the Mancini accountant and he turned out to be a middle-sized, hook-nosed figure wearing a red sports shirt and tartan linen trousers. We shook hands, and he led us outside to an enormous black Cadillac with darkened windows. The driver, who was introduced to us as 'Leftie', wore dark glasses and had a strong Italian-American accent.

Emma and I sat in the back as we drove through the city while Wolfie treated us to a running commentary on the beauties of Las Vegas. He was obviously proud of his home-town. We peered out of the windows at the gaudy hotels, restaurants, and shopping centres that lined the Strip. Everything was lit with unremitting neon light. Emma, who, as a small child, had experienced the kind of Sunday School education which would have delighted John Pilkington, said that it reminded her of Heaven – 'The darkness is no darkness with Thee and the night is as clear as the day,' she quoted. This remark pleased Wolfie very much.

When we arrived at our hotel, the Ziggurat, two attendants dressed as Eastern potentates in robes and turbans opened the door for us. They took possession of our luggage and led us with much ceremony into the hotel foyer. Wolfie accompanied us to the reception desk where we were signed in and were given a golden key for our room. One of the attendants carried our bags across the hotel lobby to the tower where we shot up to the twentieth floor in a gilded glass elevator.

Then we followed Wolfie down a long corridor to our suite. It had an incredible view towards Cleopatra's Palace, the hotel where Sir William Dormouse had had his blackjack difficulties. The room itself was vast. There was a golden fountain playing in one corner surrounded by a positive jungle of green plants. At the other end was a gigantic bed with four Babylonian golden lions on both sides guarding it. The walls were decorated with Assyrian bas-reliefs depicting hunting scenes. In the corner were two large white sofas and a marble table with a vase holding at least two dozen tiger-spotted orchids. There was a huge bowl of fresh fruit and a couple of boxes of chocolates. 'This is our best room', Wolfie smiled. 'Luigi and Sylvester allocate it only to their most honoured guests.'

'Golly,' I exclaimed.

'Gosh,' Emma added.

'Our pleasure,' Wolfie said as he walked towards the door. 'After such a long flight you'll need a rest and a shower. I'll be back at half past eight to take you to dinner. Unfortunately Luigi's away on business until tomorrow evening so we'll be going to Sylvester's house. He and his wife are sure looking forward to knowing you. Now everyone wants you to enjoy yourselves. They've put down a thousand dollars worth of credit so you can try your luck at the tables downstairs. And Sylvester asked me to present this to your lovely wife.' He bowed and handed Emma a plain white envelope. Inside was a thousand-dollar token for Saks Fifth Avenue. They'll be expecting you in the shopping mall. Just tell them you're Luigi's guests.' Emma and I looked at each other as he closed the door. What, I wondered, was going on?

After a brief nap, Emma and I dressed and explored the hotel. It was unbelievably flossy. We examined the casinos, the lounges, the artificial lake surrounded by golden fluted columns and the gigantic sailing ship modelled on an Assyrian dhow which transported guests to various parts of the hotel. It was hard to imagine how money could have been spent more lavishly and, by English standards, more tastelessly. There was even a show starring no less a celebrity than Sir Louie Loon. He was billed as playing a mauve piano sitting atop a lighted moon. Later we sat in a black marble bar where we were served colourful cocktails by a waitress in a sequinned gold toga and matching turban. The turban was considerably bigger than the toga.

'You realise we can't accept the casino credit or that shopping token, don't you Emma?' I said.

She laughed. 'I was afraid you'd say that. Why do I have to be married to Mr Integrity? I know . . . it looks too much like bribery. How are you going to return them without offending the Mancinis?'

'I thought I'd say that the English tax authorities were ferocious about that sort of thing and I hoped he'd understand.'

Emma nodded. 'Yes. That sounds all right . . .'

We were waiting at the appointed time in the lobby. The black Cadillac appeared from nowhere and we climbed back inside. Leftie told us that Wolfie would meet us at Sylvester Mancini's house with his date. Emma was instantly curious. 'Who is Wolfie's date?' Leftie grinned. Her name apparently was Divine de la Rue and she was a student at the casino training school.

We left the city behind and drove into the magnificent desert mountain landscape. Beside a large lake, Sylvester's neo-Italianate house was surrounded by palm trees; the entrance was lined with marble statues of Roman gods and goddesses. As we pulled up the drive, an attendant opened the car door and led us into a black and white marbled hall where Sylvester and his wife Gina were waiting for us. Both were rotund and olive-skinned. Sylvester was wearing a shiny grey suit with an open-neck shirt; his ambitiously blonde wife was splendid in a tight silvery trouser suit.

They led us into a large sitting room with a double-height vaulted ceiling. The carpets were white, the upholstery black and there were long velvet curtains in a leopard-skin pattern. The walls were covered in large rococo gold frames. It was a little overwhelming to discover that they all contained oil reproductions of well-known Italian Old Masters.

The four of us sat on two matching sofas while another servant served yet more champagne in tall fluted glasses. Sylvester caught me looking around. He laughed. 'Not bad for an orphanage brat!' he said. I remembered that the Vice-Chancellor had said exactly the same thing when we went to visit Sir William in Shropshire. I wondered what those two had suffered as children. Sylvester then went on to tell us that he had just spoken to his old friend Flanagan who hoped we were having a good time.

He was interrupted by the entrance of Wolfie and Miss de la Rue. They were quite a pair. She was a least ten inches taller than he, but this was partially accounted for by the red high heels she was wearing. Her appearance could only be described as spectacular. She wore, for want of a better term, a red glittering top and a matching skirt. The top barely covered her enormous breasts and the skirt would have been a reasonable-sized belt. Emma, in her elegant black frock looked as covered up as a pious Muslim wife beside her.

Sylvester was an excellent host. He introduced everyone and explained that he thought we would like to meet Divine de la Rue because she had just started her course as a trainee croupier at the King Midas Casino College.

'Is that the name of your training school?' I asked.

'Sure is! You're learning a lot aren't you, sweetie?'

'Yes, Mr Mancini,' said Divine de la Rue.

Dinner was served in the adjacent dining room. The black and white theme continued, but this time the velvet curtains were tiger-striped. The glass table was supported by four golden reproductions of Botticelli's Venus rising from the waves. I could see that Gina Mancini was interested in art. We ate the largest, thickest, tenderest steaks I had ever encountered. 'Luigi has them specially flown in from Kansas,' Sylvester informed us. They were accompanied by baked potatoes overflowing with sour cream and a green salad. I wasn't sure what Emma would think of this menu.

I was placed between Divine and Gina. Both ladies were wearing pungent scents which fought a rearguard battle with each other in the air around me. 'So,' I turned to Divine and tried not to look down her cleavage, 'you're studying to be a croupier, is that right?'

'I started last month,' she infomed me in her soft little voice.

'And do you like the college?' I said rather desperately.

She looked puzzled, but answered readily enough, 'Oh yes . . . I love everything in Las Vegas, don't you?'

'And where do you come from originally?'

'Well . . . we moved around a lot. I was born in Smoke City, Arkansas.' She batted her eyelashes at me.

'That's a long way away.' I said. She was unlike any student I had ever met; more like a ten-year-old playing at being an adult. Mary and Rosalind were far better company.

'And you take courses?' I persisted.

'Well I've only just started . . . what we try to do is please the customers,' she said.

Sylvester leaned over and winked. 'That's the Mancini motto. No one ever went broke pleasing the customers!'

I wondered how intellectual curiosity and academic freedom fitted in to this philosophy. While I was pondering this, dessert was served. It consisted of three gigantic scoops of ice cream, peach, chocolate chip and coffee crackle. While tackling this, I asked Wolfie about the modes of assessment used in the King Midas Casino College.

'The course is very practical,' he replied, 'We don't want to bother the girls with too many papers and things.'

'Are there equal numbers of male and female students?' asked Emma. Divine looked bewildered and glanced at Wolfie for guidance.

'We plan to show you around the training school tomorrow,' he said, and with that we had to be satisfied.

The next day was New Year's Eve. In the morning, Emma and I had a delicious breakfast in our room. Then we set off at ten o'clock to meet Wolfie at the front desk. He was to conduct us round the Mancini college of casino management, also known as the King Midas Club.

When the black Cadillac drew up outside the hotel, Wolfie was disconcerted to find Emma with me. 'Gee,' he said, 'I kind of figured that a lady like you would prefer the shopping mall. Don't you like Saks Fifth Avenue? I can always change your shopping voucher for another store.'

I explained that although we were very grateful indeed to the Mancinis, the British tax authorities would not allow us to accept such a gift. It sounded lame even to me, but Wolfie had no trouble with the explanation. 'Those bastards,' he said. 'I know . . . nothing but trouble.'

The college was located about half a mile from the hotel. Leftie drove us down the neon-lit Strip in complete air-conditioned comfort while Wolfie commented on the buildings that we passed. All the hotels appeared to be owned by the Mancini organisation, as well as most of the buildings in between. Beside me, under her breath, Emma started humming the theme of the *Godfather* films.

The training school was down a side street. It was a square whitewashed building of three storeys. There was an enormous canopy in front of the entrance and a huge black man, dressed as an African tribesman, opened the door to us. Wolfie addressed him as 'Brutus'. The tribesman called him 'Mr Goldberg'.

We were ushered into what looked like a plush London gentlemen's club. There was a thick red carpet on the floor. The walls were of rich oak panelling. There were clusters of marble pillars at every corner and the moulding on the ceiling was picked out in gold. Directly in front of us, in a custom-made niche was a life-size reproduction of the Venus de Milo; the sculptor had replaced her missing arms and they were held out as if she were about to embrace the incoming clients. Emma began to giggle. I wondered if we could possibly match such splendour in the old squash courts at St Sebastian's. I thought it improbable.

We went through large gold-ornamented doors into a casino filled with roulette wheels, blackjack tables and slot machines. There was a constant clatter of coins and canned Muzak. As it was early in the day, there were few customers and several of the students were sitting around with little to do. I am used to undergraduates, but I had never seen anything like them. They were wearing what was presumably a Mancini uniform – brief gold costumes which might have been suitable for exhibition ice-skating if their tights had been thicker and their blouses less skimpy. I felt I was in a room of young women, all of whom had been given their younger sisters' clothes.

Divine de la Rue extricated herself from a conversation with another huge African tribesman and came forward. She smiled at Wolfie extravagantly and shook hands with Emma and me. We were invited to sit at a blackjack table and Divine nimbly dealt us a hand of cards. She had clearly learned a lot in the time she had been training. She demonstrated how she managed the pack and what she said to encourage the punters to bet. Emma was fascinated and asked her if she had always had the ambition to be a croupier. I was not sure if she understood the question or if she had not heard it properly. She looked at Wolfie rather than Emma when she made her reply. 'I just want to please the customers,' she said.

When she finished her demonstration, she rose from her seat to fetch us drinks. Wolfie patted her on her bottom as she passed. I was astonished. I would certainly have been accused of sexual harrassment if I had done such a thing to my students.

While we waited for our drinks, Wolfie led us to the casino office. The gentlemen's club theme continued. There were capacious red leather armchairs, oak panelling and a huge partners' desk. On the wall were a series of photographs. They all showed a large man of Italian appearance shaking hands with one recent president of the United States after another. 'That's Luigi,' said Wolfie. 'He's a big contributor to all the presidential campaigns.'

Emma was puzzled. 'He seems to support both the Republicans and the Democrats,' she observed. 'Which side is he on?'

'He's on the Mancini side,' said Wolfie, giving me a big wink. 'As long as they don't stand in the way of the business, he's happy with anyone! All those big-shots have fund-raising dinners in Vegas and Luigi makes sure he's the biggest contributor. Every time . . . He says it's an investment. He's right! We've never had any trouble from any of them . . . It's the same thing with the stars. We've got that Englishman here at the moment, Sir Louie Loon . . .'

'I noticed,' I said.

'You wanna hear him?' he asked, 'I can easily get you tickets.'

'I don't think so . . . we don't really care for his sort of music . . .'

'I agree,' said Wolfie, 'but you've got to give it to him. He's made a lot of money and he's even met all the royals at Buckingham Palace . . . He's quite a guy . . .'

Divine returned with our drinks. She was as adept at serving as she was at dealing cards. Emma and I had both asked for orange juice, but Wolfie had bourbon. The beverages were served in tall glasses full of ice and decorated with mint, lemon and a small parasol. I noticed that Divine had brought no drink for herself; quite unselfconsciously she had become a waitress, melting into the background.

Then Wolfie took us on a tour. A few students were being given practical instruction by men in dark suits, but there seemed to be no classes as such. Indeed, there were no lecture rooms. I was expecting to see departments dealing with subjects such as Accountancy, the History of Gambling, the Mathematics of Probability and Tourist Management, but I could see no sign of any of them. When I asked about a library, Wolfie told me it was upstairs. We would see it later.

Then we were guided to a wood-panelled elevator. It was old-fashioned with a cage and it was operated by yet another African tribesman. This one was called Marcus. On the walls were prints of safari hunting scenes. On the next floor we walked down a plush corridor to a room filled with television monitors. There were several gentlemen in sharp, shiny suits and slicked-back hair who were watching everything. One of them was introduced to us as Shorty. Since he was well over six feet tall, I gathered the name was intended to be ironic. Apparently he was in charge of security in the casino.

'Glad to know you,' Shorty said extending his hand, but without diverting his gaze from the monitors. 'I've got a bastard down there who's cheating.'

I looked over his shoulder and thought of Sir William Dormouse and old Mrs Catnip. 'You mean he's counting cards?' I asked.

'Nope . . . nothing like that. Look, you can see. He's got a friend standing behind the dealer and he's holding up a mirror.' I stared into the screen and caught sight of a flash of light. Then there was a commotion. As I watched both men were grabbed by a group of tribesmen and they disappeared. Within a minute it was as if they had never been.

'Gotta go to the office and nail 'em,' grunted Shorty and, followed by two acolytes, he left the room.

'What about the library?' I asked brightly.

It was next door and it was not quite what Emma or I had expected. There were many more DVDs than books and they were all pornographic in content. They were even classified under such headings as 'art films', 'sado-masochism', 'girl-on-girl' and 'classics'. In the last section I found a copy of the *Decameron* and the *Memoirs of Fanny Hill*, so, in all fairness, there was some nod to culture. I took a deep breath. 'That isn't quite what I meant, Wolfie. I don't know who this is for, but I was expecting something a bit more, uh . . . academic for your students.'

'Oh this is the guests' library. The students aren't too hot on reading and writing, are you sweetie?' He turned to Divine de la Rue who was pattering behind us on her high heels.

'I just want to please the customers,' said Divine again.

'So how do you to assess the students if they don't read and write?' I asked. My head was spinning, but I was doing my best to adjust my ideas of a college education.

'Well that's your job,' said Wolfie. 'That's why they're going to St Sebastian's, to get their BAs.' He made an expansive gesture with his hand. 'Luigi wants all his employees to be graduates. That's the point . . .'

'But how have you ensured up to now that they achieve the requisite standard?' I asked.

'We have a rule. You've gotta please the customer. If there are no complaints, then they've done good.' He winked at me again.

'I think St Sebastian's is going to demand a little more than that . . .' I began, but Wolfie interrupted.

'Time to go upstairs,' he said. He seemed embarrassed. Turning to Emma, he suggested that she wait in the library. 'It's quite comfortable there. Plenty to read . . .'

'Oh no! I want to see upstairs,' Emma was robust. 'I'm finding it all most interesting.' Wolfie was not happy, but he summoned the elevator again and we proceeded on our journey upwards.

When the doors opened, a curvacious redhead wearing an exceptionally brief chambermaid's outfit and extraordinarily high heels was waiting for us. She had a feather duster in her hand and she wriggled as she smiled at us. She led us down a dimly lit passage which was painted a deep red. It was like going back into the womb. We were ushered into a sitting room lined in leopard skin velvet. There was a small bar at one end and there were several soft sofas and armchairs. Rather tasteful erotic paintings lined the walls.

'Shall I bring in the girls?' asked our hostess, looking doubtfully at Emma.

'Just get us a drink, sweetie,' commanded Wolfie. The chambermaid busied herself at the bar. She was as adept at the task as Divine had been.

'Oh but we would like to meet the students,' I said.

'I imagine this is where they learn tourist management skills?' asked Emma, entering into the spirit of things,

'Sure do!' said Wolfie. 'But they're busy at the moment.'

From his tone, I did not feel I could ask exactly what they were busy doing so I started a conversation on the logistics of bringing students over to St Sebastian's for a semester. Wolfie was uneasy throughout. He waved the chambermaid away as soon as we were furnished with further drinks and looked at his watch.

'Gotta go soon,' he said. 'Leftie's gotta pick up Luigi from the airport at twelve so I'll take you back to the Ziggurat first. You'll be having dinner with him at eight in the Hanging Gardens Restaurant. It's on the top floor of the hotel.'

'I'm sure we will enjoy it, said Emma.

When we returned to our hotel room, Emma and I had a serious talk. 'You can't go on with this, Felix,' she said. 'That was no more a training college than the Moulin Rouge is. It's a brothel with a casino attached.'

I nodded. 'I think you upset things rather. Wolfie was all set to let me have my pick of the girls on the top floor . . .'

'Good thing I was there then! The whole thing's deplorable. What are you going to tell Flanagan?'

I shook my head. 'I just don't know. He's quite determined. I don't think he's going to be deterred. Honestly, the next thing will be a degree in Pole-Dancing. How in the world did I get mixed up in this?'

Emma was sitting on the bed flipping through the Ziggurat promotional magazine as we talked. She stopped. 'Oh, God No!' she said, pointing to an article.

'What's the matter?' I asked.

The article was entitled 'The Best New Year Ever' . . . 'It describes how for New Year's Eve women are supposed to wear rabbit ears and men sparkling top hats,' my wife informed me.

'Dear heaven!' I shuddered.

'Look at the picture.' There was a large photograph of a group of Ronald and Nancy Reagan look-alikes all kitted out with celebratory head-dresses.

'Perhaps they'll provide everything in the restaurant. What does the magazine say about the Hanging Gardens?'

'It's impressive. It's been awarded four stars by some French gourmet. It's also incredibly expensive . . .'

By a quarter to eight Emma and I were ready for dinner. Emma wore her best chocolate brown velvet evening dress, which matched her eyes, and I climbed into my dinner jacket. We had to catch the Assyrian dhow to take us to another part of the hotel and another glass elevator took us up to the restaurant. Wolfie and Sylvester were waiting for us. Emma was indeed given a pair of rabbit ears on a velvet head-band, and the three of us were furnished with the requisite top hats. I was glad neither my students nor my theological colleagues could see us. Then we were taken to be introduced to Luigi Mancini.

He turned out to be a large, dark-haired figure wearing a bright red bow tie and a cummerbund. Standing in the centre of a group of Italian-looking men, he was flanked by two dodgy-looking figures who were probably bodyguards. I was not drawn to him, but he was certainly civil. He shook hands with me; then he bowed to Emma, kissed her hand and said, 'Welcome to Vegas.'

'Thank you for having us,' I replied.

He put his arm around my shoulder and guided me to a nearby plate glass window as Wolfie introduced Emma to the other guests. The city sparkled below. 'You see those hotels?' he said pointing to all the gigantic buildings around us. 'We built them; we own them; and now your university is going to train us to manage them. Vision! That's what it takes! Vision!' He lifted up a glass of champagne. 'To the future!' he said.

At dinner I was seated between him and his wife Frankie. She was a tall brunette with a bouffant hair-style and bright red fingernails. She was wearing a low-cut white dress and sported the biggest diamond ring I had ever seen in my life. I wondered if it could possibly be real. She asked me if I had tried my luck in the casino.

'No,' I said. 'Luigi very kindly offered to start us off with a thousand dollars' worth of chips, but the tax authorities in England won't allow us to accept that sort of gift.'

She smiled understandingly. 'The tax people aren't easy,' she said.

I looked at the menu. The food was French and clearly exquisite. I thought I might as well enjoy myself and told the waiter that I would have whatever my wife chose. She knew my tastes. Frankie was amused. 'Gee,' she said, 'it's lovely when married people know each other's feelings. Luigi always depends on me to choose his clothes.' I looked at the red cummerbund and thought it would be more tactful not to comment, so I smiled instead.

She was very easy to talk to. She explained exactly how everyone around the table was related to everyone else. 'Except Wolfie of course. He's not Italian, but you've got to have a Jewish accountant. They're so sharp . . .' She stopped herself, looked at me and went red.

I laughed. 'I am Jewish, but I'm not sharp. I was always hopeless with money. I don't think Luigi would want to employ me in that capacity.'

She smiled back at me. 'Well Wolfie's dad worked for Luigi's dad so there's a long family connection there too. He's an only child, you know, and he's always lived with his momma. Old Mrs Goldberg was nice, but she sure kept Wolfie under her skirts if you know what I mean.'

'No chance of his getting married then?'

Frankie chuckled. 'Oh Jeeze no! She saw off any girl real fast. I gave up fixing him up with dates years ago. But things may be different now. She had to go into a nursing home a couple of months back and I don't think she'll last much longer. Wolfie's such a good son. He visits her every day, but she doesn't know him any more . . .'

'So he's ripe for the picking?' I suggested.

'Sure is!' grinned Mrs Mancini.

The food was superb. Emma chose well and I enjoyed every mouthful. However, I was surprised to notice that neither Sylvester nor Luigi was eating any dish advertised on the menu. They both had huge steaks which looked identical to what we had eaten the previous day at Sylvester's house. Presumably that was what they liked and they were sticking with it.

After dinner, there was dancing. The band was excellent and I thought of Magnus on his cruise. I wondered how he was getting on with his twin tasks of waltzing with the octogenarians and finding out about Crispin Chantry-Pigg. The whole trip to Las Vegas was certainly an experience, but I was not sure that I wanted to repeat it. I found the company disconcerting.

Finally midnight struck. We had drunk too much champagne, been doused in bonhomie and streamers and had wished each other a Happy New Year repeatedly. It was time to go to bed. Next day we were going home. 'Well,' said Emma, as we were undressing, 'an interesting couple of days . . . New Year with the Mafia . . .' and she started to hum the theme from the *Godfather* again.

I was very much afraid she was right.

CHAPTER EIGHT

Father Chantry-Pigg is Unwell

We left Las Vegas the next morning. Wolfie and Sylvester saw us off at the airport and we parted with expressions of mutual esteem. We had already arranged that they would be visiting the university in March with Luigi for the annual St Sebastian's Feast. We hoped that the old squash courts, the site of the new Golden Arrow Casino, would be ready for the laying of a foundation stone. In my own mind, however, I was determined to bring the whole absurd enterprise to an end.

By the time we arrived home, there was very little of the Christmas vacation left. While we'd been away, Imogen had had a very successful few days at the Women's Refuge. She felt that she had a better grasp of the whole issue of domestic violence and was ready to write her dissertation. To her relief, there had been no further visit from Helga Flanagan. I always felt miserable when it was time for her to return to Cambridge, but I knew that she was happy there and, from all accounts, was doing very well.

Emma had a great deal of work to do. She was immersed in a new programme on Lenten cookery and she needed to spend several days in London. I was left to my own devices. As soon as the new term started, I made an appointment to see the Vice-Chancellor to tell him about our adventures in Las Vegas. However, Flanagan was currently away at a meeting of the Vice-Chancellors' Association, and his secretary told me I'd have to wait until the following week.

Therefore it was not until the Monday that I arrived in his office. In an affable bellow, Flanagan shouted at me to come in and I found him bubbling over with enthusiasm. 'I've just got rid of that boring bloke, Ralph Randolph,' he said.

Ralph Randolph was the Professor of Chemistry. I had hardly ever spoken to him, but I knew him by sight. He was a rather dour figure, invariably dressed in a dark suit and emitting a strange, vaguely metallic smell. 'Is he old enough to retire?' I asked.

'Man has no vision!' pronounced Flanagan. 'No idea at all! We can't go on with Chemistry. It costs a fortune and it attracts fewer and fewer students. So I gave him the opportunity of a life-time. I offered to redecorate all those space-consuming laboratories and start a brand-new degree programme: Celebrity Studies. He isn't exactly a ball of fire, but even he couldn't fail with a project like that . . . But he's got no imagination. He said that if he couldn't teach chemistry, he would go elsewhere. So I accepted his resignation before he had a chance to change his mind.' Flanagan roared with laughter.

'What are you going to do with the other two chemists?' I asked.

Flanagan wrinkled his brow. 'Don't know yet! They've all got tenure dammit, so I can't just throw them out on their ears. I'll have to think of something . . .' Then the sun came out and he turned his attention to me. 'Just the man I wanted to see,' he said. 'I've got something to show you.' He picked up a large piece of paper which was on his desk and handed it over. 'This came from that artist fellow, what's-his-name, Julian Bosie, this morning. It's just a preliminary sketch to make sure we like it!'

I found myself gazing at a very realistic picture of St Sebastian being pierced with arrows. He had a body builder's physique and there was an expression of ecstatic torment on his face. 'Jolly good, isn't it?' the Vice-Chancellor was admiring. 'It'll be quite an eyeful when it's twelve feet high and hanging in the Great Hall.'

I took a deep breath. 'It's certainly memorable,' I said.

Flanagan sat down behind his desk. 'Now tell me all about Las Vegas. How did you get on?' he asked. 'Was Sylvester hospitable?'

'Oh yes.' I could at least be enthusiastic about the trip. 'Yes. We were treated royally and I met Luigi, his brother-in-law, who is in charge of the whole Mancini empire. Everyone was extremely kind and generous and they gave us a delightful time.'

'Splendid!' boomed Flanagan, 'Well that's all settled then! I knew you were just the bloke for the job.'

'Well . . .,' I began hesitantly. 'It's not quite as straightforward as that . . .'

'How do you mean . . . not as straightforward?' The Vice-Chancellor frowned. 'I hope you're not going to be a wet blanket, Felix. We can't afford to let this opportunity slip through our fingers. There're plenty of other universities just waiting in the wings for this. What on earth's troubling you?'

'Well for a start . . . there isn't really a training school to go into partnership with . . .'

'What do you mean . . . there isn't a training school. Sylvester told me quite specifically that they have a fair-dinkum training school. Absolutely the best. It's called the King Michael Club or something.'

'The King Midas Club.' I hesitated. 'Yes, Emma and I visited it.'

'Well there you are then!' said Flanagan.

I was determined to make my case. 'But it isn't a training school. There's a small casino, but there are no lecture rooms and the library is not for the students. It's just a collection of pornography for the guests.'

'Pornography, eh?' Flanagan was interested.

'The girls do learn the practical skills of being a croupier and they all seem to know how to serve drinks and things like that, but the top floor is a brothel! It's not a college!'

Flanagan laughed, 'Really Felix, you do exaggerate . . .'

'Honestly, I'm not. Emma came with me to see the place, and they were embarrassed and tried to keep her downstairs. But she insisted on visiting everywhere and we were asked if we wanted to look over the girls. We can't possibly go into parternship with them.'

'And did you select a girl?' Flanagan leered at me.

'No, I certainly didn't. Emma was there.'

Flanagan gestured for me to sit down in the armchair opposite his desk. 'You shouldn't worry about it,' he said. 'What they do in Las Vegas needn't concern us.'

'But, Vice-Chancellor,' I protested. 'I don't think you've got the picture. It was just like the *Godfather* films. For all I know, they may be dealing in drugs and they're certainly running a prostitution skam.'

Flanagan was growing impatient. 'Well that means there's all the more for St Sebastian's to do on the academic side. Perhaps we can insist that the students stay for two terms rather than one?' He thought about this for a moment and then shook his head. 'I don't think Luigi Mancini would take it. He's paying us a couple of million as it is.' He turned his attention to me again and he spoke sternly. 'You must understand, mate. When I took this university on it was looking bankruptcy in the face. The government is giving us less and less money and is insisting that we attract more and more outside funding if we are to survive. The Mancini organisation *is* outside funding. We can't afford to turn down this chance and there's an end to the matter.'

Suddenly the frown left his face and he smiled. 'Come on Felix. I know you can do this for the university. Las Vegas needs us and we need Las Vegas and before very long there will be super-casinos all over the United Kingdom as well. It's only sensible to get in on the ground floor. I know you have your reservations, and quite right too, but you must see this as an opportunity, a wonderful opportunity, to clean up the gambling industry. Think of it as a moral challenge!'

'But . . .,' I protested.

'No buts! It is all arranged! Luigi Mancini is due here in March for the St Sebastian's Feast. The plans will proceed as agreed.' Flanagan stood up. 'Now I must go. I'm supposed to address the Rotary Club weekly luncheon. I'll have another word with the Planning Officer for you.' I noticed that Flanagan was wearing a Rotary pin in his lapel. He walked me to the door, patted me on the shoulder and sent me on my way. I knew when I was defeated.

Later that afternoon, I met my Kant class for the first session of term. Both Mary and Rosalind were in superlative form. They had clearly put the traumas of the previous months behind them. Afterwards, I went to the Senior Common Room for a cup of tea. The room was unusually full and I found myself sitting next to John Pilkington. He was entertaining the former Dean, Wanda Catnip. Pilkington frowned as I sat down. 'I understand you've been in Las Vegas.' he said. I wondered if this were common knowledge. Wanda looked surprised, and I explained that the university was exploring the possiblity of setting up a degree in Casino Management.

'A thoroughly reprehensible idea,' Pilkington commented.

I pointed out that it was the Vice-Chancellor's scheme, and that I had been deputed to organise it. Then, anxious to change the subject, I asked Wanda about her mother. 'I met her in the St Sebastian's bingo hall when I was doing some research for the new project.'

Wanda became very tetchy. 'I can't understand it,' she said. 'All Mother seems to want to do is play bingo. She goes with that cleaner, Mrs Brush. She's been a thorough nuisance about it.'

'Is your mother interested in gambling?' Pilkington asked.

Wanda shook her head. 'To begin with it was just a little outing for her, but she's become more and more preoccupied with it. I can't understand the attraction.'

'She seemed very homesick for her old home in Leeds,' I said.

Wanda became pink in the face. 'Mother is absurd. She keeps whittering on about wanting to move into an old people's home with her friends . . .'

'Wouldn't that be a good thing if she'd like it?' I asked.

'Nonsense!' Wanda was very brusque. 'Daddy bought that house to be security for me. It's ridiculous to sell it now and lose all that capital just to satisfy a whim. It isn't as if the government will pay for her to have residential care. The house would have to be sold and Mother probably wouldn't like the home anyway.'

'It's very good of you to look after your mother as you do, Wanda,' said Pilkington sanctimoniously.

'Well, as you know John,' responded Wanda Catnip, 'I was never one to shirk my duty . . .'

A few days later, I was sitting in my office looking up information about the Mancini organisation on the internet. There was a knock on the door and it turned out to be Magnus back from his trip. I was delighted to see him. He was deeply tanned and was carrying a large package. 'Hello,' I said, 'you look as though you had a lovely time.'

Magnus slumped into one of the plastic chairs I used for seminars. 'Exhausted!' he sighed. 'Danced out! Talked out! Dined out! I never want to see another octogenarian as long as I live!'

'How is Pushkin?' I knew that Magnus's cat did not like being left with cat-sitters.

'Cross!' said Magnus. 'He's sulking and he has a touch of cystitus. I know that wretched girl didn't buy him his favourite cat litter whatever she says . . .'

'Anyway,' he continued, giving me the package. 'I brought you a present.' Inside was an African mask of a fat green frog. It looked uncannily like Flanagan. 'Got it in the Caribbean,' he said. 'Couldn't resist.'

'That's very kind. But really Magnus, where can I hang it? Surely not in my office.'

'I thought you might wear it for departmental meetings. Give our colleagues a scare!' he said. Then he handed over the new copy of *Private Eye*. 'Now, I've got something important to show you. Turn to page twenty-three.'

There was a small heading which read 'High Principals.' Underneath was written:

There's a new scandal at St Sebastian's University. The notorious friar Brother Chantry-Pigg has recently been found in its venerable precincts. Still in his brown habit, he has taken over the college chapel. He was exiled from his friary in Oxford supposedly to to escape the attentions of the ex-wife of the famous French film director, Jacques Bousset, whose *En Bon Point* was an international hit. However, rather than remaining loyal to his vows of solitary monasticism, he is now, unbeknownst to the brothers, actually living with Mme. Bousset in a million-pound executive home. As his 'housekeeper' she cooks him extravagant meals and attends full-time to his comfort. It is clear that the fragrant Danielle Bousset has changed her taste in men. *En Bon Point* was a celebration of rotundity. The Holy Lusty-Pigg is skeletally thin.

Magnus smiled slyly. 'Good isn't it?'

'Really Magnus! You go too far!'

'Ah, but you haven't heard the full story. When I was on my cruise, I had plenty of time to do research about our friend. Harry's pal the Bishop of Bosworth seemed to know all about the errant brother: apparently he's notorious in clerical circles. There have been a string of minor scandals involving rich women. Danielle is one of a long line. She first moved to England to avoid publicity from the French newpapers, who were giving her no peace. After her divorce she took a job in a hospital in Oxford where she worked as a radiographer. It was there she met Chantry-Pigg when he thought he had broken a toe tripping over a croquet hoop.'

'Harry told you all this?' I asked.

'Most of it . . .'

'What in the world did she see in him?'

'No accounting for tastes,' Magnus grinned. 'Maybe the attractions of fat men wore off. I understand she's very religious and the Roman Catholic Church let her down badly. Maybe the dear old Church of England can do better.'

'Yes, I read about that on the internet. They didn't hesitate to give Jacques Bousset an annulment to his marriage. Was he fat by the way?'

'Gross I understand. *En Bon Point* was his fantasy: lithe young girls chasing after enormously fat men.'

'After he won his Oscar, they apparently did.'

'Life imitates art! But the point is, Chantry-Pigg and Danielle became close. He was never in his friary. So the ecclesiastical authorities hoped to avoid the occasion of scandal by sending him to us.'

'Really! It's too much! We're not a dumping ground for delinquent clergymen . . .'

'I agree. But unknown to his order, Danielle bought a house in

St Sebastian's on the proceeds of her divorce. She now seems to spend her time cooking for our chaplain.'

'And nobody knew anything about it?'

'They do now!' Magnus smiled like a snake. 'Everyone reads *Private Eye* and even the Church of England will have to do something about the situation. I've known the assistant-editor for years and he was delighted with the story!'

Clutching his magazine, Magnus went off to his office; we planned to meet for lunch at one.

When I arrived in the Senior Common Room, he was sitting at a table with Patricia Parham. They were both bent over the article, giggling. I ordered a cheese and onion roll and a bag of crisps and joined them. 'Have you seen this?' Patricia asked.

'Magnus showed me.'

'It was the talk of the Senate meeting this morning,' she said. 'Apparently, Chantry-Pigg has already sent in a doctor's note saying he is suffering from stress and will be off for several weeks . . .'

'Did the Vice-Chancellor say anything?' I asked.

'Not formally, but the rumour is he's delighted. He thinks the article'll help with recruitment and put St Sebastian's on the map. He's also threatening to approach Mrs Bousset for a donation and enlist her to give a series of lectures for a new degree course he's dreamed up in Celebrity Studies!'

'Typical! That man never disappoints!' declared Magnus. 'By the way, how's the casino going, Felix?'

'Don't ask! The Vice-Chancellor is working on the Planning Officer to develop the squash courts site, and the Mancinis are coming in March for the St Sebastian's Feast. Emma and I have just got back from Las Vegas. It was quite a trip!'

On my way back to my office, I passed the chapel vestry. There was a neat sign on the door which read, 'Father Chantry-Pigg is unwell'.

There was a message waiting for me on my answerphone from the Vice-Chancellor's secretary: Flanagan wanted to show me something, and he asked if I could come to see him straightaway. What I wondered had happened?

I found the Vice-Chancellor standing in front of the largest, most baroque gold frame I had ever seen. It was propped across his sofa and it took up half his room. 'Look,' he said, handing me a letter, 'this is the surrounding for the St Sebastian portrait. It arrived this morning along with this note . . .'

The missive was typewritten on extraordinarily thick cream paper. At the top was an engraved crest of a large fish standing in an upright position on a scroll. Inside the scroll was a motto – *Heb Porpoise, Nid Pwrpas.*' The letter itself read as follows:

Dear Professor Flanagan,

After we last spoke, I commissioned this frame from one of my people in Virginia. I hope you like it. Both Julian and I feel it will suit the new St Sebastian portrait very well. Julian has been working hard and the picture is now in its final stages. As you may know, he is one of the most talented American portrait painters working today. There are examples of his work on display in the Virginia House of Representatives, the Virginia Senate House, the Porpoise Museum Sweetpea, Sweetpea College and several other public buildings in the state.

In my view the new portrait is one of his finest pictures to date. It is representative of his style and I hope you and your university will be as pleased with it as I am. As I mentioned to you over the telephone, I wish to donate both the portrait and the frame to your university as a charitable gift. This will have some tax implications and I will be sending you the requisite forms to complete in due course.

We plan to be in London for the second week of February and would very much like to see the portrait hung. Would it be possible to have a little unveiling ceremony? We will be sending you the finished article next week so it should be with you by the end of the month. It will be an easy matter for any picture dealer to stretch the canvas and put it in the frame.

In London we will be staying at the Dorchester. Before that you should continue to contact me in Sweetpea. Both Julian and I very much look forward to meeting you,

With best wishes,

Thomas Jefferson Porpoise
(Thomas Jefferson Porpoise VI)

'You're going to want me to organise the unveiling ceremony,' I said.

'I was hoping you'd suggest it.' Flanagan was all charm. I reminded myself firmly that he was a bully and a wife-beater. 'You'd better liase with Mr Porpoise to see which day is most convenient for him,' he continued. 'Then we'll have a little party. Cake and sparkling wine should be enough, but we must keep the old bloke happy.'

'What are you going to do with the frame in the meantime?' I asked. It really was gigantic.

'The porters will come and hang it in the Great Hall. I'm expecting them any minute . . . and we'll exile all my boring pre-decessors to the Senior Common Room.'

As we were speaking, the Head Porter and his spotty young assistant came into the room. Even they were rather daunted by the size of the frame. 'Well I 'opes we can get it through them doors . . .' the Head Porter remarked. 'And 'ow are we supposed to 'ang it on the walls? That's what I want to know. It'll bring down all that there oak panelling.'

The Vice-Chancellor was very soothing. 'I'm sure you'll manage, Mr Thomas,' he said. 'I always know I can count on you.'

'Well I does my best, Sir, as you know. Look out there, young Kevin. Don't 'it the corner. This is Art, this is!' And the two of them staggered off in the direction of the Great Hall.

'Tell them where to put it, would you mate,' said Flanagan to me and left us to it. I followed the pair down the corridor and we spent an exhausting afternoon hoisting and fixing St Sebastian's new acquisition to the Victorian woodwork of the Great Hall.

The next couple of weeks were uneventful. Crispin Chantry-Pigg failed to reappear and Mrs Sloth reverted to her old standard of incompetence in the library. On the one occasion I spoke to her, it was obvious that she had been crying. I was returning some books and I thought I might as well broach the subject. I asked her as Trustee of the Chapel if she had any idea when Father Chantry-Pigg was returning to work.

'I don't know and I don't care,' was Mrs Sloth's pastoral response.

'I think *Private Eye* may have given the wrong impression,' I said, trying to pour oil on troubled waters. 'It may be that Madame Bousset really is only Father Chantry-Pigg's house-keeper. We don't know for certain . . .'

'Oh that woman! She's so rich! No one can compete against her!' She dumped a pile of books onto the counter and disappeared into her private little sanctum.

As promised, the famous picture arrived at the end of the month. I did not see it. I arranged for a picture-framer to come in to fit it into the frame and he and the porters were closeted in the Great Hall for a whole morning stretching the canvas and putting it up. Meanwhile a blue velvet curtain had been hung in front of it so it could be revealed in all its splendour at the unveiling ceremony.

All the pictures of previous Vice-Chancellors had been transferred to the Senior Common Room, much to the dismay of the academic staff. As Magnus remarked, it was a sure-fire recipe for indigestion. The Great Hall had been emptied of chairs. It was swept and polished under the supervision of Mrs Brush and then the door was locked. There was no entry to anyone. The whole university was agog to see the new work of art.

Thomas Jefferson Porpoise was scheduled to arrive at four o'clock on the afternoon of the 10th of February. The Vice-Chancellor and I were waiting at the front entrance in the biting cold to receive him and, sure enough, a silver-grey Rolls-Royce drew up in front of us as the cathedral clock struck the hour. Thomas Jefferson was exactly as I remembered from Sweetpea. He was probably in his mid-seventies, with white hair and a slim figure. Julian Bosie was also slender, but his hair was gold. He had dressed for the occasion in an artist's smock and a Parisian beret. He would have fitted in nicely among Crispin Chantry-Pigg's troop of incense-swinging acolytes.

Flanagan was effusive to the pair. He enquired about the success of their trip and, on hearing that they were intending to visit Sir William Dormouse in Shropshire, he embarked on an enthusiastic account of our visit. I wondered if Thomas Jefferson Porpoise had thought to purchase a few hot water bottles. Given the capaciousness of his car, I thought it probable that he was bringing his own generator to combat the cold of the castle.

We led our visitors into the Great Hall where a large number of academics were already assembled. The Vice-Chancellor introduced the pair to Registrar Sloth and to Dean Parham. I was amused to notice that Patricia had made no effort whatever with her appearance. Then it was time for the opening ceremony.

I melted into the background and found myself standing beside Magnus, Patricia and her partner, Judith. I noticed several of my theological colleagues, including John Pilkington, dotted about the audience. Then Flanagan, who was standing between Thomas Jefferson and Julian, struck a glass with a spoon and began his speech:

'Ladies and Gentlemen,' he said, 'today marks the beginning of a new era in the history of our university. During the Victorian period our founding-fathers created an institution whose mission was to spread the good news of the Gospel to far-flung parts of the earth. We, the inheritors of this great tradition, have a similar goal: to enlighten the world with wisdom and knowledge. It is in this spirit that we are launching several new degree programmes. One of our most exciting ventures is our new degree in Casino Management in partnership with the King Midas Casino College of Las Vegas. As you all know, the government is intending to establish super-casinos throughout this country in imitation of the network already established by our American cousins.' Flanagan bowed in the direction of Thomas Jefferson, who smiled back. It was clear that the two had already achieved a profitable understanding.

'We here at St Sebastian's,' continued Flanagan, 'will make our contribution to this endeavour by providing training of the very highest quality to those who find their life's vocation in this most specialised industry.' I thought momentarily of Shortie, Wolfie Goldberg, Leftie, Divine de la Rue and the African tribesmen.

Flanagan was enjoying himself. 'We have a very exciting plan for redeveloping the old squash courts into a state-of-the-art casino and you will be delighted to know that I heard only this morning that the university architect has just been granted full planning permission for his designs. In the meantime this historic Great Hall will be playing its part. Not only will it act as a forerunner for our future casino, but it has now been recognised as a licensed venue for marriage and commitment ceremonies.' I looked over at Pilkington and saw him wince. So much for his petition . . .

'These wonderful life-enhancing ceremonies will be watched over, dare I say presided over, by this magnificent portrait of our patron saint which is soon to be unveiled. May I introduce to you all our honoured guests, the world-famous philanthropist Mr Thomas Jefferson Porpoise VI and his young protegé, the distinguished portrait-painter Mr Julian Bosey. Thomas Jefferson is a most generous patron of the arts, and it is his wish to donate this portrait to the university. This is an extraordinarily generous gift and each and every one of us who is part of St Sebastian's is deeply in his debt. I have asked him if he might be willing to say a few words before we actually see the portrait.'

'Oh God!' said Magnus, 'More oratory . . .'

Thomas Jefferson Porpoise was not backward in coming forward. In his soft Southern drawl he began, 'Friends. It is a great pleasure for both of us to visit your august institution and Julian and I are surely honoured by the kind things your President has just said about us.'

Magnus closed his eyes. 'I did not vote for Flanagan for President!' he said.

'To my mind,' Thomas Jefferson continued, 'this portrait is an inspired work by one of the most talented young artists of our generation. I know my young friend will not be embarrassed if I tell you that he is generally recognised as one of the greatest portrait painters working in America today. It is a particular privilege to be able to give something like this to one of the foremost educational institutions of Great Britain, a country to which we, as Americans, owe so much. I feel real joy to think that this painting will grace this beautiful hall for hundreds of years to come. May it be an inspiration to the young people who study here and, in its small way, contribute to the friendship, the very warm friendship which already exists between our two wonderful nations.'

Then he stepped forward and pulled a purple cord. To my great relief, the curtains covering the portrait parted. There was a hush as the assembled audience stared at the canvas.

The figure of St Sebastian stood in its full twelve feet of glory. It was obvious that Julian Bosie had used his own face for a model. It was a very competent likeness. The body, however, belonged to someone who took a daily dose of steroids and spent every waking hour lifting weights in a gym. Every vein and every muscle stood out in sharp relief from the bright pink flesh tones. At strategic intervals, arrows skewered bank notes to the body and streams of blood glistened redly from the wounds. Behind the head was a gold halo and the face, uplifted to Heaven, bore an expression of orgasmic torment.

'Bugger me!' said Magnus.

Patricia and Judith started giggling uncontrollably. I looked over to Pilkington to see his reaction. I was not disappointed. He went purple, spluttered to several theologians standing nearby, and stormed out of the room. Several members of the Theology department followed close behind. I realised something needed to be done fast. I caught Magnus's eye and together we began to clap. Patricia and Judith followed our lead and soon the whole room was applauding wildly. Bosey swept off his beret and made a tremendous bow. Thomas Jefferson and Flanagan were thrilled by the audience reaction and smiled at each other. Then it was time for the wine and cake to be served.

Afterward, Magnus invited Patricia, Judith and me for a drink in his office. As usual there were books and papers scattered everywhere. I swept a pile of Hebrew grammars off the sofa and Patricia and Judith sat down. Magnus and I took the armchairs opposite. 'So,' he smiled as he poured out glasses of sherry, 'what did you think?'

'That is the most camp picture I have ever seen,' Judith pronounced.

'Bloody marvelous', enthused Patricia. 'I'm going to send a photograph to *Gay Post*. It'll be a sensation! The university will become a mecca for homosexual and lesbian commitment ceremonies. We'll be famous everywhere.'

'You think they'll like it?' I asked.

'Like it? They'll love it. A twelve foot muscular St Sebastian shot with arrows! It's irresistable.'

'I hope you're right,' I said doubtfully.

'Take my word for it,' Patricia was very positive, 'there'll be queues. Ceremonies, three or four of them, every weekend. People'll come from abroad to be committed in front of that thing. Just think of the photographs! We'll be world-famous, believe you me!'

'Not quite the mission our founders had in mind,' I said.

'Perhaps not,' grinned Magnus as he refilled our glasses, 'but a toast to the future nonetheless: let St Sebastian's bugger the world!'

'I think it's a case of the world being buggered at St Sebastian's!' corrected Patricia.

Patricia was as good as her word. On the cover of the next edition of *Gay Post* there was a photograph of the St Sebastian portrait. Inside there was an illustrated article about the beauties of the campus and the Vice-Chancellor's new venture into commitment ceremonies. Immediately enquiries flooded in from gay couples throughout the country and even abroad. Within a fortnight, the Great Hall was solidly booked for every weekend until Christmas. There was also a sprinkling of week-day reservations.

I soon heard from Flanagan. He was intoxicated with the success of his project. Given the triumph of Mixed Blessings, he had decided to use the Great Hall exclusively for the ceremonies. There would be no room for the new casino even as a temporary measure. Therefore there was pressure to rush through the redevelopment of the old squash courts. He had given instructions to the university architect to complete the final details. Luigi Mancini and Sylvester would lay the foundation stone on their visit for the Founders' Day Feast at the end of March. I was told to liaise with the Mancini organisation and go about purchasing roulette wheels, blackjack tables and slot machines. Inevitably the Mancinis had their own source and were anxious to facilitate a handsome discount for us.

In the meantime, I was setting up a programme of courses, making use of colleagues in the Economics, History, Statistics and Business Studies departments. It was hard to imagine Divine de la Rue and her fellow-students in their skimpy costumes applying their minds to such subjects as Management Accountancy, the History of Gambling and Classical Theories of Chance, but I persevered.

Amidst all this activity, Magnus arrived in my office one afternoon. He was clutching an email from Harry. The Bishop of

Bosworth had sent further news of Brother Chantry-Pigg. Apparently the Friary had held an official ecclesiastical investigation in response to the *Private Eye* article. Chantry-Pigg had been cleared of all charges of sexual misconduct. It was said that Madame Bousset had been willing to swear under oath that they were not lovers. She insisted that she was trying to support the wonderful work of the chaplain within the university. She had merely wanted to make sure that the friar was properly looked after.

'In a million pound house on a diet of smoked salmon and caviar!' said Magnus. I had told him what I had observed in the town's delicatessen.

'Poor wretched woman,' I said. 'She was a slave to Jacques Bousset during their marriage and I suppose that's the only relationship she can imagine with a man.'

'Even if they weren't sleeping together,' commented Magnus, 'it certainly looked as if they were. And the sheer hypocrisy of pretending to be a celibate priest when your living conditions are, at the very least, potentially scandalous, can't do the Church of England any good.'

'But did they let him off the hook?' I asked.

'No,' said Magnus with relish. 'They got him on financial grounds. Apparently the Friary had been paying Chantry-Pigg an allowance for board and lodging. They thought he was renting a simple bed-sit from a respectable local landlady. Instead, he was living on the fat of the land with Mrs Bousset and was pocketing the money. So they're insisting that that money is to be paid in full to Danielle.'

'To her that hath shall be given!' said I.

'And to avoid further gossip and fulfil the conditions of his stipend, Chantry-Pigg now has to move out and rent a room in a hall of residence. He also has to have his meals in the student refectory . . .'

I giggled. 'That'll be a change for him!'

'Serve him right,' Magnus declared. 'Pompous shit!'

'Well all those nice young men who follow him about will like having him around, but I shouldn't think he'll enjoy a student bedroom. It'll be quite a change. Poor Danielle Bousset! She doesn't have much fun in life.'

'Anyway,' said Magnus, 'the story is he's coming back on Monday . . .'

That Sunday Emma and I got up late. We were having our orange juice and croissants in the kitchen when there was a knock on the front door. It turned out to be Magnus. He was carrying three copies of the *Sunday Inquirer*. 'You'll be interested in this,' he said, handing over the newspapers.

'What on earth are you doing with that rag?' asked Emma incredulously. 'It's the worst tabloid of the lot.'

'Just look,' Magnus grinned.

On the front page was a photograph of my students Mary and Rosalind in evening dresses. They were standing back-to-back under the banner headline: 'Secret Life of College Chaplain'.

'Holy shit!' I said.

'Read on.' Magnus was highly delighted.

Brother Chantry-Pigg, an Anglican friar and chaplain of St Sebastian's University has been harassing his young charges in no less a place than the college chapel vestry.

The *Sunday Inquirer* has been given a tape recording of his attempted seduction of one of the university's undergraduates, the lovely Miss Mary Philpot. A second year student, she is as good as she is beautiful. She is an active member of the Chapel Society and the University Choir.

When she rejected the friar's sexual advances, he can be heard shouting at her on the tape saying: 'Don't be a silly girl. You know you want it. You know you do. Stop wriggling. Do what you're told . . . Come back you stupid little bitch!'

The luscious Rosalind Hotchkiss – also a second year student – told the *Sunday Inquirer* that this was not the first time that the randy Brother had attempted to seduce her friend:

'He did it before. And we complained to the university authorities. Our tutor was very kind . . . .'

('That's you,' pointed out Magnus . . .)

'But nothing could be done. He said that it was our word against Chantry-Pigg's and there simply wasn't enough evidence. But

148

when we produced the tape-recording, in spite of the support of our teachers, the university authorities still refused to act.

'We complained officially, and there was a hearing. It was presided over by the Visitor of the university, the Provost of St Sebastian's Cathedral. He turned out to be a friend of the Chaplain and he insisted that tape recorded evidence was inadmissable.

'He made sure that nothing happened. He even demanded that we handed over the tape and tried to get us expelled from the university.'

However the resourceful Miss Hotchkiss had made a secret copy and she handed it over to the *Sunday Inquirer*. To ensure its authenticity, your *Sunday Inquirer* has given it to one of the country's leading sound laboratories. One of their voice recognition experts has compared the tape with a recording of one of Rev. Chantry-Pigg's sermons (on the importance of virginity no less!) and has pronounced it a hundred per cent authentic.

'It would be one chance in two hundred million that the two voices were not the same,' he told us.

Chantry-Pigg is a member of an Anglican religious order and is the great-grandson of the Second Lord Blanding, a well-known philanthropist in the in the time of Queen Victoria. It is a pity that the friar cannot follow his noble ancestor's example. There is also madness in the family. The present Lord Blanding is a cousin. He unfortunately is confined to a mental hospital. Two years ago he threatened his gamekeeper with a hatchet.

The *Sunday Inquirer* has attempted to contact both Brother Chantry-Pigg and the Provost of St Sebastian's Cathedral. Both were unavailable for comment.

The whole episode raises serious questions about our universities. In good faith and at great expense, we send our sons and daughters to receive the best possible education. We have a right to be sure that they are not molested by lecherous teachers. The fact that Chantry-Pigg is a Reverend makes the situation even worse. It is a betrayal of trust and the *Sunday Inquirer* wants to know what our institutions of higher education are doing to make sure that this kind of thing never happens again.

As we were enjoying this effusion, the doorbell rang again. Mary and Rosalind were standing on the doorstep looking sheepish holding two more copies of the newspaper.

'We've seen it,' I said, leading the girls inside. 'Dr Hamilton just brought us a copy.'

'We thought you'd better know,' Rosalind said.

Emma provided more orange juice and gave the girls croissants. Magnus looked quizzical. 'What I want to know,' he said, 'is how the *Sunday Inquirer* got hold of this disgraceful story . . .'

Mary looked embarrassed, but Rosalind was quite untroubled. She started on the tale. 'We saw the article about Father Chantry-Pigg in *Private Eye*, and I remembered what you said about going to Clifford Maxwell . . .'

'You know I handed over the tape at the trial,' Mary was hesitant, 'well Rosalind had kept a copy . . .'

'And I was jolly glad I did,' said Rosalind stoutly. 'So I looked up Mr Maxwell in the Yellow Pages and we made an appointment to see him. He had a really posh office in Mayfair. I got a bit nervous, but he was interested in our story. He thought he could do something with it. He took us to lunch in a fancy resturant nearby.'

'Where?' asked Emma.

'It was called Maximilian's. The food was lovely.'

'He must have thought you were worthwhile,' said my wife. 'That's one of the most expensive restaurants in London.'

'I wondered,' Mary was wide-eyed. 'There weren't any prices on the menu . . .'

'Anyway,' continued Rosalind, 'he told us that it was a good story and he wanted to see if he could sell it to the *Inquirer*. He said he'd act as our agent, but that he would take forty per cent of whatever we were paid . . .'

'Forty per cent!' Magnus was astonished. 'I'm in the wrong profession!'

'He called us the same day to say that the newspaper wanted us to be photographed.'

'And so you were,' I said.

'But it wasn't what they really wanted. They tried to make us go topless, but we weren't going to.'

'I should think not.' Emma was indignant.

'Well Mary wouldn't anyway.' Rosalind was honest, 'I wouldn't have minded if the money was good enough, but I thought it would spoil the story. "Innocent young girls molested by a flirty friar . . ." '

'Rosalind!' Emma was prudish about that sort of thing.

'Well they offered to pay us a lot more if we would.'

Magnus brightened. 'How much more?' he asked.

'Forty thousand each . . .'

'Bloody Hell! I'd do it for half.' Magnus obviously envisaged a new career for himself.

'I don't think you quite have Mary and Rosalind's assets,' I pointed out.

'Well, we didn't want to. So we only got half. We have to give Mr Maxwell eight thousand pounds each . . .'

'That'll pay for your lunch,' remarked Emma dryly,

'But we still get twelve thousand each and that will clear our university debts.'

'Great!' I said.

'I'd say it was! Jolly good article! Enjoyed every word!' Magnus was eating his croissant and his sweater was decorated with crumbs. 'Can't see the friar reappearing after this. Scuppered by the press! Just what he deserves!'

'The Provost is bound to be in trouble, too,' I reflected.

'Oh . . . he'll get away with it. They'll promote him again to keep him out of trouble.' Magnus did not think much of the workings of the Established Church. 'That type always slides through things. Friends in high places! He'll be all right! . . . Very delicious croissants,' he remarked, reaching for the last one. 'Does anybody want this?'

The next morning I made an appointment to see Flanagan to discuss plans for the Mancini visit and the new Golden Arrow Casino. The estate manager was anxious to know how the building site should be set out for the foundation stone ceremony.

When I arrived in his office later in the day the Vice-Chancellor was holding a golf club and was trying to putt a golf ball into a glass next to his wastebasket. 'Want a go, mate?' he asked. He was wearing a golf hat with the insignia of the St Sebastian Golf Club.

I declined, but was curious about this sudden interest. 'Had a brain wave,' he announced as the golf ball missed the glass and banged into the wastebasket. 'What we need is to expand into Recreation Management. We have all these playing fields which are underused. I thought we could hire them out to various local organisations.'

I resisted the urge to point out that the playing fields were there to encourage our students to play games. We were meant to believe in a healthy mind in a healthy body. But Flanagan was in full flow.

'I called the Secretary of the Golf Club last Friday and he gave me lunch at the club on Sunday. He was very keen. They could do with more space. I suggested we went into partnership. The university could offer a diploma in Professional Golf. He loved the idea!'

Was there no limit to the Vice-Chancellor's schemes? The university was no longer offering degrees in Chemistry or Philosophy. Instead we were peddling Casino Management, Celebrity Studies, Professional Golf and Commitment Ceremonies. I wondered where it would end.

'Anyway,' Flanagan continued, 'He gave me the hat and a golf club plus a ball. Can't seem to get the hang of it though!'

'But we've never done Sports Studies. I shouldn't think anyone knows anything about Professional Golf.' I said.

'Well we'll have to learn. Go on a course or something. Academics are meant to be intelligent after all. I've also got a couple of dance schools who want to go into partnership with us at the moment, so we'll have to branch out into that whole area. Perhaps I can get those prima donnas in the Drama department away from all that Shakespeare stuff and teach what people really want to know. Anyway Felix, let's get down to business . . .'

Flanagan spread out several architectural drawings on his desk and explained about the plans for the casino. Amongst the papers was a photograph of a silver trowel for the foundation ceremony. He clearly was intending to do the thing properly.

On the sofa I noticed a copy of the *Sunday Inquirer*. 'You saw the article?' I asked.

'Yup . . . loved it! Just what that canting hypocrite deserved!

The bloody Provost was on to me demanding the girls' expulsion, but I pointed out that if he'd done his job properly at the hearing, it would never have come to this. Anyway I've had a word with the Archbishop. The Provost is not long for St Sebastian's. They'll find a way to kick him upstairs again!'

'So the girls aren't in trouble?'

'In trouble!' Flanagan laughed. 'Quite the reverse! It'll do the university a power of good. Applications will go up. Mark my words! Those little sheilas did looked stunning. Do you know how the newspaper got the story?'

I explained about Mary and Rosalind's visit. The Vice-Chancellor was impressed. 'Clifford Maxwell! Really! I didn't know those two had it in them.'

'They're very good philosophers,' I observed mildly.

Flanagan brushed this aside. 'They have a real flair,' he said. 'What we need to do is to invite them to be tutors for the new degree in Celebrity Studies.'

'Tutors?'

'Student "involvement" is the new buzzword. It saves on staff costs. Send them an email. We don't have to pay them. We call it work experience and they can put it on their curriculum vitae.' The Vice-Chancellor took off his hat, straightened his tie, and walked me to the door. 'Exciting times, mate,' he said as he sent me on my way.

I had agreed to meet Magnus in the Senior Common Room at four. We arrived together, ordered tea and tea-cakes, and looked for a place to sit. Pilkington was by himself in the corner reading the *Times Higher Educational Supplement*. 'Come on, Felix,' Magnus said smiling. 'Let's see what he thinks about the *Sunday Inquirer*.'

Pilkington looked up as we joined him. He made a brief nod in our direction and turned back to his newspaper. Magnus was not to be deterred. 'Heard the news about Father Chantry-Pigg?' he asked.

Pilkington nodded. 'A great pity,' he said.

'Absolutely,' responded Magnus, winking at me. 'Seducing students! It just won't do.'

Pilkington winced as Magnus took a rumpled copy of the article out of his pocket. 'You've seen the piece?'

Pilkington muttered that he had heard about it from his secretary. 'Well, then,' Magnus began, 'you need to be fully informed. He's a member of your department, after all. Let me go through it with you.'

Before Pilkington could object, Magnus began reading the page in a loud voice. Heads turned in our direction. When he finished, he grinned. 'Quite a little escapade, don't you think? Chantry-Pigg won't be able to stay on after this.'

Pilkington nodded gloomily.

'It's sad for his fan club of nice young men. What will they do without the chaplain to dance attendance on?' I said.

Magnus was very robust. 'With the success of the commitment ceremonies, perhaps they can hire themselves out as bridesmaids,' he suggested.

Pilkington was not amused, 'Don't be absurd, Magnus,' he said in a very stuffy tone, 'those ceremonies are a disgrace!'

'Well,' I pointed out, 'St Sebastian's is desperate for money and apparently there are very few nice places for weddings . . .'

'And after all,' said Magnus triumphantly, 'we all know Buggers can't be Choosers!'

CHAPTER NINE

The Very Worst Sort of Cad

Magnus was right. Crispin Chantry-Pigg was not seen again in St Sebastian's. Within a few weeks, the rumour went round that one of his cousins had given him a cottage in Devil's Bridge, Wales. He was to be employed as site supervisor of one of her caravan parks. It seemed a sad comedown after an existence in Winchester Close with the ex-wife of a famous film director.

Meanwhile, arrangements were being finalised for the Mancini visit to the university. Invitations to the St Sebastian's Feast had been sent out, and programmes for the laying of the foundation stone were being printed. The Vice-Chancellor was in contact with Sir William regarding his speech. He was to be driven down just before the dinner by young Will Dormouse, his eldest grandson. It was felt that he was too old to stand around in the cold for the building site ritual.

Also the first commitment ceremony had taken place. Over a hundred guests flooded the university. I was on my way to class when I saw two young men in white suits passionately kissing each other. Then guests threw confetti over the happy couple as they ran to a yellow Saab convertible which was decorated with multi-coloured helium balloons. I thought it all looked delightful.

One afternoon I ran into Mrs Brush. She was mopping the floor outside John Pilkington's office. 'Can I have a quick word?' she asked. 'It's about Elsa Catnip. I'm worried about her.'

'Is she all right?'

'Well . . . to tell you the truth, she's had a bit of a problem with her gambling.'

'She's lost money?' I was concerned. I did not think Wanda Catnip would be indulgent about paying her mother's debts of honour.

'No . . . it's just the opposite. She keeps winning. And those in charge are beginning to look suspicious. She's not sure whether to go back.'

'Look, Mrs Brush,' I said. 'That isn't a crisis. All she has to do is lose once in a while. That's what I suggested when I first spoke to her.'

'But Elsa hates losing . . .'

'Well, there's no alternative. She must bite the bullet occasionally if she doesn't want to be thrown out of the place.'

'Don't you think they'll catch on?'

I shook my head. 'I'm sure they won't,' I said.

Later that day I had a telephone call from Mrs Catnip herself. She was very apologetic about ringing, but she said she needed to see me. We arranged that she should come after Mrs Brush had finished her work. At five there was a knock on my door and the two ladies arrived. Mrs Catnip was wearing a dark blue coat and a red woolly hat. I made them both a cup of coffee and they sat down opposite my desk.

'It's so kind of you to see me, Dr Glass,' Mrs Catnip began. 'I know how busy you are, but I'm at my wits' end.'

She took a deep breath and started on the story. 'I know Mavis told you that I had a bit of trouble with the casino last week. The dealer got rather angry when I won ten games in a row. And he summoned the manager. Well, I told them I was just learning how to play and got lucky. But they suggested I go back to bingo.'

'But they'll continue to let you play for the time being?'

'I think so, dear. And I know I've got to lose a bit sometimes, but it's harder than you'd think . . . But the real problem is that I wanted to go back to Leeds. You see, there are at least six casinos in the city and I could go round them all so they wouldn't remember me . . .'

'Well why don't you?'

Mrs Catnip looked awkward. 'Well you see, dear, I'm eighty-six and I can't really manage on my own. I can't carry the shopping any more and the coal is too heavy to bring in. That kind of thing. I wanted to move into the Sunset Residential Home. It's just down the road and I've got lots of friends there . . .'

'Well, what's the problem with that?' Sadly, from my earlier conversation with Wanda, I knew the answer all too well.

'I'd have to sell the house and Wanda becomes so angry if I even suggest the idea. I hoped maybe if I won enough at the blackjack, I might be able to pay for the Home myself. But I can see that no manager is ever going to let me win that kind of money . . .' Poor Mrs Catnip looked as if she were going to cry. 'I suppose I've just got to stay with Wanda in St Sebastian's, but I miss my friends so much.' She dabbed her eyes.

'Look,' I said, 'I think the situation is easier than you think. Could you manage in your own house if you had a little extra help?'

Mrs Catnip brightened. 'Oh yes dear, I could easily. But help is very expensive. It would be at least a hundred pounds a week. There just isn't enough from my husband's pension . . .'

I took out a notepad and wrote down some figures. 'First of all,' I began, 'you'd be able to get a Care Allowance. People your age are entitled to it. That's at least forty pounds a week on top of your existing income.'

Mrs Catnip looked doubtful, 'Are you sure dear? I don't want to take charity.'

'It's not charity. You're entitled to it like your old age pension. I got one for my own mother. It's for anyone who needs help so that they can stay in their own home if at all possible.'

Mrs Catnip was not slow on the uptake. 'So I'd only need to win an extra sixty pounds more every week.'

'Would that be possible?' I asked.

'I could do that easily . . . if I went to a different casino every time then it would be less than forty pounds a month overall from each of them. They wouldn't mind that . . .'

'Well there you are then! But remember, you've got to lose sometimes. Otherwise they'll get suspicious like they did here . . .'

The two ladies gathered up their coats and handbags and I walked them to the entrance. Mrs Catnip looked much happier. As they left, I gave them both invitations to the St Sebastian's Feast. Mrs Brush said that she couldn't be there because she had to make tea for her husband, but Mrs Catnip was interested. 'Do come,' I said. 'I'll introduce you to Sir William Dormouse. He's a great blackjack player just like you.'

As time drew near for the Mancini visit, the university became increasingly busy with arrangements. Luigi Mancini, Sylvester, and Wolfie Goldberg were flying into Heathrow and had hired a chauffeur and car to meet them. They would come up to St Sebastian's for the university festivities a day early, and were booked in to the best rooms in the White Hart Hotel. The invitations to the Feast had been sent out. Flanagan had asked Emma for advice about food and she had offered to host a dinner party the night before in our house. She was currently working on a programme about French provinical cuisine and thought this might be a good opportunity to try out several new receipes.

On the day of the Mancinis' arrival, the university flag was raised over the Clock Tower. A small party had assembled before the Old Building including the Vice-Chancellor, the Registrar and myself. Just before four o'clock a vast white stretch limousine pulled up in front of the university. It completely blocked the street.

The chauffeur opened the doors and slowly Sylvester, Luigi and Wolfie emerged from the depths. The Vice-Chancellor, wearing his academic gown and hood, stepped foward. He hugged his old friend, and shook hands with the other guests. Luigi was very affable. He slapped me on the back and drawled, 'How're ya doing Felix?' Sylvester and Wolfie seemed equally glad to see me.

I remarked that St Sebastian's was a long way from Las Vegas. 'Sure is!' said Luigi, looking about him at the grey street. 'You oughta get more street lighting round here!'

The Vice-Chancellor ushered the party into his office where sherry and canapes were served by waiters dressed in white uniforms emblazoned with the university crest. There was a hushed silence as Flanagan expressed his gratitude to the Mancini organisation for their generosity towards the university and made an expansive gesture towards various architects' plans which were displayed on the walls. Luigi nodded and looked pleased when he was told about the dedication ceremony that had been arranged for the following day. Then it was time for the limousine to take our guests to their hotel.

Dinner was scheduled for eight. In addition to Luigi, Sylvester, Wolfie, the Vice-Chancellor and Helga, Emma had invited Registrar Sloth and Joy Pickles to make up numbers. I felt a little awkward about asking Joy. She had never acknowledged the flowers that I had sent her, but in the event she seemed quite happy. She came wearing a very low-cut yellow dress which looked as if it were too small for her. Emma looked disapproving, but, compared with Divine de la Rue on a similar occasion, her costume was almost in good taste. Sloth appeared very grey and middle-aged beside her.

I was relieved that Helga sported neither dark glasses nor any form of body cast. As usual she was quiet and looked constantly to Flanagan for approval, but she slowly relaxed in Emma's company and seemed to be enjoying herself.

The Mancinis were the last to arrive. It was with enormous difficulty that the driver squeezed into our street and parked the white limousine in front of our house. I foresaw that I would have trouble with the neighbours later, but, as soon as they were dropped off, the car inched its way out again.

When Emma opened the front door to the Las Vegans, Luigi kissed her hand, thanked her for her gracious hospitality and presented her with an enormous bunch of red roses. We did not have a vase big enough to contain them. Once everyone was seated, I handed around drinks and home-made cheese straws. Conversation was easy. Sylvester and Flanagan entertained the company with a flow of childhood reminiscences. It was all very jolly although I knew that the jovial stories concealed a great deal of hardship and misery.

We then went in to dinner. The new conservatory looked beautiful with Emma's flowers and table decorations. For the first course, she had made a wonderful dish with fresh scallops and garlic. This was accompanied by an excellent chilled white Burgundy.

Wolfie was seated next to Joy Pickles. She listened sympathetically as he told her that his aged mother had just, as he put it, passed on, after being moved into a nursing home. The local rabbi, Max Rhinestone, had conducted the funeral and over two hundred people had been present. To my surprise, Joy seemed to understand the intricacies of Jewish funeral customs. Her own father had died recently and had been buried according to the Orthodox rite in Golders Green.

'I didn't know you were Jewish, Joy,' I said. I wondered if her family knew about her relationship with Sloth.

Joy looked self-conscious. 'Well we're not religious,' she fiddled with her knife, 'but we do support Israel and my family have always belonged to an Orthodox synagogue.'

The main course was a rich pheasant casserole. There were roast potatoes and a variety of vegetables with a thick dark claret to go with it. This was followed by a selection of French cheeses, all at the perfect state of ripeness. Pudding was a delectable French tarte tatin served with crème fraîche. The English guests enjoyed every mouthful, but I noticed that Sylvester and Luigi pushed their food around without eating much. It was clear that what they liked was steak. Emma had observed this too and when the apple tart was served, she offered them as an alternative large servings of Häagen-Dazs chocolate ice cream fresh from the freezer. They loved it.

Throughout dinner Flanagan dominated the conversation with his descriptions of the future Golden Arrow Casino Training College. 'We were going to start off using the Great Hall, but due to the Mancinis' generosity,' he smiled at Luigi, 'the Hall can now be used solely for weddings and commitment ceremonies.'

Luigi was puzzled. 'Weddings I know about,' he said, 'but I don't know about commitment ceremonies?'

When the Vice-Chancellor explained that in the United Kingdom it was possible for gay couples to commit themselves legally to one another, Luigi was troubled. 'You mean they get hitched up? You gotta priest who does this?'

'They don't actually get married,' Flanagan soothed his visitor. 'They dedicate themselves to each other and it means that they become each other's next of kin.' He took a Mixed Blessings brochure out of his pocket and passed it to Luigi who put on a pair of gold spectacles. He scanned it, shook his head, and passed it over to Sylvester.

'You know,' Luigi leaned back in his chair, 'it's not exactly how we do things. There was this kid, Tony Brocca. He grew up with me in the Bronx. A skinny guy. Anyway, after doing a little bit of this and a little bit of that in New York, he moved to the Florida Keys and started up a deep sea fishing business. He went into partnership with some Mexican. He tried to keep it a secret that the two of them were sorta more than business colleagues, but it got around. His family was sore as hell. The last thing I heard was that his brothers went down to see him and he ended up hanging from the rafters in an old smoke-house.' Looking at the Vice-Chancellor he grinned: 'For me you unnerstand, I'm as liberal as the next guy, but if you want to do that sorta thing in the U.S. of A., you sure don't tell anyone about it.'

I wondered if I should have invited John and Maureen Pilkington to the party rather than Sloth and Joy Pickles. Pilkington and Luigi would have seen eye to eye in the matter of gay rights.

The following day a buffet lunch had been organised in the Great Hall for the Mancinis and a few other honoured guests from the university. Magnus was in high dudgeon because he was not included. The Vice-Chancellor insisted that all academic staff wear their gowns. At twelve-thirty the Mancinis' white limousine arrived and Luigi, Sylvester and Wolfie were first led into the Vice-Chancellor's office for drinks.

Flanagan had placed a Victorian gong in the corner of his room. When the cuckoo clock behind his desk struck one, Registrar Sloth hit the gong three times and announced that luncheon was served. We all gathered up our things and filed into the Great Hall. There a very splendid buffet of both cold and hot food had been arranged in front of the St Sebastian portrait. We helped ourselves and sat at several small tables. I found myself next to Helga who smiled at me timidly. Then Luigi took the chair on my other side.

As he worked his way through his lunch, our guest kept glancing up at the portrait and was plainly fascinated by it. 'Hey,' he said, through a large mouthful of boeuf bourguignon, 'who's that guy? Quite a physique! No wonder all the poofters love him!'

Helga giggled. When I told him that Sebastian was a saint and a martyr, Luigi hastily crossed himself. Then he asked how he came to be pierced all over with arrows. I tried to explain that St Sebastian had lived in the third century in Italy and it had been a time when Christians were persecuted. I said that the university and town were named after him. Then I pointed out that the arrows had not actually killed him. 'Fortunately,' I told Luigi, 'he seems to have attracted the attention of a kindly widow who looked after him until the wounds healed.'

'So he liked women even though he was a saint,' commented our guest approvingly.

I said that I wasn't sure about that, but I did know that eventually he was clubbed to death by his enemies. Luigi was interested in this. 'Clubbed to death, huh?' he said. 'My cousin's boy got himself beaten to a pulp the other day.'

Helga and I expressed concern for the unfortunate young man, but Luigi was not sympathetic. 'He got himself involved with the Ferretto gang, so what do you expect? My cousin was always too soft with him. I'd've given him a job. Family's family after all! But no, he wanted to strike out on his own and that's what happened. Dumb kid!'

Helga asked how the boy had annoyed Mr Ferretto's people. 'I dunno,' said Luigi. 'Some drug deal or other went wrong I expect. Alberto Ferretto always was a mean bastard.' I was not sure how to react to this story. Fortunately it was very far away from St Sebastian's University in the respectable home counties of England.

Luigi continued to gaze at the painting. 'You got the name of the artist?' he asked.

I explained that the portrait was a gift to the university from an American benefactor, a millionaire from Sweetpea, Virginia. It was painted by a young friend of his whose name was Julian Bosie. The Vice-Chancellor, I was sure, had his address.

'Maybe he'd do a few dozen of these things for our casinos!' Luigi suggested. 'Could he paint Cleopatra in her barge or a coupla gladiators fighting or the walls of wherever-it-was falling down?'

I caught Helga's eye and we shared a moment of agonised mirth. Then I got a grip of myself. 'I'm sure he'd be very pleased with the commission. He's still young and making his way.'

'Good!' said Luigi, 'Then we can screw down the price a bit . . .'

After lunch the whole party made its way to the site of the old squash courts. The original corrugated iron shacks had been taken down and there was rubble everywhere. However, a path had been cleared through the mess and there was a small area in the middle where the first stone was to be laid. Flanagan, looking as broad as he was long in his Vice-Chancellor's gown and hat, stepped foward carrying a blue box. Luigi, placed on his right, towered over him. A student dressed in a maroon velvet gown and hat was on the Vice-Chancellor's left. He held up a brass trumpet and played a few bars of Purcell's voluntary. It was the signal for everyone to gather round and look attentive.

I had seen enough of the Vice-Chancellor on these occasions to recognise that he adored being in the limelight. With a flourish, he stepped onto a wooden box which had been strategically placed in front of him. 'Friends,' he began. 'We are gathered here today for a milestone in the history of our beloved university. Over a hundred years ago our founders envisaged that the college they created would become a light to the nations. And so it was. The missionaries who were trained in these buildings travelled all over the world bringing knowledge and civilisation wherever they preached. We live in a different age with different aims and different values, but we still have the same strong sense of dedication. We too, in our own way, will enlighten the world.'

He looked round at the assembled company and with a bold gesture pointed towards Sylvester and Luigi. 'You see before you the two newest and very possibly the greatest benefactors this university has ever known. They share our vision. They have taken the trouble to leave their huge business empire in Las Vegas to be with us on this unique occasion today. Each and every one of us should be grateful to the Mancini family which has made this new enterprise possible.'

He dropped his voice and assumed a more conversational tone. He sounded more Australian than ever. 'As some of you may be aware, Sylvester Mancini and I go way back. We were good mates together many years ago in Australia and I can tell you we two cobbers got into some hair-raising scrapes.' There was obsequious laughter from the audience. 'I would never have believed in those days, and neither, I promise you, would any of our teachers, that Sylvester would distinguish himself as a business man and would become a leading light of the vast Mancini empire led by his cousin and brother-in-law, Luigi.' He doffed his cap in Luigi's direction and Luigi nodded back. 'We are truly honoured that Mr Luigi Mancini himself could be with us this afternoon and we welcome him to St Sebastian's most warmly.'

At this point everyone clapped, but Flanagan was not finished. He held up his hand. 'We at St Sebastian's University are delighted that a new partnership has been formally launched between our institution and the Mancini-sponsored King Midas Casino College in Las Vegas. My distinguished colleague Dr Felix Glass has visited the college and came back with glowing reports about its innovative educational programme.' Figuratively I wiped my brow. I told myself that one qualification for being a Vice-Chancellor was an ability to be economical with the truth.

'You will be aware,' Flanagan continued, 'that the British government has recently promoted the idea of super-casinos throughout the country. It is to be hoped that this bold initiative will bring about the regeneration of all our great cities. We at St Sebastian's are determined not to be left behind in this visionary project. Our vocation is to contribute. We have introduced a new degree in Casino Management under the direction of Dr Glass, who is himself an eminent academic and the author of several well-received books.' I though briefly of my latest, *Kant's Critiques Revisited*, languishing on the shelves of academic bookshops, priced at sixty pounds a copy.

'Our new venture,' continued Flanagan inexorably, 'will provide casino training at the very highest level. It is a new degree and is the first of its kind in the United Kingdom. Our aim is to be a centre of excellence in this field. With the help of Mancini Enterprises, within a couple of years, we will be sending out trained experts to all the countries of the civilised world. The Golden Arrow Casino Training College of St Sebastian's University will be world-famous and it is all going to take place here, on this very spot. Now is the moment I know we have all been waiting for. I call upon upon Mr Luigi Mancini to lay the foundation stone of this great new venture.'

The Head Porter, who was standing nearby, handed Luigi Mancini a square piece of stone approximately the size of a small loaf of bread. Luigi placed it on a row of bricks which had already been laid and everyone clapped. Then the Vice-Chancellor took a silver trowel with a bone handle out of the blue box he was holding and handed it to Luigi. 'This,' he said, 'is a small token of our appreciation for your generous involvement in our exciting new joint venture. The trowel reads "Presented to Mr Luigi Mancini on the occasion of his laying the foundation stone of the Golden Arrow Casino Training College of St Sebastian's University. *Per Fortunam ad Prosperitatem.* Through Luck to Wealth".'

Luigi was very taken with the gift; he patted the new foundation stone with it and sliced it through the air several times. Then he shook hands with the Vice-Chancellor and there was more clapping. As I looked around, I noticed that Wolfie Goldberg was standing near the back. He had placed himself next to Joy Pickles and they appeared to be talking rather intimately.

Drinks before the Feast were scheduled to take place at seven o'clock in the Senior Common Room. Over seventy guests had been invited. One of the first to arrive was Sir William with his grandson, young Will. He was dressed in a somewhat frayed dinner jacket and rumpled notes for his after-dinner speech protruded from his pocket. He looked in excellent health, although he walked with the aid of his stick with the silver dormouse handle.

Young Will deposited his grandfather into my care and disappeared to the student bar. He was anxious, as he put it, to sample the local talent.

Just as I had levered Sir William into a chair, Wanda Catnip and her mother entered. Wanda looked like thunder. 'It was ridiculous of you to invite Mother,' she said. 'I don't know what she thinks she's doing here, but once she had the invitation, there was no stopping her!' Then she disappeared in the direction of the ladies' lavatory leaving her mother behind.

I sat Mrs Catnip next to Sir William and introduced them. They may have been born in different sectors of society, but they were much the same age and I knew they had a common hobby. 'Sir William,' I said, 'you might be interested to know that Mrs Catnip read the book about blackjack strategy that Harry gave you. And I understand she's doing very well indeed at our local casino.'

Sir William brightened. 'Good show!' he said. 'I always like to hear about those casino sharks getting their comeuppance.' I had a quick chill of foreboding as to what he would say in his after-dinner speech. However, having found another blackjack fan, he was not going to sit chattering idly. He reached into the pocket of his dinner jacket and said in the most gallant manner possible, 'I'm delighted to make your acquaintance Madam. I happen to have brought a pack of cards with me. I thought some-one might like a little game after dinner. You wouldn't care to have a go before the guests arrive, would you?'

Elsa was thrilled. 'Well I'm just a beginner, dear,' she said, 'But, yes. If you like, I'll play a hand or two with you.'

I helped the two old people move their chairs around one of the Senior Common Room tables and I cleared away the glasses and napkins. 'Would you like to be dealer? What about seven games with you as dealer and then seven games with me?' suggested Sir William.

'Very well,' said Elsa Catnip. She rummaged in her capacious bag and brought out a matchbox. 'Let's play for matchsticks,' she said, 'it makes it more interesting if we have chips.'

'I say, why not?' Sir William was not one to turn down a sporting proposition.

Elsa divided the matches between the two of them and the contest began. By this time Wanda had come back into the room. Her temper had not improved and she took me on one side. 'I understand you've been encouraging Mother in this ridiculous folly, Felix,' she accused me. 'She tells me that she wants to go back to live in her house in Leeds and she'll support herself on the proceeds of blackjack playing.'

I shrugged my shoulders. 'Perhaps you'd better take a look at her card-playing skills before you make a judgement, Wanda,' I suggested.

Mrs Catnip dealt the first hand. People were coming into the Senior Common Room and a crowd began to assemble around the two players. Sir William did very well. By the time he had finished his seven games, his pile of matchsticks was considerably the larger.

'See,' said Wanda Catnip. 'She's absolutely hopeless. Look how much she's lost!'

'She's not playing yet,' I said. It was clear that Wanda had no idea of the rules of blackjack. ' She's the dealer. Wait and see how she does in the next group of games.'

Then the two of them swopped roles. Mrs Catnip had made good use of her time. She knew exactly where the cards lay. She won every one of her seven games and Sir William's pile of matches was decimated. There was a ripple of applause and Wanda looked uncomfortable. 'Beginners' luck!' she said.

It was Sir William's turn again. Mrs Catnip dealt out the cards with her old work-worn hands. By this time Sir William had played himself in. His record was as impressive as Elsa's. There was a breathless hush among the onlookers and again they broke out clapping as he won every one of his seven games.

'Well done, dear!' said Elsa Catnip.

But there was no doubt that she was equally good. She had no trouble winning all her matches back when she played her hands. The audience was enthralled and the entertainment might have lasted all evening if the Head Porter had not announced in a loud voice, 'Pray silence for the Registrar.'

Sir William shook Elsa's hand and bowed. 'Well done, Madam,' he said. 'You're quite a gel!'

Elsa smiled shyly as the Registrar clinked his glass. 'Our honoured guests were regrettably detained,' he informed the company, 'but they now have arrived. The Vice-Chancellor has taken them straight into the Great Hall. Would you all please make your way there and find your places. Seating plans have been put on the notice boards near the door.'

Led by Registrar Sloth, the guests filed out of the Senior Common Room. They went across to the Great Hall where a horseshoe table had been arranged in front of the St Sebastian portrait. I noticed that Joy Pickles was wearing an elaborate red dress with a deep décolletage. She left Sloth's side without a backward glance and, all smiles, moved into her place next to Wolfie Goldberg.

The Vice-Chancellor was at the head of the table with Luigi Mancini on his right and Sir William on his left. Emma and I were seated several seats down across from one another. On the other side of Luigi was placed the Provost of St Sebastian's Cathedral. It was the first time I had seen him since his exposure in the *Sunday Inquirer*. He looked even sleeker and more self-satisfied than usual. It had been announced in *The Times* that very morning that he had been appointed Suffragan Bishop of Puddlethorpe and that he would be taking up his new position at the beginning of August. I remembered what Flanagan had said about the Archbishop kicking him upstairs. There was no doubt that our Vice-Chancellor knew the ways of the world.

The Provost said the St Sebastian's Latin grace before we sat down. But I was diverted by Sir William. He was looking flustered, almost angry. Had he perhaps been unsettled by the game with Elsa? I did not think this probable. He came from a culture which emphasised the importance of being a good loser. Anyway, he had enjoyed himself. Perhaps he had mislaid his speech? But no, I could see it was still in his dinner-jacket pocket. I was mystified. Something was very wrong, but I had no idea what it could be. As the Feast went on, Sir William did not calm down. I hoped the food and drink would have a soothing effect on him, but, if anything, he became more agitated. He kept glancing angrily in the direction of Luigi Mancini; then he frowned, shook his head and clicked his tongue. He left most of his dinner uneaten although I noticed that he did take several glasses of wine.

Flanagan, on the other hand, was having a splendid time. He and Luigi had quickly established a rapport and they were telling each other stories and roaring with laughter.

Apart from Sir William, it seemed to be a successful dinner. The food was good. The Great Hall, lit by candles, looked dark and romantic. The waiters were unobtrusive and each course succeeded the previous one seamlessly. Over us loomed Julian Bosie's portrait of our patron saint, but in the shadowy light even that monstrosity looked rather elegant.

After the raspberry pavlova, coffee was poured out and port was circulated. Flanagan stood up, tinkled his fork against a plate and raised his glass. 'Ladies and Gentlemen,' he declared, 'The Queen!'

There was a loud scraping of chairs as everyone stood and said in unison, 'The Queen!' Then we all sat down again and there was a general air of relaxation. However, Flanagan was not to be cheated of making a speech.

He began by welcoming Luigi Mancini, his brother-in-law Sylvester and the Mancini accountant Wolfie Goldberg to St Sebastian's. This was a great occasion, he said, because it was the inauguration of an extensive building project to house the new Golden Arrow Casino Training College and to launch a full degree programme in Casino Management. The Mancini organisation from Las Vegas was funding this huge initiative in conjunction with its own training school, the King Midas Casino College in Nevada. There would be a constant exchange of students (I thought momentarily of Miss de la Rue), and both institutions would be enriched by the mutual contact.

Then the Vice-Chancellor turned to his neighbour on his other side. Sir William looked straight ahead as Flanagan leaned towards him and embarked on a lengthy introduction. Sir William, he said, was an important landowner in Shropshire, well-known for his enlightened attitudes towards his tenants. He was a scion of one of the noble families of England. One only had to look at him to see that he was a top bloke, both a sportsman and a gentleman. Then he gave a brief account of our stay in the Dormouse castle and he made a joke about the lack of central heating. Sir William smiled wanly. At the same time he emphasised the warmth and generosity of Sir William's hospitality and his enthusiasm for this new venture at St Sebastian's.

When Flanagan finally wound down, Sir William raised himself to his feet. He had taken the script of his speech out of the pocket of his dinner jacket, but he left it untouched beside his port glass. Clearly he was intending to speak impromptu . . .

'Vice-Chancellor, Ladies and Gentlemen,' he began. 'It is an honour to be with you this evening. What your Vice-Chancellor has initiated is a very excellent plan, very excellent indeed! There is no doubt that the government will be successful in its determination to establish super-casinos throughout the British Isles. Jolly good idea, in my view! Nothing wrong with a game of cards or two! Keeps people off the streets! And quite right to involve the university in the early stages. Train people properly from the beginning, that's the thing! Then we know that all the games will be sporting and above board . . .

'Now, when I was a schoolboy, I played quite a bit of black-jack. There wasn't much else to do in school in those days to tell you the truth. None of this modern emphasis on examinations. You either got wet and muddy playing rugger or you sat cosy and warm in front of your study fire having a flutter or two. Jolly good fun it was . . .

'More recently I have become a serious player. I know some of you watched me have a few hands with that lady sitting over there.' He pointed with his long bony finger at old Mrs Catnip who was placed far down the table. 'Let me tell you, she was a worthy opponent! Probably the best player I have ever come across.' Sir William bowed in Elsa Catnip's direction and raised his glass. 'My congratulations, Madam. First rate if I may say so! There should be more like you!' Everyone took this as a cue for a round of applause. Mrs Catnip looked confused for a moment. Then she got to her feet and made a shy little bow before sitting down again. Her daughter, who was sitting opposite, looked almost apoplectic with fury.

Sir William returned to his theme: 'So you see Vice-Chancellor, I fully support this admirable initiative of yours and I have every confidence that the St Sebastian's Golden Arrow Casino and the degree course directed by Dr Glass will be a triumph for the university. And so it should be . . .'

If only he had stopped there, all would have been well. But he had not finished. There was a long pause while he looked down at Luigi Mancini who was smoking a very large cigar and drumming his fingers on the table. 'However I must warn you Vice-Chancellor,' continued Sir William, 'I believe you have made a very serious error. One hesitates to accuse a fellow-guest, but I'm afraid there can be no mistake about this. That individual who is sitting beside you, Signor Mantovani or whatever he is called, is not a person you should be associating with. I've met him once before and I have incontrovertible evidence that he is neither a gentleman nor a sportsman. Indeed, Ladies and Gentlemen, I can only describe him as the very worst sort of cad!'

There was a hush in the Great Hall. This was not the kind of speech the company had been expecting. The evening was certainly turning out to be interesting. After a moment Sir William continued his tirade. 'It is only right that you all should know the basis of my accusation. I will tell you the full history of our acquaintance. Last summer I took a short holiday in Las Vegas with my daughter whom many of you may know, Victoria, the wife of Professor Harry Gilbert. We stayed at the Cleopatra's Palace Hotel and I was anxious to try my hand at blackjack!

'I had recently read a most interesting and excellent book, which I hope will be required reading in your new Casino Management Degree programme. It is called *How to Win at Blackjack in Ten Easy Lessons* and it is written by an American mathematician, Dr Ernest Ripper. Well I was anxious to try out his recommendations and strategies which involved observing very carefully which cards had been played. And I have to say, it was most effective. I spent an evening in the Cleopatra's Palace Casino and, though I say it myself, I was doing very well. Indeed, I had high hopes that by the end of my holiday I would have made enough money to install central heating in my house and your Vice-Chancellor would never again have had to borrow a hot water bottle to keep himself warm at night.' There was a ripple of laughter around the room. Everyone was fascinated by Sir William's narrative.

'After a couple of hours, I was just getting into my stride and was starting to win a great deal of money. I claim no credit for this. It was merely the result of the application of the principles as explained by the splendid Dr Ripper. But then I was rudely interrupted. The manager of the casino, instead of being pleased to see an elderly guest enjoy himself and win a well-earned thousand or two, decided to intervene.

'My stack of chips was undoubtedly increasing and indeed reaching significant proportions when several very sinister-looking . . . well I can only describe them as thugs, surrounded me. It was most unpleasant. They were all wearing ill-tailored shiny suits and they all reeked of some very vulgar, cheap hair-oil. Without a by-your-leave, they had the audacity to frog-march me into some tart's boudoir of a backroom where I was confronted by the very rascal, Vice-Chancellor, who is sitting on your right-hand side this evening.

'He insisted I sit down and one of his appalling henchmen

offered me a glass of whisky. I thought I was being poisoned. It was totally unlike any whisky I had ever drunk in my life before. It tasted even worse than the stuff we used to brew up in the officers' mess just before we embarked on the D-Day landings in the last war.

'Then this fellow had the impertinence to tell me that card counting was banned. He said it was against the rules. And then he expelled me from his casino, and told me that I would be debarred from any premises he owned for life.' Sir William paused at this point in his story. The memory had made him quite angry and he wiped his flushed face with a large white handkerchief.

'As you can imagine, Ladies and Gentlemen,' he continued, 'I was profoundly shocked. I always understood that our American allies, like ourselves, believed in free enterprise and personal initiative. I should have remembered my experience in the army. We always used to say amongst ourselves that the Yanks couldn't be depended on. Rotten bad soldiers they were. Kept getting upset! Totally unreliable! In my view we'd have won the war much sooner without them!

'Still I mustn't get diverted from my subject. I was appalled at my treatment. Damned unsporting is all I can say! Just because that bandit there was going to have to pay out a pound or two in winnings, he stopped me from playing. I can only call that being a bad loser, a rotten bad loser!' He turned the full force of his fury onto Luigi Mancini who sat as if he had been turned to stone. 'Sir,' he said. 'Your conduct is a disgrace to your profession! It is not cricket and it simply will not do!'

Having made this pronouncement in a voice of thunder, he turned back to Flanagan. His manner softened. 'So you see Vice-Chancellor, I have a duty to warn you against this criminal. For the sake of your own reputation as a gentleman and to save your university from dishonour and disgrace, it is vital that you break all ties with him immediately. I am sure you are innocent in this matter and you had no idea of the snake in the grass you were harbouring, but, before it is too late, I must beg you to sever the connection.'

At this point, Luigi stubbed out his cigar. He stood up and gestured to Sylvester and Wolfie to follow him. Without a backward glance the three of them marched down the length of the Great

Hall and disappeared out of the far doors. They left a stunned silence behind them.

Then Flanagan came to his senses. He sprang to his feet and gave chase. 'Wait!' he cried. 'Just wait a moment!' But it was too late. The three men had hurried down the steps of the Old Building and had climbed silently into the white stretch-limousine which was waiting outside. As the Vice-Chancellor arrived on the pavement, the great car was already speeding round the corner and in a couple of seconds it had disappeared from view. Flanagan was left in the chilly street gazing after it.

The dinner broke up soon afterwards. Sir William seemed blithely unconcerned that he had wrecked the evening. Indeed, he appeared to feel that he had done the university a good turn. Flanagan was plainly furious. He barely said goodnight to his guest and he hustled Helga none too gently into his Mercedes-Benz.

For the next few days rumours circulated around the university. Firstly, we heard that Helga was in hospital. The story was that she had tripped on the stairs and had fallen, hitting her head against the bannister. What was certain was she had bad concussion and possibly even a fractured skull.

Meanwhile all the plans to build a casino were put on hold. The Vice-Chancellor had tried to contact Luigi at the White Hart Hotel after the Feast, but there was no one there. The Mancinis had ordered the limousine to drive directly to London where the whole party had stayed at the Connaught. The very next day they caught a flight to Las Vegas from Heathrow. Sylvester, however, had telephoned to say that the Mancini organisation was no longer interested in establishing any sort of partnership with St Sebastian's.

I received a note from the Vice-Chancellor's secretary. He did not blame me for the debacle – mercifully he did not know that I had already heard of Sir William's adventure in Las Vegas. He merely expressed regret that things had gone so badly. He was angry with Sir William. He felt he had been ungrateful and tactless. In the light of the lack of sponsorship, he could see no way that the proposed degree in Casino Management could now be established. This meant that I would have to revert to my original responsibilities and he would be informing Dr John Pilkington, my Head of Department, of this fact.

It also emerged that Joy Pickles had left St Sebastian's. Wolfie Goldberg had telephoned her from London and she had joined him the next day and had flown with the Mancinis to Las Vegas. We heard that Sylvester had arranged for her to be given a job as the new administrator of the King Midas Casino College. I felt a certain satisfaction at this. With Joy's level of efficiency, it was highly unlikely that the school would ever recruit any more 'students'. The Registrar however was disconsolate and was taking time off work.

When I next saw Magnus in the Senior Common Room, he was reading a copy of the *St Sebastian's Gazette*. On the front page was a picture of Luigi Mancini and the headline: 'Scandal Dogs Uni Casino'.

'So,' he said, 'we're not going in for gambling after all.'

'It seems not,' I said.

'Pity . . . still Sir William's speech was, by all accounts, quite a tour de force . . . .'

'That's one way of putting it,' I agreed.

'And I hear the Vice-Chancellor has taken it out on poor Helga?'

'That isn't the official story,' I said cautiously. 'But I fear it's all too probable.'

'But he'll have other plans.' Magnus was not wasting pity on Flanagan. 'And what about you, Felix?' he asked, 'Are you going to have to go back to teaching all the undergraduates?'

'Yes . . . Pilkington has informed me that next term I revert to my original schedule. He added a typically moralistic note that it was a pity I ever left it.'

Magnus dunked a shortbread biscuit in his coffee. 'How many contact hours a week are you supposed to do?'

'Seventeen.' I took a deep breath. 'It's only for one term now, but I feel bad about it. It means that the students are short-changed. I just can't give them the attention they deserve.'

Magnus had no illusions. 'Well we all know that in the modern university, the students come a very poor second to the imperative of making money,' he said.

CHAPTER TEN

The St Sebastian's Ghetto

The following week, I received an email from Pilkington outlining in further detail my duties for the rest of the year: I would be required to teach all my old philosophy courses, assess all the essays and dissertations, and serve as the first marker for all the exam scripts. This meant that the summer term would be incredibly busy. However, my load would diminish the next year because there would be no first-year students. He also informed me that there would be a departmental meeting on the Wednesday of the last week of the spring term.

I had not been very conscientious about attending the Theology department meetings – partly because I had been busy with my Casino Management activities, but mainly because nothing was ever discussed that concerned me. This time it was clear that Pilkington was cracking the whip. I telephoned Magnus to suggest we went together, but it turned out that he had deliberately arranged a dental appointment to conflict with the meeting. I therefore foresaw a very boring afternoon.

On the Wednesday I arrived just as proceedings were about to begin. Pilkington started by going through the minutes of the last meeting. From them I learnt that the department had agreed to establish a new Centre for the Study of Religious History.

I was surprised. I had heard Pilkington express scorn for what he called the 'old-fashioned fixations with world religions' and this new centre seemed like a very daring venture for the St Sebastian's theologians. I had a brief fantasy of courses on Indian Religions, New Age Activities, Primitive Magic and Eastern Esoterica. I was soon disabused.

Pilkington reminded us that this initiative was being proposed by the Church historians in the department. It would focus on the development of Christianity from ancient times to the present. All those engaged in this area of teaching and research would be expected to contribute. Already other leading Church historians from universities in Britain and abroad were being contacted to lend their names as research fellows to give the whole enterprise prestige and credibility. The whole department had voiced its strong support for this new development and it was hoped that it would attract funding from a wide variety of ecclesiastical bodies.

However there was a hitch. Pilkington told us that he had had a protest from an unexpected quarter. The Professor of Sociology at St Sebastian's, Ahmed al-Haidari, had somehow got wind of the project. He had invited Pilkington to lunch and had told him that, as a practising Muslim, he found the initiative offensive. It implied that Christianity was the only true religion.

At that point, for the first time since I had known him, Pilkington attempted a joke. He smiled bleakly and said, 'It's nice to find that even a sociologist can sometimes get the right idea.' Everyone but me chortled and it was clear that we were going to move onto the next item of the agenda with no further discussion. Professor al-Haidari's intervention was going to be ignored.

I was not happy about this and I put up my hand. Pilkington made as if he did not see me, but one of the Old Testament lecturers pointed out that I was wanting to say something. Pilkington sighed. 'Yes Felix . . .,' he said.

'John,' I began, 'I'm afraid I don't understand this. It seems to me that Ahmed is right. Why is this centre to be called a Centre for the Study of Religious History if it focuses exclusively on

Christianity? That's a category mistake. Why not call it a Centre for the Study of Christian History? Surely that would be more accurate?'

Pilkington was not going to argue the matter. He was dismissive. 'All of those who have been involved in the establishment of this centre have agreed on the name. We have spent a great deal of time on this and have talked it over thoroughly,' he said. 'We believe that the title will be an asset in helping us attract outside funding for research projects so I don't think we should waste any time discussing it any further.'

I did not drop the subject. 'But,' I objected, 'it makes no sense to call it a Centre for the Study of Religious History if the only thing to be studied is the Christian tradition. What about Judaism and Islam and the other world religions?'

'We're not a Religious Studies department,' snapped Pilkington. 'As you know, it is a matter of pride that here at St Sebastian's we have not been infected with the whole Sixties pluralist virus. As a matter of policy we don't teach non-Christian world-views. So it's obvious that when we refer to religion, we mean Christianity.'

'It's not obvious to me,' I said. 'And it's misleading.'

My colleagues were becoming impatient. Pilkington shrugged his shoulders. 'I think as usual you're in a minority of one, Felix,' he declared and he passed on to the next item. This happened to be arrangements for the installation of a coffee machine next to Wendy Morehouse's office.

I was incensed by Pilkington's attitude. After returning to my room, instead of concentrating on marking the waiting piles of essays, I spent a couple of hours writing a parody of a well-known Christian hymn. The original verse went:

'The Church's One Foundation
Is Jesus Christ Our Lord.
She is His New Creation
By Water and the Word.
From Heaven He came and Sought Her
To be His Holy Bride.
With His Own Blood He Bought Her
And for Her Life He Died.'

It was a hymn we used to sing frequently in Westminster Abbey when I was at school. I hadn't thought of it for years, but I remembered liking the tune. My version went as follows:

'Religion's One Foundation
Is Christianity.
The Faiths of Other Nations
Don't make the Category.
From All Their Works Defend Us
Preserve Us from their Texts.
We Know these Faith Pretenders
Are Naught but Heathen Sects.'

Though Liberals Argue plainly
For Hindu, Muslim, Jew
And Keep Repeating vainly
That They're Religions too.
Our Faith will never Falter,
Truth's Trumpet still will Sound.
It's on the Christian Altar
That true Religion's Found.'

I felt better after composing this ditty and went over to the Old Building to see Magnus. He had only just returned from the dentist. His face was swollen and he looked like a hamster. He was also feeling exceedingly sorry for himself. 'Bloody dentist,' he complained. 'I'd almost rather spend the afternoon with Pilkington. First she gives me a school-ma'amish lecture about not using dental floss properly. Then she fishes about inside my mouth and finds three enormous holes. She pokes a couple of agonising injections into me and then she gets to work with her damned drill. It was over an hour of complete misery. And when we at last came to the end, then she charged me four hundred pounds for the privilege of torturing me! Honestly, by that time I was expecting a supportive letter from Amnesty International!'

I sat down on his sofa and I told him what had happened at the departmental meeting. As I went through the story, I felt myself becoming angry all over again. How dared Pilkington suggest that the only religious history was Christian history? It was outrageous!

'I told them they should call it the Centre for Christian History,' I grumbled, 'but Pilkington wouldn't listen. He was absolutely determined. And his lack of respect for Professor al-Haidari's views is a disgrace. Ahmed is a distinguished scholar and a very nice man. He even took Pilkington out to lunch . . .'

'I wonder where they went,' mused Magnus. 'I believe he's rather rich. I could do with a good lunch myself after my ordeal!'

There were times when Magnus was infuriating. I tried to drag him back to the point. 'It's misleading to call it a Centre for Religious History if all the other religions are excluded. And it's insulting.'

'To you?'

'Not to me. But it demeans other faiths. Do Pilkington and the others really believe there is only one religion?'

'Oh I should think so. He's a fearful bigot underneath. But you're not going to change him. And it's not as if anyone is ever going to take any notice of their stupid centre.' Magnus had few illusions about his colleagues. He had worked with them for a very long time.

'They're always having these idiotic initiatives,' he continued. 'And they always fizzle out after a couple of years. It's just an attempt to attract money from learned foundations and to persuade the powers-that-be that St Sebastian's has a thriving research culture, whatever that is . . . It also keeps them busy writing letters and having committee meetings rather than actually getting down to doing any work. When all's said and done, Pilkington has only ever written one book and that was a modification of his PhD thesis. I know he's been commissioned to contribute the volume on the pastoral epistles to one of those dreary sixth form Bible Commentary series. He's been at it for at least five years. He's had three terms' study leave dedicated to the project and there's still no sign of the finished product . . .'

I laughed. 'Oh well . . .,' I said. 'Could you manage a cup of tea if I made it?'

Magnus leant back in his chair and, while the kettle boiled, I read him my new version of 'The Church's One Foundation.'

'We used to sing that at Winchester,' reminisced Magnus. 'Rather a jolly tune, I remember. Your version's better. Why don't you send it to Pilkington? It might cheer him up!'

'Maybe I will,' I said recklessly. 'Perhaps he'd think better of the whole business.'

After we had drunk our tea, Magnus announced that it was time for sherry. He got out a new bottle and poured me a generous drink. By the time we had come to the end of our second glass, the conversation had become more and more hilarious as Magnus suggested a variety of new lines and verses for my 'hymn'. The upshot was we emailed all the members of the Theology department and sent them a copy of my composition. I told myself there was still a chance they might reconsider their centre's title.

The next morning there was a letter from Pilkington marked Private and Confidential waiting for me in my pigeonhole. I had a sense of foreboding. What was he going to tell me this time? The note read as follows:

Dear Felix,

As you are aware, a new lectureship in Church History has recently been established and we are in the process of making an appointment. There are several excellent candidates whom we will be seeing soon. There is, however, a problem about accommodation. There are no spare rooms in the Arts Block. This means that the new lecturer would have to have his office elsewhere. It is important that the person appointed is able to be integrated into the department smoothly. For this reason I have decided to allocate your room to the new appointee. As the only full-time philosopher in the department, it is not vital for you to be located with the theologians and it is clear from your attitude that you are making no attempt to adjust yourself to the department's ethos.

I have therefore contacted the Estates Manager about spare rooms. It appears that Harry Gilbert's former office in the Old Building is currently being used for storage. This will be allocated to you and I have arranged for the maintenance department to transport all your items there as soon as possible. In any event, your current room must be empty by the start of the summer term.

Please confirm that you have received this letter. I should only add that I, and many of your other colleagues, found your recent communication about the Centre for the Study of Religious History highly offensive and hope for your own sake that it will not be repeated.

Yours ever,

John
(Dr John Pilkington, Head of the Department of Theology)

I was very upset by this missive. I had had the same room ever since my arrival at St Sebastian's. Why should I move out now? Irate, I telephoned Patricia and explained the situation. 'You're the Dean,' I said. 'Can't you intervene?'

There was a pause. 'I'm sorry, Felix,' she said. 'It really is John's responsiblity as Head of Department to decide on rooms. I don't think I can interfere. He's already complained to me about your poem. I thought it was funny, but he was furious. It was stupid of you. You should have known that he has absolutely no sense of humour.'

Later in the day I went to see Magnus. He opened the door wearing a bandage around his head. 'Are you OK?' I asked.

'I was extremely damaged by that damn dentist.' He spoke with dignity. 'The pain was excruciating and it is only now beginning to wear off. I thought it best to take precautions. I didn't want to sit in a draught.'

Magnus swept several books off an armchair and gestured for me to sit down. 'You won't believe this,' I began. 'I got a letter from Pilkington this morning, and he tells me I have to change rooms.'

'Change rooms?'

'I'm being expelled from the Arts Block. It's all supposed to be because the department's getting this new lecturer in Church History. I asked Patricia about it. But she said she couldn't do anything since it was up to the Head of Department. Really, she says, it's because Pilkington is so furious about my hymn. Anyway I've got to move.'

'Where are you going?'

'Pilkington said I could have Harry's old room.'

Magnus was enthusiastic. 'But that's over here! How excellent! Harry loved his room. Of course, it was full of his antiques and oriental carpets. But the Arts Block is awful. I always refused to go. The architecture's much better here.'

'But, Magnus, they're throwing me out. Everybody will know the real reason. It's all because I don't fit in.'

'Would you want to fit in with that lot? Think of it as a promotion. Onwards and upwards. . . .!'

'Honestly, Magnus. You just don't see it. This is just what happened to my grandparents during the last war. As Jews they were ostrasised. They were forced to move from their beautiful big house in central Berlin and were crammed into a ghastly apartment with two other families in a slummy suburb. That's why they fled to London after Kristallnacht. Pilkington's just like the Nazis. He wants his department to be Judenfrei. That's what it comes down to . . .'

Magnus readjusted his bandage. 'I say, old chap,' he said, 'I think you're going a bit over the top. The Old Building isn't a ghetto – after all the Vice-Chancellor and the Industrious Sloth have their offices over here. And so do I for that matter.'

'It's insulting.' I was determined to sulk.

'I think you'll like the idea when you get used to it,' consoled Magnus. He searched around for his sherry bottle. It was concealed by a pile of papers behind his phallic statue. He poured out two generous glasses. 'L'hayim!' he said, using the traditional Yiddish toast. 'Here's to life in the St Sebastian's Ghetto!'

The day after term ended and the students disappeared, I began packing up the books in my office. I had to put them all in cardboard boxes ready for the move to the Old Building. Compared with many academics, I never thought I had a large library, but there is a major difference between books sitting neatly on a shelf and books scattered in piles all over the floor. The whole task was a nightmare and took me nearly two days.

In the meantime, all the tables and chairs that were being stored in Harry Gilbert's old room had to be removed. The administrator was not happy about this because she had nowhere else to put them. For several days the corridor outside my new room was almost impassable and looked like a furniture depository. The bits and pieces were only taken away by the Head Porter and his team after the Catering Manager had intervened. He had three huge commitment ceremonies in the Great Hall, one after another, and he insisted that the Health and Safety people would not tolerate his waiting staff tripping over furniture while they tried to serve gourmet banquets.

The new room was spacious with splendid Gothic windows. Sadly it needed painting. Harry had hung a great many pictures on the walls and there were old nail marks and chipped patches of plaster everywhere.

Imogen had just come home from Cambridge for the spring vacation. Emma and I loved having her with us and I hoped she might help me redecorate. However, she was still busy with her dissertation. Her Director of Studies had been very pleased with the first draft and we had high hopes that our daughter was heading for a First. Imogen still felt that it needed fine tuning and she was making frequent visits to the Women's Refuge to consult with Jan and Liz, the paid workers, and to do further interviews with the residents.

One evening she told us what she had learnt about Mrs Flanagan. Apparently, Helga had been taken into hospital the night of the St Sebastian's Feast. She was suffering from extensive bruising, a head wound and serious concussion. When she regained consciousness, she had been interviewed by the police. They pressed her, but she had persisted in her story. She said she had had too much to drink and had fallen down the stairs hitting her head. The police told Jan that they did not believe this for a moment. The position of the blood stains in the house told a very different story, but there was no chance of bringing a successful prosecution if Helga refused to cooperate.

Jan and Liz visited her frequently in the hospital. They never ran into Flanagan. Either he was not going to see Helga at all or he came early in the morning or very late at night. In any event she never spoke of him. She was very quiet and was having to undergo a huge number of neurological tests. However, Imogen thought that she would be discharged within the next couple of weeks. The women from the Refuge were doing their very best to persuade her to come and stay with them, but, as yet, Helga had refused to commit herself.

Once the university reopened after Easter, I went in to collect my post. Amongst the usual pile of letters and magazines was an ominous envelope marked Private and Confidential. I went to my office which was now crowded with boxes and opened it. It was from Pilkington. It read:

Dear Felix,

Over the vacation period I have been drafting the department's plans for the next five years. Before term begins, I want to let you know about the position of philosophy. As you are aware, the university is committed to fulfilling its contractual obligation to the existing undergraduates. This means that we will continue to run philosophy courses for the next two years.

Your old colleagues, Malcolm Bridgestock and Jonathan Pike, have already taken early retirement. Their part-time contracts will come to an end once the current students have graduated. Since the subject will no longer be taught, there will be no further role for you at St Sebastian's. As I am sure you appreciate, your own contract specifies that you can be made redundant if the subject area for which you were appointed is no longer being taught. Since this will occur two years hence, I am recommending to the Redundancy Committee that it commences the necessary steps now so that your post be declared officially redundant when the time comes. There is no problem about the philosophy research money from the Research Assessment Exercise. It will continue to be paid to the Theology department.

'I realise that this may be distressing news, but I did warn you at the beginning of the academic year that this would be the likely outcome of the Vice-Chancellor's strategic plan. You are of course at liberty to appeal to the Redundancy Committee if you choose to do so. However, I would strongly recommend instead that you speak to the Registrar about early retirement, which will be possible once you reach the age of fifty-five. There is no doubt that you are likely to achieve a more advantageous arrangement from the administration if you accept the inevitable graciously.

I hope you have settled into your new room and find it comfortable,

With best wishes,

John
(Dr John Pilkington, Head of the Department of Theology)

This letter should not have been a surprise. I knew that I was vulnerable and the whole fiasco of the degree in Casino Management had not strengthened my case. Nonetheless seeing it in writing was a shock. I did not want to retire. As a philosopher, I felt that I was at the height of my powers. And anyway the whole thing was so unfair. I had given St Sebastian's the best years of my life. The Philosophy department was well-respected in the outside world and we had done exceptionally well in the last Research Assessment Exercise.

Then there was the personal element. How on earth could Emma and I survive without my job? Admittedly Emma earned a very good salary with the BBC, but positions in the media are notoriously insecure. If for some reason her programmes ceased to be popular, her employers would have no hesitation in looking for new talent. At least Imogen would have finished at Cambridge before I had to leave St Sebastian's, but what would we do if she wanted to embark on some expensive postgraduate training? My pension would not begin to cover the cost of law or medical school.

I searched for my telephone amongst the boxes of books. It took me fifteen minutes to find it as it was buried at the bottom of a carton of philosophical encyclopaedias. When I plugged it in, I was relieved that it was still working.

I called Magnus at home. When he answered, he told me he was having a bath. In the background I could hear running water. 'Do you think I could get electrocuted using this thing?' he asked.

'I'm sure it's perfectly safe,' I said. 'I'm sorry to ring you now, but I'm in terrible trouble. I've just received an official letter from Pilkington. He tells me that since there will be no philosophy in two years' time, he is applying to the Committee to have my post declared redundant. He recommends that instead of fighting the decision, I accept it and take early retirement.'

There was a splash. After a long pause I heard Magnus's voice. He had just lost the soap. 'Sorry, old chap,' he said, 'I'm having a bit of difficulty here. You say Pilkington wants to make you redundant? Well, I'm not surprised. The theologians are not exactly the sharpest knives in the drawer and you can't expect them to enjoy having someone like you around. You undermine their comfortable presuppositions. I don't suppose any of them liked your splendid hymn very much either. I shouldn't have encouraged you to circulate it . . .'

'But what am I going to do?' I said desperately.

'Well you'll be in your mid-fifties once the last of the philosophy students leave. Won't you have had enough of St Sebastian's by then? After all, Emma must be doing quite well and you'll get an index-linked pension. You should have enough to live on. And after all, Imogen is old enough to start earning her own living. She can support her old parents. I always thought I should have had a daughter to look after me in my old age.'

Magnus was not an expert at offering consoling pastoral advice. I made one last bid for sympathy.

'But Magnus,' I protested. 'I don't want to leave.'

'Oh dear, you do remind me of Harry. That's just what he used to say.'

'Did he?'

'He kept maintaining that he liked research; he liked his students; he liked to be useful; he liked contributing to the sum of human knowledge. I did my best to dissuade him and put him in touch with reality, but he could never see it. Anyway, in the end he got a better job. Maybe you will too . . .'

'Magnus,' I tried to divert him from his flight of fantasy. 'What am I supposed to do?'

There was a pause. 'I don't know,' Magnus said. 'I never know what to do. The best thing is to wait and see. Maybe you'll win on the premium bonds like me! Ah,' he declared brightly. 'Here's the soap . . . slippery little bugger!'

For the rest of the vacation I was depressed. I slept badly. Emma insisted that we went to bed at the usual time, but I always found myself awake at three o'clock in the morning. I kept calculating and recalculating how much money we would have once I retired. The situation was not desperate. We had paid off our

186

mortgage and I had made extra contributions to my pension over the years. We would still be reasonably comfortable as long as Emma could keep her job. But I could not overcome the feeling of unfairness. It nagged at me and I found myself fantasising about taking revenge on Pilkington and his smug disciples.

Just before term began I volunteered to drive Imogen back to Cambridge. I had tried not to trouble her with all my difficulties, but I found myself compulsively discussing the situation round and round with anyone who would listen. Imogen was always gentle and sympathetic with me but I feared that I had ruined her vacation. In any event she was still preoccupied with her dissertation which was due to be submitted in the middle of May.

After leaving her in her college, I drove back to St Sebastian's, but I was not concentrating on the road. I was nearly home when I landed at a busy intersection. Without looking properly, I pulled out directly in front of a black Peugeot. There was a screech of brakes, a moment in which time seemed to be suspended and then I heard an enormous crash. I had suffered a direct hit broadside.

The other driver was all right. He jumped out of his car to speak to me. I knew it was all my fault and I said so. Then I realised that I was in excruciating pain and I could not move. I was trapped inside the car and it was a full fifteen minutes before an ambulance, the police and a fire engine arrived at the scene. The firemen pried open the door. The paramedics could not have been kinder, gentler or more reassuring. I was carried out on a stretcher and placed in the ambulance. The siren was activated and within a very few minutes we had arrived at St Sebastian's Hospital.

I do not remember very much of the details. I was taken immediately into the accident and emergency room where I was X-rayed. The doctors were concerned that I might have damaged my spine, but all was well. Only my pelvis was fractured. It was broken in two places. Later I was wheeled on a trolley to one of the wards where my hip was placed in traction. Emma had been contacted straightaway. She arrived in the emergency room and stayed with me, holding my hand, while the doctors did their investigations. Then she went upstairs with me and helped the nurses settle me in the ward.

'Poor Felix,' she said stroking my hand. 'Tell me what happened?'

I explained about the accident and asked about the other driver. 'He appears to be fine,' she said. 'Just a few scratches.'

I was relieved. 'How long do they think I'll be here?' I asked.

'The doctors said at least ten days. But then you'll need to rest at home for about three months. They don't want you to put any pressure on the hip for six weeks. But you'll be able to walk with a crutch.'

'I'll have to get sick leave,' I said. 'Someone else will have to teach my classes next term.'

'That's their problem,' Emma said stoutly. 'Let Pilkington worry about it.'

The next day Imogen came down from Cambridge by train. Emma had tried to dissuade her, but she needed to be reassured that I was all right. In the event she was more upset than I was. She was tearful and Emma and I had to tell her again and again that it was not her fault. She was not to blame that I had driven her back to the university. I had been careless and that was the end of the matter. The important thing was to be thankful that the damage had not been more serious.

Later that afternoon, Magnus arrived carrying a bunch of tulips and a box of chocolates which was already opened. One of the nurses found a vase and he offered her a chocolate. 'Looks like someone has already had a few,' she said.

'Couldn't resist on the way to the hospital.' Magnus was not embarrassed. 'I didn't have much lunch and I must keep my strength up.'

So,' he said, putting the sweets on my bedside table, 'you've had a bit of a crash.'

'Not just a bit, Magnus. I could have been killed.'

'Well, you seem to be in one piece. Jolly relieved to see you sitting up. Actually, you don't look bad at all.'

'I'm going to be off work for three months,' I said.

'Three months, eh? That'll put the cat among the pigeons. Someone else will have to mark your exams . . .'

'And finish off the courses . . .' I pointed out.

'Serve them right!' said Magnus.

'Yes it does actually!' I remained very angry about Pilkington's letter. 'I'm still really pissed off. This accident would never have happened if Pilkington hadn't written to me the way he did. I wasn't concentrating properly all because of him.'

'Don't worry about it, old chap.' Magnus helped himself to another chocolate. 'The important thing is that you're going to be all right.'

Imogen came to see me once more before returning to Cambridge. She was buzzing with news. 'You'll never guess. I've just bumped into Jan and Liz from the Refuge. They were going to fetch Helga Flanagan. Apparently she admitted a couple of days ago that it was the Vice-Chancellor who caused her injuries. He always hits her when he gets drunk. She still refuses to testify to the police against him, but she at last accepts that if she goes back to him, he will probably do it again in a few weeks. So she's going to stay in the Refuge for a short time until she's really well and then she's going to think about what to do next. Jan and Liz are just off to rescue her dog from the Flanagan house while the Vice-Chancellor is at the university.'

I smiled at my daughter. She was so young and enthusiastic and idealistic. I wanted to protect her from disappointment so I felt I had to warn her. 'Are you sure she won't change her mind and go back?'

Imogen shrugged. 'It does happen, but Jan thinks not in her case. She really does seem to have turned the corner. She sees that her husband is a drunken bully. It's all happened too many times before and this really was the last straw.'

'I hope so,' I said.

Magnus was a faithful visitor. Emma stayed with me for most of the day, but she needed to continue with her work so Magnus came every afternoon. On my fifth day in the ward, he arrived looking very smug. 'I've had a brain-wave!' he said.

'Really?' I wondered what wild plan he had thought of now.

'You're going to be very bored if you're away for three months. But you're not going to want to concentrate on philosophy. It's too much like hard work.'

'So what are you suggesting?' I asked.

'You need to do something amusing. Something that will keep your mind occupied, but is not over-taxing. Why don't you write a novel?'

'A novel?' I was surprised. I was the author of several books, but I had never tried my hand at fiction.' I've got nothing to write about.'

'Ah,' Magnus said, 'but I have. I'm going to tell you a story. It's the perfect plot and you're going to fictionalise it. It's about a conspiracy on campus, St Sebastian's very own campus conspiracy . . . .'

That was how my career as a novelist began. On his subsequent visits to the hospital and when he came to see me at home, Magnus told me the full story of Harry Gilbert's troubles and the real reason why he left the university. I was gripped and I knew other people would be too.

Emma, Magnus and Imogen were not my only visitors. A couple of days after my accident, I was greeted by an attractive middle-aged woman in a white coat. It was Danielle Bousset.

'I saw you when you came in when I did your X-ray. I wasn't sure if you'd recognise me so I waited a bit before coming to say hello. We met after Crispin Chantry-Pigg's inauguration service,' she said in her attractive French accent.

'Of course I remember you.' I was a little embarrassed to see her, but I took my tone from hers. 'How kind of you to look in on me!'

'Let me see your charts.' She picked up the documents at the end of my bed and studied them. 'Yes . . . that's what I thought. It's a nasty fracture, but in no way life-threatening. You'll be completely well in a few months.'

'I'd forgotten you were a radiographer,' I observed.

Danielle sighed a little. 'It's clearly what I do best. As you know, I've had my difficulties.'

'How long have you been here?' I asked her.

'I started once Crispin left.'

I took a deep breath. 'Look,' I said. 'I'm really sorry about what happened. I don't know if you know, but I was involved. Those two girls were my students. I feel bad if I caused you unhappiness.'

Danielle gave a little Gallic shrug. 'You did me a favour,' she said. 'You probably know, it isn't the first time I've been deceived. I genuinely thought Crispin was a good, holy person, and I wanted to help him in his work. Of course I knew he had a weakness for good food and he had a taste for luxury, but we all have our faults. They seemed such minor failings. . . .'

She paused for a moment and then she continued. 'He lied to me about those two young girls, you know. He told me that he'd been accused, but he insisted that they had set him up and that they were psychologically disturbed . . . And then it all came out in the newpapers. I realised that I'd always be a bad judge of men. If I was serious about helping people, I had no alternative, but to go back to my profession.'

'Well you've certainly helped me,' I said.

'That's kind of you to say so. Please don't feel guilty about what happened. I had to find out what he was like sooner or later . . .'

She was just about to rise from her seat when Patricia and Judith arrived in the ward. Judith was carrying a pretty pot of blue hyacinths and looked as impeccable as ever. Patricia, on the other hand, appeared to have slept in her clothes for the last week. I introduced Danielle to the pair and the three of them sat down together for a few moments.

I offered round the remains of Magnus's box of chocolates. Danielle and Judith both refused, but Patricia took two. We had a general chat about what was going on in the university and in the town. Judith happened to mention that she was on duty at the Women's Refuge that night. Danielle was interested. She said that she had always wanted to contribute to that kind of enterprise. Then she told the pair that she was the ex-wife of the film-director Jacques Bousset. They nodded sympathetically; they said they had read all about it. Judith offered to introduce her to Jan and Liz. The Refuge was always in need of new helpers and she was sure Danielle would be welcome. The upshot of the discussion was that Judith and Danielle arranged to meet each other in the town that very evening.

On the day I went home, Emma made me my favourite dinner and we had a lovely evening together. For the next week I prac-tised with my crutches, trying not to put weight on my left hip. I soon became quite nimble. Meanwhile, I established a routine. After I dressed every morning and manoeuvred myself down the stairs, I worked in my study on the new novel.

Over the years I had written both articles and books dealing with philosophical topics. I had never before attempted fiction. When Magnus visited me in hospital, I had made notes about Harry's misadventures. The details were appalling. This was to be the raw material, but, at the same time, it was going to have to be fictionalised. I had no wish to find myself in the libel courts.

I decided on the title straightaway. 'A Campus Conspiracy' had a nice, alliterative quality. I also made up my mind that the book was going to be published anonymously. I was not keen to be an author-celebrity, even if such a thing were possible. Then the characters must be protected as well as myself. All the people had to have new names and different attributes. The university also had to have a different title, location and geography. I found the power intoxicating. Here was a world that could be manipulated at will. People would behave exactly as well or as badly as I chose. It was life as it ought to be rather than life as it really is. For the first time in my existence I realised that fiction is far more interesting than fact . . .

The first step was to draw up a comprehensive plan; I had to know where it was all going. That was what I had done with all my other books and I saw no reason for a novel to be any different. I calculated that there would be fourteen chapters and the whole volume would be about eighty thousand words. So far, so good. Then I took the plunge. I knew something about campus novels. I had always been a fan of C.P. Snow, Kingsley Amis, Malcolm Bradbury and David Lodge. The stories tended to start at the beginning of the autumn term and they finished in the summer, echoing the academic year. I remembered the splendid first sentence of Bradbury's *History Man*: 'Now it is autumn again; the people are all coming back.' I tried to create the same mood. 'Term had begun,' I wrote, 'A slight fog covered the grass . . .'

The first chapter almost wrote itself. I was bewitched by my own creation. I hadn't realised before I began that it was to be a comic novel – in fact I thought that I was temperamentally more suited to tragedy – but this turned out not to be the case. As I described how an over-sexed undergraduate attempted to seduce an elderly professor into giving her credit for an essay she hadn't written, I found myself chuckling uncontrollably.

I knew the story would become darker. The protagonist would be accused of sexual harassment; his colleagues would gang up against him; they would try to force him into early retirement; there would be series of disciplinary meetings; the Dean, Head of Department and Vice-Chancellor would all try to bully him into submission. He would win some battles and he would lose others. Even at the end his triumph would be equivocal. It sounded grim. Yet somehow, whenever my mind played with the material, I was overwhelmed by the intrinsic humour of the situation.

As soon as I had finished the first chapter, I read it to Emma. She was outraged by the hero's plight, but she giggled throughout. I was encouraged and thought the time had come to find a publisher. I had no idea where to look. All my editors in the past were specialists in non-fiction. Where was I to begin? Casually, between bursts of writing, I surfed the web. Within a few minutes I had come across a familiar name.

Several years earlier I had advised an old friend on a book when he was working for a prominent university press. I had heard that he had since set up on his own. In his new venture, he was publishing novels as well as academic tomes. I grabbed the telephone. He was out, but his secretary told me that he would return my call in the afternoon. A few hours later he was on the line. I described what I was doing and he was enthusiastic. 'Send me the first chapter and the outline of the book,' he said. 'I'll let you know.'

I received a contract from him the following week. Emma and I were still eating our breakfast when the post flapped through the door. At the top of the pile was a large white envelope. Inside was a typewritten letter informing me that they would be delighted to take my novel. I was to be paid a small advance and they were looking forward to receiving the complete manuscript as quickly as possible.

Emma was delighted. She was used to dealing with the mass media. 'That was really quick!' she said. 'The publisher liked it!'

For the first time I had doubts. 'But do you think I can actually write this book?' I asked.

'You've already done the first chapter and most of the second.' Emma was a great one for sticking to facts.

'But I've got twelve and a half more to go. What if the characters don't do what I want them to?'

She laughed. 'They haven't any choice,' she said.

The next day Emma told me that she had been discussing my book with one of her fellow-producers at the BBC. Her colleague was in the throes of a steamy transatlantic love affair with a Hollywood movie moghul. To enliven the intervals between sexual acrobatics and long aeroplane flights, she told him about my hero's troubles. Apparently he was enthralled. He said it was just like the quarrels in a movie studio. Via his lover, he requested that I send him the first chapter together with an outline of the book as an email attachment. He wanted to discuss it with a friend.

Emma was very amused. 'What is the difference between Hollywood and St Sebastian's?' she asked.

'I don't know,' I said. 'What is the difference between St Sebastian's and Hollywood?'

'In St Sebastian's the arrows are metaphorical, but in Hollywood, they're merely fake,' she said.

'A distinction without a difference,' I told her.

Meanwhile I received a Get Well Card from my colleagues in the Theology department. I was half-expecting this. I knew it was something the secretary organised. Sure enough, the confection when it arrived looked as if it had been chosen by Wendy Morehouse. Her signature was also in a prominent position. I examined the object carefully. Even theologians I had barely spoken to had written a short personal message. However, there was one glaring omission. John Pilkington must still be angry with me about my 'hymn'. He had not signed the card. I smiled wryly at this; Christian forgiveness is much preached, but not always practised.

A few days afterwards I had a telephone call from Mary and Rosalind, my clever philosophy students. Emma invited them to call round and they arrived punctually at four o'clock clutching a very nice potted cyclamen. We had a good chat. They told me that they were preparing for their exams and I assured them that I expected them to do outstandingly. Then I asked them about their plans after they had graduated in a year's time. I hoped they might consider doing their doctorates in Philosophy. They had other intentions . . .

'A lot has been happening since we last saw you,' Rosalind began. 'Since our pictures appeared in the newspaper, several firms phoned us about becoming models.'

'Models?' Emma was horrified.

Mary blushed. 'Not the kind who advertise in telephone kiosks. Fashion models,' she said.

'Anyway,' continued Rosalind, 'We chose one agency. They paid for a portfolio of photographs and we've both been taken on their books. We had several engagements over the vacation including one in Greece. It was great!'

'What about your course?' Emma was not happy with what she was hearing.

'Well they'd like us to drop out of the university now, wouldn't they Mary?' Mary nodded.

'But we're determined to finish next year. We don't want to leave without a degree and they're willing to wait. Then we'll do it full time. The money is unbelievable and you travel the world.'

I sighed. I knew philosophy could not compete, but I was reluctant to let them go. They were amongst the best I had ever taught. 'You don't want to consider being research students?' I suggested. 'One day you could teach in a university.'

Hesitantly they explained that they could not see any future in the subject. 'We know they're going to shut down the Philosophy department here, and the same seems to be happening in other places,' Rosalind pointed out. 'It doesn't look as if they'll be any proper jobs in the future.'

'There will still be universities,' I pleaded.

'Yes,' said Mary, 'but they're going to offer different subjects. You know we've been recruited to help on the Celebrity Studies course next year for work experience?'

I nodded. 'I had heard that.'

'Well,' continued Mary, 'with our background we're far more likely to be offered a job in Fashion Presentation or Modelling Studies or something like that. No one is interested in the philosphy of Kant or Hegel or the English empiricists And frankly I'd far rather be a good fashion model than spend three years on a doctorate only to be stuck teaching a nonsense subject like that.' She was a highly intelligent young woman.

'The money is certainly better!' Rosalind reminded me,

'And the locations are definitely more glamorous!' concluded Mary.

When the girls left, I sat in my study and looked out of the window. Emma's ornamental cherry trees were in bloom and the sun was shining. I should have taken pleasure in the scene, but I had been saddened by my students' visit. When I was Rosalind and Mary's age I had been delighted at the prospect of postgraduate study. Three years later, I had been overjoyed when I was appointed as a lecturer at St Sebastian's.

That time was over. Soon the Philosophy department would no longer exist. Like Chemistry it would disappear. Instead there would be Celebrity Studies, Highland Dance, Professional Golf and who-knows-what-else. The university had found committment ceremonies and foreign partnerships far more worthwhile than earnest enquiry and serious scholarship.

It seemed that financial profitablity had become the only criterion of success. Alf Flanagan himself had only been appointed to St Sebastian's because he perfectly understood the signs of the times. He was a wife-beater. He drank too much. He made no claims for outstanding erudition. None of that mattered because he did know how to make money. Ultimately that was the only thing that counted . . .

CHAPTER ELEVEN

Diversification's the Name of the Game

Even though I was not going in to work, Emma thought it was important that we try to follow our usual routine. This meant that I continued to accompany her once a week to the supermarket for our major food shop. Every Monday evening we drove to the St Sebastian's Waitrose and parked the car. Emma took charge of a trolley. I hobbled behind on my crutches and tried to dodge undisciplined children and their inattentive parents. Several weeks after my accident on one of our expeditions I bumped into Mrs Brush. She was excavating the frozen food section and I stopped for a chat.

'How are you?' I said, as Emma headed off to the dairy department.

'Why hello, Dr Glass,' she acknowledged me. 'I did hear about your accident. Are you better now?'

I explained that the doctors were pleased with my progress, but that I would be on sick leave through the whole summer term. 'Are you still going to bingo?' I asked.

'Oh yes,' Mrs Brush nodded, 'I still go every week, but it's not so much fun now Elsa's left . . .'

I was interested. 'Did she really return to Leeds after all?' I asked

'Yes,' said Mrs Brush. 'In the end she was determined and she told that daughter of hers she was going. Not that Professor Catnip minded. As long as the house wasn't sold, she didn't care tuppence what happened to her mother . . .'

'When did she go?' I tried to pull Mrs Brush back to the facts.

'Oh nearly two months ago. Soon after that dinner. She had a lovely time with that posh old fellow. A real gentleman he was, she said. It gave her back her confidence. I had a postcard from her just the other day.'

'Really?' I was eager to know more.

'Yes. She got that Care Allowance you told her about. They pay her every fortnight and someone comes in every day to keep an eye on her.'

'And what about the blackjack?'

Mrs Brush laughed. 'She told me that last week she won more than two hundred pounds. She's got a mini-cab which takes her to a different casino every week and she does try to lose sometimes. I don't know how she does it. I never seem to win at bingo . . .'

As we spoke Mrs Brush hooked out four large packets of oven chips. I was surprised that she needed so many. 'I'm doing some shopping for Dr Sloth,' she explained. 'I used to clean for Dr and Mrs Sloth when they lived together and I took on both houses when he joined that little trollop Joy Pickles.'

'I heard that Dr Sloth was in a bit of a bad way.' On his last visit, Magnus had been full of the fact that the University Registrar was looking very unkempt and down-at-heel.

'He is!' Mrs Brush became expansive. 'You wouldn't believe it. Yesterday I found he'd put his best grey suit in the washing machine. It was completely ruined. I didn't know what to do. He mopes about all day. Sometimes he doesn't even go into work. Often I find him asleep in his armchair and he's never even gone to bed . . . I don't know how they're managing at the university without him . . . and the state of the house now you wouldn't believe! Dirty dishes everywhere . . . I thought that Joy was bad, but it's even worse now she's gone . . .'

'Really?' I was fascinated by this glimpse of middle-class angst.

'Poor man . . . I knew that girl was no good. And she's gone off with someone else I hear . . .'

'Yes. An American accountant from Las Vegas.' I thought Mrs Brush might as well know the truth.

The Theology department cleaner was not one to let such a detail escape her. 'Las Vegas! . . . Well I never! . . . Like in the films!'

'Maybe Dr Sloth ought to go back to his wife,' I suggested.

'That's what I keep telling him. But between you and me, I think he's too embarrassed to ask.'

'Perhaps someone ought to have a word with her. It sounds as if he needs rescuing.'

Mrs Brush looked thoughtful. 'I see her every week . . . perhaps I should give her a little hint . . .' And with that she put her oven chips into her trolley and trundled off.

One afternoon a few days later I was working away at the adventures of Harry and Victoria when the telephone rang. Emma was upstairs in her study and she answered it. 'It's for you,' she shouted down. 'Someone ringing from America.'

I struggled with my crutches and went to the telephone. 'Hello,' I said.

'Is this Felix Glass?' The voice was loud, with a strong New York accent.

'It is,' I replied.

'Well my name's Mark Margolis; I'm an agent at Goldfarb and Goldfarb in Hollywood. I'm a friend of Kate Fitzgerald who works at the BBC with your wife. I think you know that Kate sent me the first chapter of your novel and the outline of the rest.'

I realised this was the famous transatlantic lover. He sounded as if he had a great deal of energy, but I wondered what he was telephoning me about.

He got to the point quickly. 'Look,' he said. 'I'm pretty sure we've got a winner here. I'm having lunch at the Los Angeles Country Club tomorrow with the Head Producer at Pacific Studios. I want to make a pitch. Is that OK with you?'

'Pitch?' I asked. I had a vision of my new friend rolling out a very long green cricket pitch somewhere in the Californian sunshine.

'Yea. That's the way it works.' Max Margolis was certainly enthusiastic. 'I'll tell him the plot over lunch. And if he's interested I'll give him all the stuff you sent. Then we'll take it from there.'

I was astounded. 'Seriously? You think there might be a film in it?'

'Well it's early days yet. It all depends who they can get. But it's looking good. I'll get back to you as soon as I know something. Let me give you my telephone number and my website address. You'll want to look me up.'

'Golly,' I said. I found a pencil and wrote down what he told me.

'Sorry,' he said. 'Got to go! There's someone on the other line.' The telephone went dead.

I was stunned. Could *A Campus Conspiracy* really become a film? This was a world I knew nothing about. Certainly no Hollywood agent had ever rung me about *Kant's Critiques Revisited*. In any event the novel was not even written yet. I was only about a third of the way through. Yet they seemed to be thinking of casting the main parts already . . . Who would they want for Harry, I wondered. Who could play Wanda Catnip? And what about Magnus? When all was said and done only Magnus could play Magnus. Anyone else was inconceivable. It was all too fantastic.

Nonetheless it was a fact that a real-life Hollywood agent had been in touch on the telephone. He was intending to discuss it over lunch with someone from a major studio. Probably it would come to nothing. But then again, one never knew . . .

When I told Emma she was as amazed as I was. 'I don't believe it,' she said. 'Well this'll certainly give you another interest beside that stupid university. You understand how it works, don't you?'

I was forced to confess total ignorance. My publishing ventures in the past had never involved Hollywood. However, my wife was good at money and she seemed to have a perfect grasp of procedure.

'If you get an option,' she explained, 'it won't be that much.

Probably considerably less than a year's salary from St Sebastian's. The real money comes from receiving a percentage of the box-office profits . . .'

'A percentage of the box-office profits?' I interrupted. 'But I've only just started on Chapter Six. I haven't even got to Wanda Catnip and the gorillagram yet. And that's the central scene of the book.'

'People sell film rights before they've written a single word,' my wife informed me. 'In fact, you're rather slow on the uptake . . .'

The next week a large white envelope arrived by special delivery. It was marked 'Goldfarb and Goldfarb' on the front in large gold letters. Inside there was a typewritten letter from Max Margolis and two detailed contracts. The letter read:

Dear Felix

Great news! I had lunch with Sherman Fish from Pacific. He loved the idea and wanted to see the outline and first chapter. I heard this morning that they want to buy the option on the book. Once it's finished, they'll hire someone to do a screenplay. But don't worry, I'll insist that you're to be involved throughout. They're willing to give you $50,000 now. I tried for more, but that's the best I could do. They know you're a first-time author and that's always a disadvantage.

I'm including two contracts with the letter. The first one is for me to act as your agent. As you will see, I take 20% on all earnings. It's the standard form I give to all my authors. Please read it through carefully and if you are not happy with anything, get in touch.

The second contract is with Pacific, outlining the agreement about the option. It also includes sections dealing with a wide range of other issues including a percentage of the net returns on the film. Again, please give this your full attention and let me know if there is anything you feel needs changing.

Both contracts should be signed and returned by special delivery. Once they arrive, I will inform Pacific that they should send me the check. I will take my percentage and forward the rest to you. The whole process should take about three weeks from when you return the documents.

I hope you are as excited about this project as I am. We are only at the first stage, but I have high hopes that a first-rate movie will emerge from all this. We are on our way!

Sincerely yours,

Max Margolis,
(Goldfarb and Goldfarb)

Emma was in London working on a new programme about Japanese food so I couldn't consult her. I rang the BBC, but she was unavailable. I would have to wait until she came home. I then telephoned Magnus at the university.

He was in the process of writing a damning review of a new book about Assyrian archaeology and he was full of it. The book was by a professor at Wellington University who had been a postgraduate contemporary at Oxford. They had lived next door to each other in the same college lodgings.

'Frightful nuisance he was too!' Magnus was in a reminiscent mood. 'He had a girl-friend called Norah who played in a brass band. She insisted on practising whenever she came to visit him. I told her that I had no objection to her playing the strumpet in his bed. That was up to her. But it was a bit much if she insisted on playing the trumpet as well . . .'

'Look Magnus,' I interrupted. 'I've got something to tell you. You'll be interested. I've heard from an agent in Hollywood. He's just sold the film option of *A Campus Conspiracy* to a major studio.'

Magnus did not believe me. 'Very funny, Felix! And I suppose they're asking Robert Redford to play Harry!'

'Honestly Magnus, I'm not making it up. I've just got a letter from this agent . . .'

'What agent?'

'Somebody who is going out with a friend of Emma's at the BBC.'

'And they offered you a contract?' Magnus was incredulous.

'I just got it in the post. I'm going to be paid fifty thousand dollars for an option on the book. Then if they decide to turn it into a film, I'll get a percentage of the box-office returns.'

'Bloody hell!' he said. 'What about me?'

'What about you?' I did not know what he was talking about.

'But it was me who told you all about Harry. It's my story really. Didn't you tell your Hollywood agent that I should have a share?' Magnus sounded aggrieved.

'I didn't think of it. After all, I'm doing all the work. And I've changed it all quite a lot.'

'But the original idea was mine.'

'It's really Harry's story,' I said defensively. This was all becoming too complicated.

There was a pause. Then Magnus laughed. 'You're probably right. I'd never get round to writing it all up. Don't worry about it, old chap. I'll be content to bask in your reflected glory . . .'

'It's good of you to take it that way, Magnus,' I said hesitantly.

'You can promise me one thing though.'

'What's that?' I did not want to commit myself to something I would later regret.

'If they're looking for someone to play my part, you might suggest that they audition me. I'm a very complex character and I've always fancied myself as an actor. I did quite a lot at Winchester . . . my Polonius was much admired . . . I don't want them to pick someone like Al Pacino. He'd mess it up for certain.'

I agreed that Al Pacino would not be the ideal choice for the Magnus character, but I pointed out that I had only sold the option. We were still a very long way from the film actually being made.

Before Emma arrived home, I dug out a bottle of champagne from the cupboard under the stairs and I put it in the fridge. Then I sat down to wait for her return. At six o'clock I heard her key in the door. 'What's this for?' she asked as I popped the cork.

I handed her the letter from Goldfarb and Goldfarb. Emma put on her spectacles, sat down and read the contracts through from cover to cover. 'Good grief!' she said. 'Fifty thousand dollars for the option! That's not at all bad for a beginner.'

She seemed quite happy with it all until she came to the clause about box-office returns. She was on to it immediately. 'Ohh!' she frowned. 'The sneaks! I suspected they'd want to give you a percentage of the net returns. Two per cent sounds very generous, but these people employ some very sharp accountants. They'll bump up expenses and calculate it so there are no net profits at all. Writers always lose out that way. I'm not going to have it!' She took a pen out of her handbag, crossed out '2% net' and substituted '1% gross'. 'Let's see what the accountants of the Pacific make of that! It's not unreasonable . . .'

I knew better than to argue with my wife about financial matters. She was far shrewder than I. Instead I handed her a glass and poured out the champagne. 'Well what do you think?' I asked.

'I think your colleagues at St Sebastian's will be furious,' she said.

Time marched on. Every day I went into my new study and worked on *A Campus Conspiracy*. I loved it. The story ran away with me and each day I found myself producing between two and three thousand words. When she was at home Emma could hear me laughing over the manuscript. The whole experience was totally different from writing my previous philosophical books. Then I had pondered every word and had compulsively written and rewritten. Sadly, there were still no plans to market *Kant's Critiques Revisited* as a paperback and the hardback sales (at sixty pounds a time) were not overwhelming.

By the end of May, the novel was nearly finished. My predominant feeling was one of sadness that the story was ending. Everything was coming together: Wanda Catnip had been humiliated; the Vice-Chancellor had been made to look foolish; Magnus was the toast of the old ladies on his cruise ship; and Harry had got his job in Sweetpea, Virginia. It only needed the final couple of chapters set in America and a last ironic twist at the end.

My hip was also much better. I felt more secure when I moved around the house and I was sure the doctors would be pleased with me. I could not wait to shed my crutches.

One afternoon Magnus came over to see us. He was so overcome with mirth that it was some time before he could speak coherently. Emma was at home and she provided the three of us with tea and home-made Swiss roll. Once Magnus had eaten two large slices of cake and was on his third cup of tea, he had recovered enough to tell us the news.

He had been over to the Theology department to hand in some student reports to the secretary, Wendy Morehouse. There, displayed over her desk was a set of wedding photographs. The bride turned out to be Joy Pickles while the groom was Wolfie Goldberg.

Apparently Wendy and Joy had always been friendly. Joy had sent the pictures because she had wanted her old colleagues from St Sebastian's to know of her good fortune.

'Well I suppose she could hardly send the collection to Registrar Sloth.' I said.

Magnus snorted. 'You should see the photographs!' They really are incredible. I've never seen anything like them. They certainly put the St Sebastian's Mixed Blessings brochure in the shade.'

'Tell us all!' commanded Emma.

Magnus settled in his chair. 'Well in the first place there were two services. The first was a civil ceremony in a small wedding chapel in Las Vegas. I don't know how American weddings work, but I suppose that made the whole thing legal. Anyway Joy wore a bright orange dress which might have been suitable for the Folies Bergère. But the real excitement was that she was given away by Elvis Presley!'

'Elvis Presley?' Emma was puzzled. 'Don't be absurd! He died ages ago.'

'It was a professional look-alike,' explained Magnus. 'Apparently in those places you can have whoever you want – Frank Sinatra, Louis Armstrong, Clarke Gable, whoever . . .'

'Presumably not Immanuel Kant?' I suggested.

Magnus regarded this remark as beneath contempt. 'Still, that's not the end. After this encounter with the great king of rock in his blue suede shoes, there was another even more sumptuous ceremony. This time religion really came into it. It was at the Ziggurat, the hotel you stayed in when you were in Las Vegas. The management closed it for two whole nights to accommodate all the out-of-town guests. The service took place on a Saturday evening so everyone was in evening dress. It was huge . . . hundreds of people . . . Joy looked like an overgrown meringue in an gigantic white confection.'

'How was it religious?' I asked.

'The ceremony was conducted by someone called Rabbi Rhinestone . . . that can't be his real name . . . It was held under an enormous canopy all draped in white lilies. It would have been ruinous for my hay-fever. And the bride was given away by no less a person than the great Luigi Mancini himself!'

Emma and I roared with laughter. 'I don't believe it,' I said. 'Well poor old Robert Sloth certainly couldn't have provided such magnificence.'

'Anyway,' continued Magnus, 'that's not the end of it. There was a huge article about it in the *Las Vegas Standard*. Wendy Morehouse had a copy of it in her desk, but she wouldn't let me borrow it. It was a whole supplement called 'The Mother of All Weddings'. There were hundreds of photographs and a run-down of all the guests. I'm sorry I couldn't bring it; you'd have adored it.'

'Perhaps it's on the internet,' suggested Emma.

I brought over my laptop computer and typed in 'Joy Pickles' and 'Wolfie Goldberg'. Immediately the article came up. Magnus had been right. It was indeed a notable occasion. The wedding dress was enormous. There was a picture of Joy standing next to her mother, Mrs Sylvia Pickles. The latter was barely visible round her daughter's layers of satin and lace. Then the happy couple were shown standing on either side of Luigi Mancini who looked rather more affable than when I had last seen him. The Elvis look-alike had been invited to the second ceremony and seemed most convincing and there was a large picture of the State Governor proposing the health of the newly-wed pair.

The guest list extended over several columns. Apparently over five hundred people were present. The Ziggurat Grand Ballroom was the chosen venue where Rabbi Earl Rhinestone (who looked disconcertingly like me!) pronounced the blessings under the extravagantly beflowered canopy. The out-of-town visitors included four presidential hopefuls, two past state governors and three ex-justices of the Supreme Court. Also listed were the representatives of various Italian-American families – the Ferretos (New York), Montadoris (Florida), Gambinis (Michigan), Calabrinis (Illinois and Pennsylvania), Rapellos (California) and Sopranos (New Jersey). The photographs extended over several pages and everyone who was anyone appeared to have been there. However, although I looked most diligently, there was no sign of Miss Divine de la Rue.

'Golly,' I sighed.

'Well,' said Emma, trying to keep a straight face, 'I hope they'll be very happy.'

Magnus had dissolved in giggles again on our sofa. We had to invite him to an early supper to sober him up.

At the end of the first week of June, Imogen came home from Cambridge. She had had a hugely successful second year. As we had all hoped, her dissertation on domestic violence had been well received and she had done well in all her other courses. In addition she had been invited to a May Ball and had obviously had a splendid time.

The next day she went over to see her friends in the Women's Refuge. She came back bringing Judith with her. We had coffee together in the kitchen and they told us all the news. Emma had just baked fruit scones. They were cooling on a wire rack and they smelled irresistible.

'Helga is about to leave the Refuge,' our daughter informed us.

'She's a different person now,' added Judith, 'and so is Helmut.'

'Who on earth is Helmut?' asked Emma.

Judith laughed. 'He's the Flanagan dog. You remember Patricia and I went to collect him from Cuckoos' Roost one day when we knew the Vice-Chancellor was at the university. He was a horrible beast at first. He was barely house-trained and he either cowered in a corner or he snapped at people for no reason at all. At the beginning we were quite frightened for the children.'

'Why was he like that?' Emma loved dogs and she hated to hear of canine unhappiness.

'Well,' Judith hesitated, 'Helga told us that Flanagan only allowed her to keep the dog because he was a present from her father. The Vice-Chancellor hated him and used to tease and torment him with food. Then when he was in a foul temper he would lash out at Helga and the dog indiscriminately. Poor Helmut just didn't know what to expect.'

'Is he all right now?' asked Emma anxiously.

'The change is amazing,' Judith told us. 'After a couple of weeks of regular living, when Patricia helped Helga train him properly, he was completely transformed. He's a lovely dog now, playful and fun. He never bites and seems completely trustworthy. The children will miss him dreadfully when he goes.'

'So Helga is definitely leaving?' I asked.

'Yes. She's just got a job as an assistant bursar at Marlborough College Cambridge.'

I was astonished. 'As an assistant bursar? But you need proper qualifications for a position like that . . .'

'She has them.' Judith was triumphant. 'You remember there was a rumour that Flanagan had tried to get a sinecure for his wife in the Bursary at St Sebastians and everyone dismissed the idea as his way of chiselling more money out of the university?'

I nodded.

'Well it was all true. She has the best possible qualifications from the University of Berlin. She graduated with the equivalent of a first-class degree in finance and she stayed on for a further year to get the German postgraduate professional accountancy diploma.'

Emma was embarrassed. 'And I dismissed her as a sad little woman who was quite a good cook, but not really very interesting otherwise. That husband of hers is a disgrace . . .'

'He was in the process of destroying her,' said Judith. 'In the end his violence was really a blessing in disguise. It enabled her to come to her senses . . .'

'Anyway,' interrupted Imogen, 'she's leaving for Cambridge the day after tomorrow. It turns out that Flanagan is away at a conference for a couple of nights, so we're going to the house to collect a few of her things . . .'

'Who's we?' asked Emma.

'Judith, Helga and me. She can't go alone. She's still frightened of the Vice-Chancellor even though she hasn't seen him since he last hit her. You know he never visited her in hospital. Not once!'

'Hasn't he seen her at all?' I asked. 'Doesn't he want her back?'

'He wrote a pathetic begging letter just before the doctor discharged her. Of course he was terrified he was about to be reported to the police.' Judith was very scornful. 'He swore that he loved her and that it would never happen again. But this time Helga wasn't having any of it. She wasn't going to hand him over to the authorities, but I think she realised that the whole cycle of violence would never be broken. This time he'd gone too far. For forty-eight hours the doctors thought she had a fractured skull . . .'

'I'm sorry Imogen,' Emma was worried, 'I do understand that Helga needs some moral support, but you've got to be careful. I don't want you to find yourself with a police record for theft or criminal damage. If you go along on this trip, you mustn't take anything out of the house yourself. And if she's tempted to destroy anything, please don't aid and abet her.'

'Don't worry.' Judith was amused. 'We deal with this type of situation at the Refuge all the time. Jan and Liz keep several pairs of rubber gloves for exactly these kinds of visitations; we tie up our hair under a cap and we all wear long sleeves. We know all about not leaving any trace of forensic evidence!'

It was nine o'clock in the evening before Imogen came home the next day. We were both worried about what had happened, but she was in the highest spirits.

'The three of us arrived at Cuckoos' Roost at half past two,' she began. 'On the way Helga told us that she absolutely hated the house. All that heavy German furniture and those ghastly cuckoo clocks were entirely Flanagan's idea. In her new flat she intends to have white walls, pale tables and chairs and be completely minimalist.'

'So what happened?' Emma was anxious about our daughter's exploits.

'Well there was very little Helga wanted. She took a few basic clothes and one or two books and bits of silver. She left all her jewellery. She told us that Flanagan had only given it to her to make it up after hitting her. She said that he could present it to his next victim. But then she insisted on going round every single one of those cuckoo clocks and removing all the weights.'

'What was the point of that?' I asked.

'The clockwork mechanism depends on them. The clocks won't go and they won't cuckoo without the weights . . .'

'What did she do with them all?' I was bewildered at this mysterious feminine behaviour.

'She put them in a big black dustbin bag. Don't look so worried – neither Judith nor I helped. The bag was incredibly heavy by the end, but she lugged the whole thing down to the front gate. It's dustbin collection day tomorrow so the whole lot will have gone by the time the Vice-Chancellor comes home!' she laughed. 'Helga thinks he'll be grief-stricken without his birds!'

'Then,' she continued, 'she found the keys to the Mercedes. She was pleased about that. She knew he was going to the conference by train, but she thought that he might have taken the keys with him. But no . . . they were there in the drawer of the hall table. The car was a present from her father so it really belonged to her. She put the stuff she'd taken into the boot and she drove it round to the Refuge. It's parked outside at this very moment and she'll drive herself to Cambridge in it tomorrow.'

Emma and I looked at each other. 'Well,' I said, 'it was a present from her side of the family, so I suppose . . .'

'Don't be a stuffed shirt, Daddy!' said my daughter.

'You haven't heard the end,' she continued. 'When she left the hospital, Helga took half the money from their joint account. That's what she's been living on – happily there was quite a lot there. Anyway, in retaliation Flanagan cancelled their joint credit cards. But yesterday she found another card. It was one they only used for holidays and they'd both forgotten about it. She came across it in the back of the silver cupboard. She wasn't sure it would work, but she tried it out by filling up the Mercedes with petrol on the way back to the Refuge. It was fine!'

I was not sure I was going to approve of the end of this story. 'So what did she do with it?'

'She thought everyone in the Refuge deserved a treat. So she booked a table at the Amalfi Restaurant for six o'clock. There were twenty of us. The two paid helpers Liz and Jan, five resident women, eight children, Patricia and Judith, Danielle Bousset who has been very helpful, me and Helga herself.'

'What about Helmut?' asked Emma.

'No . . . he had to stay at home on her bed. Anyway we had a private room. Danielle, who knows about these things, chose the wine. The children had some form of pasta and salad and ice cream and the rest of us had slap-up dinners. I had mussels followed by veal cooked in a wonderful cream and mushroom sauce. Then I had zabaglione with fresh mangos and a selection of Italian cheeses. It was yummy!'

'How much was it?' Emma could not decide whether to be amused or horrified. 'The Amalfi isn't cheap.'

'The bill was over seven hundred pounds. We had a lovely time!' Imogen grinned.

I felt uneasy. 'Perhaps I should tell the Vice-Chancellor that I'll pay Imogen's share . . .' I suggested to Emma.

'Don't be ridiculous, Felix.' My wife was having none of it. 'It's the least that man can do to contribute to the situation.'

All too soon the novel was finished. I tried to delay the moment of separation by fiddling about and rewriting the odd paragraph. But I couldn't deceive myself. The book was done. I took a deep breath, put the manuscript into a large envelope and sent it to the publisher. He telephoned back within forty-eight hours, bubbling over with enthusiasm. He was anxious that I should deal with the proofs as soon as possible. Almost before I knew it, press releases were being issued. An advance copy was sent to a prominent politician. To my amazement, he not only read it, but described it as a 'rattling good read.'

Several newspapers were intrigued by the idea of an anonymous author. Then we ran into a problem. We needed someone to talk to journalists. Eventually we decided that Emma would do the public relations for the book. She was a professional media person and would know how to cope with the press. She did a wonderful job. As a result of her efforts, there was a double-page article in the *Times Higher Educational Supplement* conjecturing who had written such a scandalous volume. The piece was illustrated by a montage of a bald-headed white male, a gorilla and a busty blond. The headline was 'Anon Brings Campus to Book.'

She also persuaded the education editor of one of the quality newspapers to take it on. In a major article, the correspondent discussed the contemporary relevance of the book. Under the headline 'In the Footsteps of Lucky Jim', it emphasised the poor standard of university management, the absurdity of the Research Assessment Exercise and the dangers of dependence on outside funding. There were also several reviews in the literary pages of the other serious newspapers.

I had never experienced anything like it. Sadly *Kant's Critiques Revisited* was still waiting for its first notice in an academic journal. In contrast, everyone seemed eager to voice an opinion about *A Campus Conspiracy*. The editor of the local paper, the *St Sebastian's Gazette* was not to be outdone. He had used Emma frequently on his cookery and leisure pages and he wanted to have an interview with her. He sent along a young reporter and she told him that an option on the book had been sold to a major American film company. The next week, a front page story appeared entitled 'Unknown Takes Book to Hollywood.' There was a nice photograph of Emma, but the young journalist had written that she did not know who the author was. We were unhappy about this and I encouraged Emma to write a letter to the editor saying that although the book was anonymous, she did, in fact, know the name of the writer. 'Oh what a tangled web we weave . . .' said Imogen when she heard the story.

Soon afterwards, my publisher telephoned me again. He was delighted with the publicity and was still exulting about the film option. By this stage it was becoming clear that the book would be a minor bestseller – Waterstone's had just placed a substantial advance order and other bookshops were following suit. It was felt that we should not let the opportunity pass. What about producing a sequel?

This idea had not occurred to me. Although *A Campus Conspiracy* was written in the first person, it was really the story of a colleague whom I had chosen to call Harry Gilbert. I was not sure that I could make up a novel with no basis in fact. My publisher was amused. I had hinted to him on several occasions that my own relationship with the university was not exactly sweetness and light. Why shouldn't the next book be centred around me? My wife thought this was a splendid idea. It would be cathartic for me to write out my feelings. I was unsure. It is one thing to write a successful novel about someone else. Could I pull off the same trick for myself? I thought about it for a few weekdays. Without any conscious effort, the shape of the new book emerged.

Like Harry's adventures, mine would also have to be fictionalised. As in *A Campus Conspiracy*, the novel's university would be called St Sebastian's, but, at the very least, all the characters' identities would have to be changed. This meant I could not use my real name. After a certain amount of discussion within the family, we settled on the central couple being called Felix and Emma Glass. The perfect title was more elusive, but it came to me in the middle of the night. It would be entitled *Degrees 'R' Us*. It would show the lengths the modern university would go to achieve solvency. In the course of time I did write the sequel and, dear reader, this is the very volume that you are now holding in your hand.

Not suprisingly the university was buzzing with gossip. There were enough people on campus who knew the original story of Harry and Victoria to ensure that St Sebastian's was recognised. But who could have written the novel? Various suggestions were made. Perhaps it was the old Vice-Chancellor who played such a prominent part in the proceedings. Could it have been the Registrar as a therapeutic exercise after he had found himself in a muddle with his ladies? It was even mooted that the original of Wanda Catnip had turned her energies to fiction during her retirement? Magnus, however, was so excited about the possib-lity of becoming a film star that he let Patricia and Judith into the secret. Soon the word spread. As far as St Sebastian's was con-cerned, I was the likely culprit.

By the first week of June several of my colleagues had tele-phoned asking if the rumour were true. I refused to confirm or deny their conjectures. There was, however, a deathly hush from my Head of Department, who had, after all, taken an important role in Harry's career. John Pilkington, in defiance of all the rules of good management, had had no contact with me since my acci-dent. There had been no card, no telephone call and no enquiry. I wondered how he would tackle the statutory Back to Work Interview when the time came.

Then, unexpectedly, I received an email from the Vice-Chancellor summoning me to see him. This sounded ominous, and I was reluctant to go. After all, I was on sick leave. I had no real obligation towards him. In the event, however, he did not want to meet in his office. Instead he invited me for lunch one Saturday at the St Sebastian's Golf Club. I did not think even Flanagan could dismiss me from my job amid the bourgeois, golf-playing citizenry of the club dining room.

In any case, I was curious to know what was on his mind. By this stage I had discarded my crutches and was able to drive the car for a short distance. I still used a stick, but it was wonderful to be able to walk on my own two feet. On the appointed day I set off at noon. The club was two miles outside the town so I took the car and I dropped in to the university on my way. I was anxious to keep abreast of my post. I parked the car and slowly mounted the steps of the Old Building. There was a crowd assembled just outside the chapel. Clearly a wedding was about to begin.

As I approached I heard shrieks of rather camp laughter. I stopped to watch the procession as it made its way round the quadrangle. First came a handsome, silver-haired clergyman. He was dressed in a white and gold embroidered cope and looked as if he were at least a bishop. He was accompanied by a couple of golden-haired little boys in white lace suplices who were swinging incense censers. Then came the two principals. It was a lesbian wedding and both brides were tall blondes in magnificent dresses. Never have I seen such glamour! Despite the incense, the scent of lilies from the chapel was overwhelming. The brides themselves were stupendous – wonderful elaborate hair styles piled up on their heads, discreet, elegant make-up, real lace veils, vertiginous six-inch high heels and perfectly manicured long pink finger-nails. This was a ceremony of the highest quality with no expense spared. I wondered what they both did for a living.

As they glided past, one bride turned to the other. She put her arm round her fiancée and said in a deep, masculine voice, 'Come on old dear, here we go!' They smiled at each other and the two of them disappeared into the chapel. There was a burst of clapping from the assembled congregation. 'Well!' I thought to myself. 'A drag wedding! I wonder what the founding fathers of St Sebastian's missionary college would have thought of that?'

After collecting a pile of letters, I limped back to the car and drove through the suburbs in the direction of the Golf Club. Perched on a hill surrounded by a magnificent golf course stretching across green fields, the Club House was an Edwardian red brick mansion with marble pillars. I caught sight of a sizeable outside swimming pool and an archery range in the distance. I had never been before. It was not the usual haunt of my colleagues – university salaries do not stretch that far.

214

I parked my old Volkswagen in the car park. It looked shabby beside the glossy Audis, Volvos and Saabs. However, I did notice that there was no outsize Mercedes-Benz. Clearly Helga had won her point over the Flanagan family motor-car. I went directly to the club house and was greeted in the hall by a porter. He was expecting me and led me into a vast Victorian conservatory filled with lush green plants. It had a very good view of the ninth hole. Seated in a large wicker armchair was Flanagan wearing his golf hat. Next to him was a white-haired gentleman with a pink face and slightly trembly hands. Both were drinking large pink gins.

'Come in, Felix, come in'. The Vice-Chancellor made me welcome and, without even asking my preference, demanded another pink gin for me. I was not used to spirits and was very aware that I was driving. I resolved to make the drink last.

'This,' declared the Vice-Chancellor, 'is Jimmy Brewster. He's the owner of Brewsters' Brewery. Brewster by name and Brewer by nature.' Mr Brewster must have heard that joke a thousand times before, but he still seemed to be amused by it. 'Now, Felix,' Flanagan began, 'how are you?'

'Much better,' I said. 'I don't need the crutches any more. And I'm feeling fine.'

'Good to hear it,' Flanagan said, clicking his fingers for the waiter. He ordered two more pink gins.

'Now,' Flanagan began, 'I've something to tell you. Jimmy here is about to retire. Tired of brewing beer, aren't you Jimmy?'

'I never liked the stuff anyway,' said Mr Brewster. His 's' sounds were very slightly slurred.

'I've just got a good slug of money from the European Union,' continued my boss. 'The university is going to take over the brewery premises and it's going to become a centre for our new degree programme in Brewing Technology!'

'Brewing Technology?' I asked. I was not sure that I had heard correctly.

'That's what I said.' Flanagan was a man in a hurry. 'As you know I got rid of that boring bloke Ralph Randolph, but I was stuck with his two remaining chemists. They both have old-style tenure and I couldn't just give them the push. I was at my wits' end. But Jimmy here came up with this brilliant idea. The chemists will continue the brewing operation and we'll keep most of the old brewery staff. That's what the European Commission cares about. Keeping jobs!'

'You can call the beer "Flanagan's Finest".' Mr Brewster wheezed with laughter at his little joke.

Flanagan was rather taken with this suggestion. 'Good idea!' he said. 'We were going to introduce Travel and Tourism anyway next year and the brewery can be the centre for all that. We'll move the Union Bar over there as well. It can be staffed by the students as part of their work experience which'll save on the salary bill. And we'll make sure it only stocks our own particular beer. It'll make a fortune! Can't lose!'

'Are you going to rechristen the bar Flanagan's?' I asked slyly.

The Vice-Chancellor paused to consider this idea. 'Well it would bring the whole thing together . . .,' he said.

Mr Brewster heaved himself up from his seat. 'Gotta go, Alf. The little woman creates merry hell if I'm not in for lunch. Good to meet you, Freddie.' He nodded at me and made his slow way to the door.

I took a deep breath. The university had abandoned degrees in Philosophy and Chemistry. We were now concentrating on Travel and Tourism, Professional Golf and Brewing Technology. How much further would things go?

'Diversification's the name of the game,' Flanagan announced. 'Got to keep moving. Can't stand still. Anyway, Brewing Technology's only one area. We're having a degree in Professional Golf. Travel and Tourism will take off, mark my words. We're already snowed under with applications for Celebrity Studies and we're only just beginning to tap the surface of Film, Dance and Drama.' The Vice-Chancellor loosened his tie and leant towards me. I could smell the gin on his breath.

'Now Felix,' he said. 'I haven't forgotten that hot water bottle.'

I felt bewildered. What had hot water bottles to do with Celebrity Studies? Flanagan, however, was in full flow. 'I'm going to reorganise the university. My predecessor's scheme was hopelessly uneconomic. We're going to group all the subjects together under three faculties. There'll be Social Science, Humanities and, most important of all, Entertainment. I want you to be the Faculty Head of Entertainment.'

'Me?' I was astonished.

'Oh yes.' Flanagan was very positive. 'I've had my eye on you from the start. And I was quite right. You've become a bit of a celebrity yourself. A Hollywood film, and a bestselling novel! That certainly puts your colleagues in Theology in the shade.'

I tried to point out that the film was by no means a certainty, but Flanagan was not listening. 'No buts!' he said. 'I'm appointing you Head of the Entertainment Faculty. It'll be the largest of the three groups. To begin with it'll have Dance, Drama, Film, Professional Golf, Celebrity Studies, Brewing Technology and Travel and Tourism.'

'What about Philosophy?' I asked quietly.

Flanagan paused for a moment and then he chuckled. 'Why not? You'd get all your Research Assessment Exercise money and it'd pay for your salary for a few years. Theology won't be pleased to lose the loot, but too bad! But when the cash runs out, you've got to raise your own salary, mind.'

For the first time I was beginning to feel that early retirement was looking like an attractive option. I made one last attempt. 'But Vice-Chancellor, you don't know what I'm like as an administrator. Casino Management was not exactly the greatest success.'

'Not your fault, mate, not your fault.' He took out his mobile telephone and put it on the table beside him. 'Sorry about this, don't want to interrupt our talk, but I'm expecting a call from Florida. Another old orphanage mate, Leroy Jones. Now he had a hell of a time with those monks. He's half West Indian and they really did treat him like dirt.'

'What happened to him?' I asked.

'Well . . . it's quite a story. He ran away from the farm when he was fourteen and the next thing we heard he'd stowed away on a ship going to America. Always did have lots of initiative did Leroy! He settled in Florida and he now owns a chain of dance studios all along the coast from Miami to Tallahassee. He calls them the Pussy Galore Clubs.'

'Pussy Galore?' I asked.

Flanagan was dismissive, 'After the James Bond heroine.'

I raised my eyebrows. I could think of another explanation. 'Anyway,' he continued. 'He wants his students to get degrees

217

and he's heard that St Sebastian's offers partnerships. That's what we're trying to arrange. He's always up very early in the morning. It's about seven in Florida and that's when he likes to call.'

At that moment the mobile on the table began to cuckoo in a manic fashion. Flanagan turned on the speaker phone and said, 'Alf here.'

A deep voice with an African-American accent responded, 'It's Leroy, mate. I've got some news for you, The partnership deal's sewn up. My share-holders are very keen. They're sure impressed with the notion of a degree in Artistic Dance. It sounds just fine! And they're prepared to finance the whole thing . . . .'

'That's great!' said the Vice-Chancellor, giving me a wink. 'Look, Leroy,' he grinned. 'I've got the new Head of the Entertainment Faculty with me now. He'll be sure to see you right, won't you Felix?' I opened my mouth and closed it again.

'That's terrific,' said Leroy. 'Now there's just one thing. One of my shareholders raised a question. He's a boring old fart and went to somewhere like Harvard himself. He didn't think a uni-versity would take us on. You do understand we specialise in exotic dancing, don't you? We advertise it as artistic, but between you and me, it sure is exotic.'

Flanagan gave a great bellow of laughter 'We're flexible, Leroy. That's the point of St Sebastian's. Our Entertainment Faculty offers all kinds of dance – ancient dance, modern dance, national dance, exotic dance. It's all the same to us. Tell them that St Sebastian's is delighted to take the Pussy Galore Clubs on board. Tell them . . .,' the Vice-Chancellor hesitated. Then his voice boomed across the airways to Florida. 'Tell them at St Sebastian's we positively specialise in Exotic Dance. Tell them . . . at St Sebastian's University . . . Striptease That's Us!'